PRAISE FOR *THE APP*

*Full of adventure ...
with real warm...*

KATHERINE WOODFINE, AUTHOR OF
THE MYSTERY OF THE CLOCKWORK SPARROW

*The Apprentice Witch is entirely more charming,
adventurous, and full of heart than a book has any right
to be. Make no mistake: there's magic afoot.*

TRENTON LEE STEWART, AUTHOR OF
THE MYSTERIOUS BENEDICT SOCIETY

A really lovely children's book.

PETER BUNZL, AUTHOR OF *COGHEART*

*[A] delightful, witty and vivid story ... I absolutely loved
Nicol's deft characterisation and evocative settings –
and it made me laugh out loud in parts!*

KIRAN MILLWOOD HARGRAVE, AUTHOR OF *THE GIRL OF INK & STARS*

*A charming tale of magic, bravery and friendship,
reminiscent of Diana Wynne Jones.*

THE GUARDIAN

*[The Apprentice Witch] takes readers on a pleasant
trip back to a simpler age ... full of witches
and spells and frightened villagers.*

THE NEW YORK TIMES

*It's a treat to be back in Arianwyn's world ... Nicol has
a really distinct brand of cosy, magical storytelling.*

FIONA NOBLE, *THE BOOKSELLER*

*... alongside the cosy feel (plenty of scones and tea by roaring
hearthfires), this is very much a story with lots of magic and
...n.*

Hot chocolate at the ready? Excellent! If, like me, you've been longing to read this, you need to settle down for a real treat! I'm proud to introduce the final part (for now!) in James Nicol's enchanting *Apprentice Witch* series. Our beloved Arianwyn is determined to discover the truth – and I want desperately to know what happens to all her friends, frenemies and rivals. I don't think I'll stop reading until I've found out! Get ready for the best witchy ending ever . . . (Afterwards, let's start the whole trilogy all over again!)

BARRY CUNNINGHAM
Publisher
Chicken House

A WITCH COME TRUE

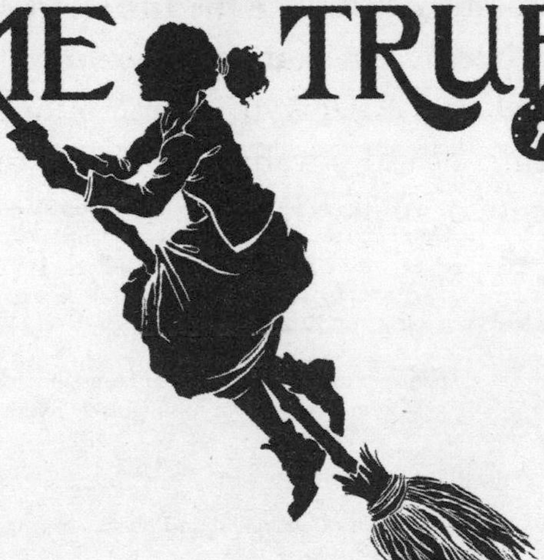

JAMES NICOL

2 PALMER STREET, FROME, SOMERSET BA11 1DS

Text © James Nicol 2019

First published in Great Britain in 2019
Chicken House
2 Palmer Street
Frome, Somerset BA11 1DS
United Kingdom
www.chickenhousebooks.com

Cover and interior design by Steve Wells
Cover and inside illustrations by Daniela Terrazzini
Map © David Wardle
Typeset by Dorchester Typesetting Group Ltd
Printed and bound in Great Britain by CPI Group (UK) Ltd, Croydon CR0 4YY

The paper used in this Chicken House book is made
from wood grown in sustainable forests.

1 3 5 7 9 10 8 6 4 2

British Library Cataloguing in Publication data available.

PB ISBN 978-1-910655-98-6
eISBN 978-1-911490-85-2

In memory of my wonderful mum
Jennifer Rose Nicol
With all my love x

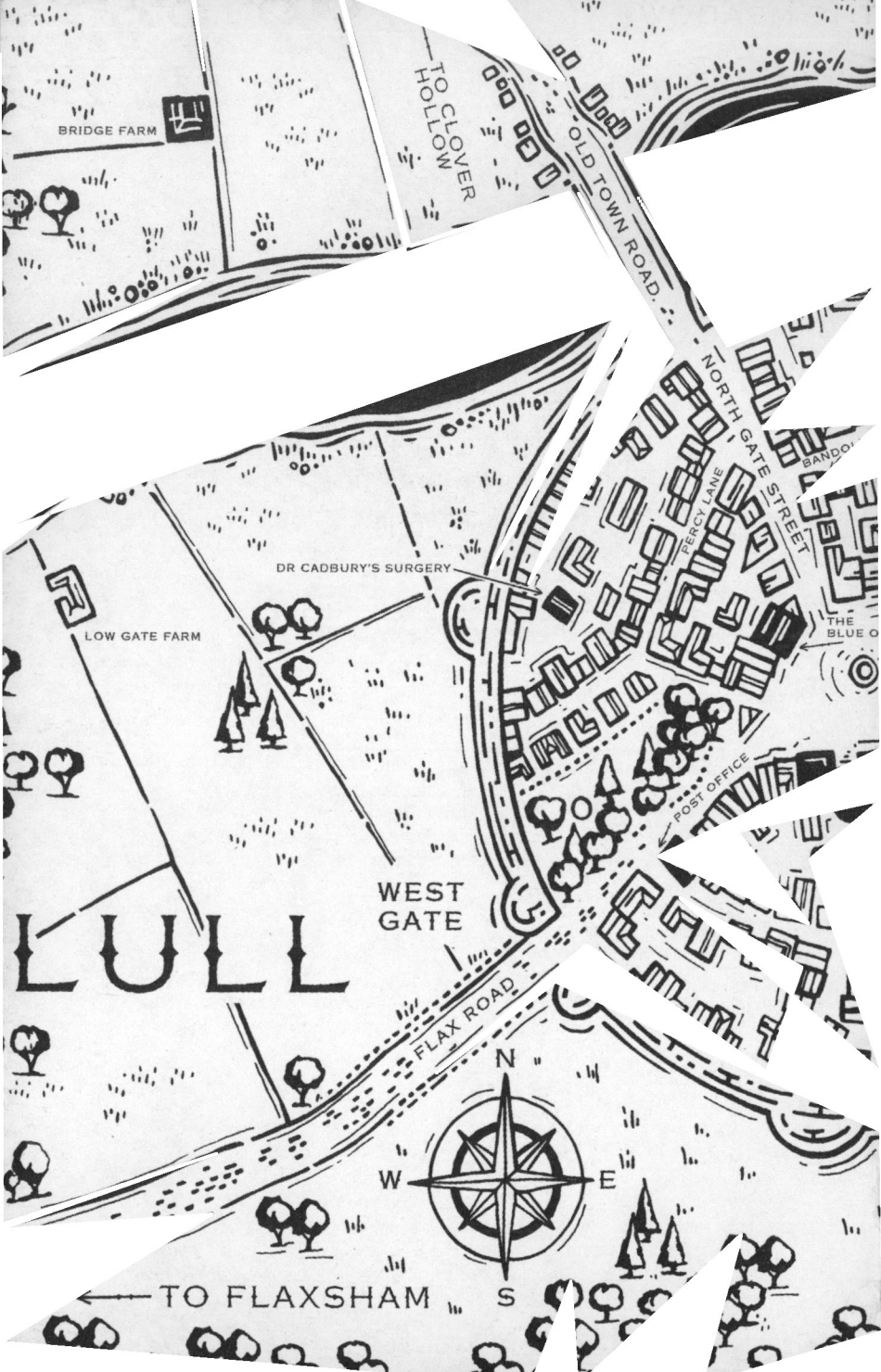

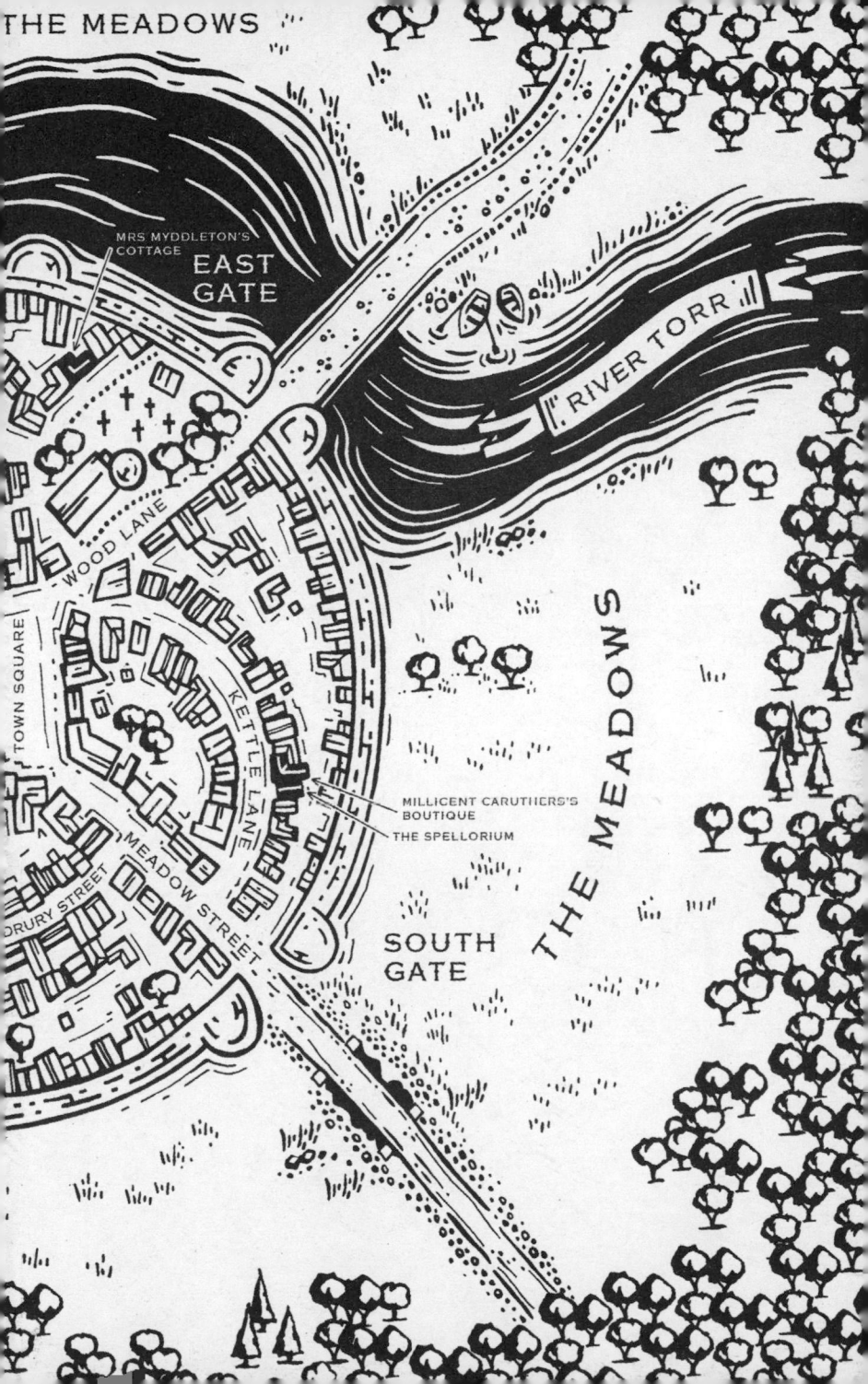

THE MEADOWS

MRS MYDDLETON'S
COTTAGE

EAST
GATE

RIVER TORR

WOOD LANE

TOWN SQUARE

KETTLE LANE

MILLICENT CARUTHERS'S
BOUTIQUE

THE SPELLORIUM

THE MEADOWS

MEADOW STREET

DRURY STREET

SOUTH
GATE

The *Quiet Glyphs* are ancient and powerful glyphs, once widely used by the witches of the Four Kingdoms. According to Estar the feyling they're now all stored inside of me, waiting to reveal themselves. Estar has promised to help identify the quiet glyphs for me as I uncover them.

I'll record all my discoveries in this notebook, a present from Colin and Salle. I'll keep it with me always, just in case.

Skygɛ – *The Shadow Glyph*

Warning – this glyph is dangerous in the hands of anyone inexperienced (my grandmother made me write that!).

The shadow glyph which has the feyling name Skygɛ (which can mean shadow, darkness and fear but can also mean obscure and protect) is a quiet glyph of immense power and was the first quiet glyph I ever

encountered. At first I assumed it had dark intentions, but the shadow glyph feeds off the doubt and fear that lives inside of us – the intention is whatever you make of it. And this is why you must hold your nerve when using this glyph: it is the fear and darkness within us that offers the glyph its power, and if you let them, these feelings can overwhelm you.
Use it with caution and care.
It is the only glyph (so far) that can defeat night ghasts.

THE NEW BOOK OF QUIET GLYPHS BY ARIANWYN GRIBBLE

Chapter 1
ST MORAG'S MILITARY SANATORIUM

'*H*ere you are, miss. This is St Morag's.' The taxi driver nodded as a church-like building came into view, squeezed between a department store and a motorcar showroom. 'Who are you visiting then?'

'My dad,' Arianwyn replied quietly, glancing once more at her grandmother's telegram.

She'd read it a hundred times on the various slow trains from Lull and at least twice in the taxi ride from Kingsport Station. The paper was all crumpled from where she had gripped it tightly. The taxi pulled alongside the pavement outside St Morag's as she read it again:

MISS ARIANWYN FLORA GRIBBLE
THE SPELLORIUM,
38 KETTLE LANE, LULL

ARIANWYN, YOUR DAD RETURNING TO
KINGSPORT TODAY COME SOON AS
POSSIBLE. HE WILL BE AT ST MORAG'S
MILITARY SANATORIUM, MARSHALL
STREET, KINGSPORT.

GRANDMA XXX

'Well, I hope he's all right, miss. Seems to be good news now the fighting in the Uris is all over and done with anyway. That'll be a shilling please.'

Arianwyn handed over the money and climbed out of the taxi. She glanced up at the high stone arches and castle-like turrets of St Morag's. The sky above had grown cloudy. She stuffed the telegram into her coat pocket and tried to shake away her unease as she raced up the steps. In a few moments she would see her father for the first time in she couldn't remember how long – shouldn't she be excited?

She *was* excited, but her stomach wobbled nervously as she pulled open the huge door. She still wasn't sure how badly he had been wounded or what his wounds even were. Would she recognize him? Would he recognize her? Would he look ill?

A sharp medicinal tang hit her as she entered the large atrium. Nurses and doctors hurried across the room into the several long corridors leading away from it, too busy to notice a young witch hesitating beside the door. 'Excuse me, I'm looking for—' Arianwyn tried quietly as a doctor approached. But he simply gave her a quick glance up and down and marched past.

Arianwyn sighed, wandering further inside. There were no signs anywhere. 'Mind out of the way!' a loud voice called and Arianwyn turned just in time to narrowly avoid being mown down by a nurse pushing a large wheeled bed.

'Sorry!' Arianwyn said, hopping to one side. 'Oh, wait, can you tell me where I can find my dad please?' she gabbled quickly. 'He's a patient here, Sergeant Gribble.'

The bed slowed and the nurse – all apple cheeks and starched apron – sighed gently. 'Dearie, we've got about seventy patients here at the moment and it's all sixes and sevens, I can tell you, what with all the soldiers coming back from the fighting. Try down there. Most of the newly arrived gentlemen are in rooms down that corridor.' She pointed down a long, whitewashed hallway.

'Thanks,' Arianwyn croaked. Her throat felt suddenly tight, as though she couldn't catch her breath. The nurse was off again, the wheels of the bed squeaking as she hurried away. 'Mind out the way, dearies!' she called brightly.

The corridor was quiet, and the only sound was Arianwyn's footsteps echoing on the high ceiling. As she drew near the first doorway, she heard a man coughing and the gentle babbling of a radio. '*In further news, the High Elder of the Witches of Hylund today declared that with hostilities in the Uris drawing to a close she would be withdrawing the majority of her witches attached to military units by the end of the year . . .*'

The door to the room stood ajar and inside a soldier sat on a bed, his face partly wrapped in clean white bandages. He had red hair, so it couldn't be her father. 'Sorry,' Arianwyn mumbled as the man glanced up and caught her looking.

The next room was larger. Several long, arched windows overlooked a drab little courtyard and a ring of chairs had been arranged around a fireplace. The bars of a small electric fire glowed a cheerful orange.

A man dozed in one of the chairs, his right arm wrapped in tight bandages and strapped securely across his chest. Although he slept, it wasn't a peaceful slumber: the small muscles of his mouth were twitching fitfully. His face was drawn and dark shadows lurked under his eyes. His sandy hair had been cropped close to his head.

'Dad . . .' Arianwyn said, her mouth suddenly as dry as a desert, her voice wavering and cracking as cool tears splashed down on to her cheeks.

His eyes fluttered open and widened briefly as he saw her waiting in the doorway. 'Oh . . . Arianwyn?' His voice was sleepy and unsure.

She nodded silently, unable to speak as her emotions got the better of her. And then she was hurrying across the room. The small space suddenly felt as wide as a universe between them. Her father tried to rise out of his chair but his bandaged arm prevented him. Arianwyn half fell, half collapsed on to him, her arms encircling his neck as she buried her face against the rough green wool of his uniform.

'My little witch!' Dad mumbled into her hair. 'I'd started to think I might never see you again.'

There was so much Arianwyn wanted to say and yet she suddenly didn't know where even to begin. The fear she had felt just a few short weeks ago – when the first telegram had arrived informing her that her father was missing – was all gone, as though that had all happened to someone else or in a story-book. And somehow this didn't feel quite real yet, either.

She pulled away, keeping her arms wrapped around her father's neck and blinking through her tears. 'Is it really you?' she asked.

Her father nodded, his grey eyes watery now. 'It's me.' He smiled and kissed her gently on the fore-head. 'Look at you, you're so tall!'

'Now this is truly a sight to stir the soul!'

A familiar voice, warm and full, echoed in the sitting room. Arianwyn turned a little and saw her grandmother standing in the doorway, a bright yellow scarf draped over her shoulders and her silver-grey hair swept up under a broad-brimmed hat.

'Gran!' Arianwyn beamed, keeping her arms around her father.

Grandmother walked over to them, placing a gloved hand on Arianwyn's curls, and leant forward to gently plant a kiss on Sergeant Gribble's head. 'It's so good to see you safe and sound, Oliver,' she said, with a contented sigh.

'You too, Maria. Thank you . . .' His voice faltered for a moment. 'Thank you for taking care of Arianwyn so well. She looks beautiful.'

Grandmother smiled. 'Oh, but you know it's Arianwyn who is looking after all of us these days.' Her eyes sparkled.

Sergeant Gribble gazed down at Arianwyn, his eyes shining with pride. But there was something else in his look, like he was trying to solve a puzzle or was seeing something properly for the first time.

Chapter 2
WAR STORIES

'Careful now, or I'll pop my stitches!' Dad cautioned, gently prising Arianwyn away. 'Well, won't you both have a seat?' he asked, suddenly sounding a little formal.

Arianwyn dragged her seat right next to her father's so she could keep a tight hold of his hand. She was afraid that he might vanish if she didn't.

'I can't believe you're back at last!' she beamed.

'I know. It feels a bit odd, I must say,' her dad replied, shifting uncomfortably in his chair.

'Is your arm bothering you?' Arianwyn asked, rising to her feet.

'A little, but it's fine – don't fuss.'

She sat down quickly and the room was quiet for a few seconds until Arianwyn jumped up again. 'Oh,

I made this for you – it's an old medical charm for pain.' She pulled a small glass orb on a long silver chain from her pocket. It danced in the air, catching the warm glow of the electric fire. 'It has two topal stones and orenta flowers in it,' she explained to her grandmother.

'Oh yes, they used to be quite popular in my day. Orenta flowers are hard to come by – I hope you didn't pay too much for them,' Grandmother said kindly.

Arianwyn offered the charm to her father who eyed it rather suspiciously. Eventually, he reached for it but then stuffed it away in his pocket.

'It won't work as well in there,' Arianwyn said quietly, a little hurt that he had dismissed the charm so casually – she'd hoped he'd be impressed.

But he didn't say anything.

After a few moments of aching quiet Grandmother stood up and said, 'I'll go see about getting us some tea, shall I?'

'Well, good luck,' Dad replied sharply. 'This is a military hospital, not the Royal Tea Rooms, Maria.'

Grandmother smiled, choosing to ignore his bad temper. 'Not that anyone would ever be fooled otherwise, Oliver – but thank you for the reminder. Back in a tick!'

Arianwyn filled her dad in on the latest news from Lull. At first she felt awkward – her dad was so quiet – but soon enough she was telling him all about how the Myddletons had had yet another snotling infestation. By the time Grandmother returned, tea things in tow, he was laughing at how young Cyril Myddleton had decided to catch the snotlings with mousetraps!

When she'd set down the tea, Gran produced a sponge cake from her bag. 'Just what's needed, I think.' She smiled.

'Yum!' Arianwyn cooed as her grandmother poured the tea and handed out the mugs – they were a little chipped and grubby but it didn't matter. She couldn't recall the last time they had all sat like this and eaten and drunk together. There was a spreading warmth in her chest and she settled back in her chair and sighed contentedly.

'It is so good to be back home. The tea is much better, for one thing,' Dad said, his eyes glinting in the light of the electric fire. For a second, Arianwyn glimpsed his old self: her mischievous and fun-loving father, the one from before the war. They sipped their tea quietly, safe and sound for the first time in years.

'Was it very hard, being away this time?' Grandmother asked eventually.

Sergeant Gribble took a deep gulp of his tea, his eyes darkening slightly. When he started to speak his voice was quiet and uncertain, as though he was afraid to say the wrong thing. 'It was very hard a lot of the time and . . . strange.' He took a deep breath and shifted in his seat, his face creasing in pain again. 'There were days, weeks even, when it felt as though there was no war, no fighting going on at all. And then weeks where there was nothing else but fighting.' He shook his head slightly, as if trying to clear it. 'The Uris is a bizarre place, even at the best of times. There was a strange feeling everywhere. Everyone could sense it – or the lack of it, really. Because it felt as though some element to the world was missing.'

'No magic,' Grandmother explained, when Arianwyn shot her a questioning glance.

She nodded, remembering how a disaster hundreds of years before had used up, or wiped out, all the natural magical energy within the Uris. There were no spirit creatures there now and no witches! But then Arianwyn frowned, remembering something her father had said in one of his letters.

'But Dad, didn't you say you had encountered someone who claimed they were a Urisian witch?' Arianwyn asked.

Sergeant Gribble sighed. 'That's what he told us . . . but I'd rather not go into that now. I did describe it all to that witch who came this morning.' He looked at Grandmother as though that might explain things.

'Who was that?' Grandmother asked; she tried to

14

keep her voice sounding light and casual, but something made Arianwyn feel suddenly nervous.

'Said she was from the council,' Dad grumbled, shifting in his seat, his tone losing some of its warmth. 'One of your lot. Don't you know her, Maria?'

Arianwyn's mind raced, thoughts tumbling over each other. Who had been here to see her father? Who else even knew her father had returned? Why were they interested in the Urisian witch? The room suddenly felt a little less cosy. The fire only offered a fake orange glow to the room, hardly any warmth at all, and the chill was curling under her coat again, wrapping around her neck and ankles, tickling along her back. She shuddered.

Deep within the hospital a bell sounded out the hour, breaking the tense silence.

'Goodness, it's very late,' Grandmother said.

A nurse appeared suddenly in the doorway and glared at them all. 'What on earth is going on here?' she demanded. 'Visiting hours ended at six o'clock sharp. You can't all be in here now.'

'I'm sorry, we didn't know—' Arianwyn started to explain.

The nurse made a small grumbling, growling noise at the back of her throat. 'Out!'

Grandmother flowed out of her chair gracefully, standing tall and statuesque in the middle of the room. 'We were not informed of the visiting hours having ended, and we are causing no disturbance.' She stepped towards the nurse. 'My granddaughter has not seen her father for several years and recently thought he had died! I will not allow you to rush them in such a manner.'

'Well—' the nurse tried to interrupt, her face reddening.

'Well nothing. I will have you know that I am a member of the Council of Elder Witches, young lady, and I am not used to being talked to in such a manner. Precisely *what* is your name?'

Arianwyn hid her smile behind her hands. Her grandmother rarely used her position on the council in such a way and she was never rude to people unless she felt they had been rude to her, but this poor nurse was getting the full works, it would seem.

'I'm Nurse Maitland . . . ma'am,' she added quickly, and curtseyed clumsily.

'Well, Nurse Maitland, we will escort Sergeant Gribble back to his room and be on our way for now.'

'Very good . . . Your . . . Worship,' Nurse Maitland squeaked and curtseyed again, before spinning on her heels and dashing off down the corridor.

Arianwyn giggled, catching her dad's eye.

'You haven't changed a bit, Maria!' Sergeant Gribble grinned.

'I don't know what you mean!' Grandmother

smiled. 'Now let's get you to bed, shall we?'

The bedroom was sparse, with two metal-framed beds shoved against the walls, thick grey blankets and crisp white sheets tucked into orderliness. Arianwyn didn't think it made the beds look at all comfortable. She steered her father's wheelchair beside one of the beds, then tugged on the blanket and sheets to turn back the covers, which took two attempts, so that her dad could slide into the bed.

He shifted himself half out of his wheelchair, his face creasing in pain.

'Here, let me help,' Arianwyn said, reaching to support him.

'No. It's fine,' he said, his voice surprisingly sharp as he batted her hand away, upsetting a pile of books and letters on the small bedside table. They tumbled to the floor. 'I'm sorry,' he added quickly. 'I didn't mean to snap, I'm just tired.'

'I know,' Arianwyn said as her father lifted his legs into the bed. Once he was settled she pulled the sheets and blankets back over him. He lay back against the pillows.

'It really is cold in here,' Arianwyn said brightly, trying to change the subject and atmosphere.

'Shall I fetch that heater from the sitting room?' Grandmother suggested.

'No, why don't we just . . . ?' Arianwyn leant over the bed and quickly sketched Årdra, the fire glyph, against the cold stones of the wall. There was just enough magic nearby to complete the spell, to make the brick glow with warmth.

'There, that might help a bit,' Arianwyn said – but her father didn't respond.

Grandmother, however, smiled warmly at her. 'I'll go see about getting us a taxi. See you out the front, OK? Goodnight, Oliver.'

For a moment, Arianwyn and her dad waited in total silence. When he finally spoke, his voice was gentle: 'I'm so pleased to be home, so pleased you are here,' he said, reaching up to pat Arianwyn's hand on the rough wool blanket. 'I've missed you and things will be better now I'm here to look after you again,' he added sleepily.

Arianwyn paused for a second. Did she need looking after? She wasn't sure. Is that what her father really thought?

She was about to reply, but saw her father's eyes were closed. He looked as though he was already fast asleep. Arianwyn turned to gather the fallen books and papers back up on to the bedside table. Amongst them were her letters, as well as some official army forms. She tucked these all back carefully as they had been, and then noticed a few photographs lying on the floor. She gathered these up. Most of them showed various groupings of soldiers, including her father, standing beside tents, marching or on parade. One was less formal, and showed a group of people standing beside the ruins of what might have been a small stone cottage. Six of the people were soldiers and two were military witches, bright silver stars pinned to a uniform of thick trousers and woollen pullovers in the traditional dark navy of the standard witches' uniform but made for trenches and marching.

In the middle of the photograph was a figure partly swathed in long flowing black robes. On the man's bare arms and bald head were swirls of black, like strange tattoos or . . .

Arianwyn turned over the photo. On the back, her father had written the names of all the people on the photograph and in bold at the bottom: 'The Urisian witch'.

Sergeant Gribble shifted suddenly in his bed, mumbling in his sleep. Arianwyn jumped and replaced the photographs alongside the books and papers. But at the last second she snatched up the photograph of the Urisian 'witch' and stuffed it into the pocket of her coat.

Chapter 3
FRIENDS & ENEMIES

'I'm just going to take these parcels round to the post office, Arianwyn. Will you be OK keeping an eye on things here?' Mr Lomax pointed to a stack of tightly wrapped, brown packages and smiled at Arianwyn, who was sitting behind the counter, reading. Mr Lomax had helped in her grandmother's bookshop in Kingsport for years, but these days he was practically running the place as Grandmother was so busy with her council duties that she didn't have time for the bookshop any more.

'Yes, of course,' Arianwyn said, glancing up from her book.

'Not rushing off to see your father?' Mr Lomax asked as he pulled on his jacket.

'We can't visit until this afternoon, hospital rules!'

Arianwyn sighed. 'I'm going to meet Grandma there later.'

'Jolly good, won't be long then.' Mr Lomax smiled and padded quietly towards the door, partly hidden behind his stack of brown paper parcels.

Arianwyn heard the door charms sound and had just turned back to her book when a shadow fell across the pages and a sharp, crisp voice sounded in front of her: 'I say, do you happen to have anything on the theatre?'

Arianwyn dropped the book in surprise. 'No, I'm sorry. We specialize in magic and—' She glanced up at the customer, expecting to see a tourist or fancy Highbridge resident who had wandered in by mistake. But standing right there, on the other side of the counter, was her very best friend in the whole wide world. 'Salle!' Arianwyn leapt from the chair, the book sliding to the floor. She dashed around the desk, toppling a pile of books that were waiting to be sorted, and grabbed Salle into a tight hug.

'Oh, Wyn, I've missed you so much!' Salle said.

'Missed you more!' Arianwyn replied.

The girls stepped apart at last, still holding tight to each other's hands and enjoying their first sight of each other for over a month. Arianwyn noticed that Salle's hair was shorter than when she had last seen her, and she was wearing a brand-new green velvet coat that glistened with beads around the collar and cuffs. She looked so confident and happy, quite unlike the tearful girl she had met on the bus to Lull, all those months before.

'What a fancy coat!' Arianwyn said, tracing the beaded pattern with her hand.

Salle turned a pirouette. 'They let me borrow clothes from the theatre wardrobe sometimes. I think the wardrobe mistress likes me!' She smiled. 'I wasn't sure if I'd manage to see you – how long are you here for?'

'I don't know. I want to stay here until I can get Dad out of that ghastly hospital – but I can't be away from Lull for too long either. Mayor Belcher was quite clear about that.'

'How *is* your dad? You know I can always keep an eye on him if you go back before he gets out,' Salle offered.

'Oh, he's OK, I think. Tired, quiet. It feels odd to see him again. But Salle, I couldn't ask you to do that for me.'

'It's no bother, honestly.' Salle smiled. 'I did learn a few things helping Dr Cadbury out you know.'

'He said to say hello,' Arianwyn said.

'He's so kind holding the job for me while I'm doing the play.'

'How is the play going? I really want to see it whilst I'm here, if I can.'

'I'll get you some tickets,' Salle said proudly.

'That would be so exciting. Perhaps we could see if Colin wants to come as well?'

'Oh ... actually, he's been twice already,' Salle said, and she blushed and looked away quickly.

Arianwyn didn't know why exactly, but she blushed too. 'Oh, I see.'

'Do you think your grandmother will want to come? Where is she anyway?' Salle peered around as though Grandmother might suddenly materialize from the bookcases.

'Council meeting, of course,' Arianwyn explained. 'And I'm sure she'd love to come. Do you want some tea? I think we might even have some of Mr Lomax's oatmeal cookies – and they're the very best!'

'Yes please,' Salle said, settling in the chair and picking up Arianwyn's discarded book.

'Keep an eye on things and I'll be back in a few minutes,' Arianwyn said as she raced to the back of the store and the stairs to the apartment above.

When Arianwyn emerged a few minutes later, pushing the door open with one leg and rushing through as the teapot and mugs rattled on the tray, she saw Salle standing very straight behind the counter, a book clutched to her chest. A tall, impeccably dressed woman stood opposite her. 'Oh, here she is!' Salle said with obvious relief as the door closed with a loud bang behind Arianwyn.

The woman turned and Arianwyn knew at once

who she was.

'Mrs Alverston,' Arianwyn said. They'd never met, but the resemblance to Gimma was clear: the blonde hair, styled just so in the very latest fashion, the hard pale eyes, the tight smile that looked a little forced.

'Oh, there you are, Miss Gribble.' Mrs Alverston moved towards Arianwyn slowly, the thick fur draped around her shoulders slipping casually down her arm.

Arianwyn met Salle's gaze and noticed her raised eyebrow.

'It is good to meet you at long last. I have heard *so* much about you.' Mrs Alverston reached out a gloved hand towards Arianwyn, who was still hold-ing the tea tray. With a clumsy clatter she set it down on a table piled with books about spirit creatures, knowing her grandmother would go through the roof if she ever found out. Then she reached out to shake Mrs Alverston's hand, realizing too late that her own was covered with ink smudges and biscuit crumbs.

Mrs Alverston smiled a small quick smile that didn't quite reach her eyes. 'Yes, well,' she said, with-out taking Arianwyn's hand, and then moved past her and turned slowly, taking in the bookcases and tables. 'What an odd little store. I was informed that it belongs to your grandmother?' She sniffed.

'Yes – that's right.' Arianwyn smiled. 'Was there a book you wanted – for Gimma, perhaps? How is she?'

When Mrs Alverston turned back to face Arianwyn, her face was creased with worry. Her eyes darkened. 'Well, I was rather hoping that you might have seen her, or that she might well be here . . .'

'Gimma? Here?' Salle asked incredulously. Arianwyn had to agree: it did seem highly unlikely. Despite everything the two young witches had been through, she and Gimma had never exactly been the best of friends.

'You see, there was something of a disagreement yesterday,' Mrs Alverston said slowly, peering into the nooks and crannies of the bookshop. 'I thought perhaps she would come here.' She fiddled with the clasp of her handbag.

Arianwyn shook her head, bemused. 'I'm sorry, Mrs Alverston. I've not seen Gimma since she left Lull.'

'Oh, Lull. That ghastly little place. If she'd never gone there, well, perhaps none of this would ever have occurred.'

A stab of fear jolted Arianwyn. 'Mrs Alverston, was Gimma wearing any charms when she left?'

'What's that?' Mrs Alverston asked.

'Her charms for the . . . um . . .' Arianwyn didn't quite know how to politely mention the charms she had fashioned for Gimma to keep her hex infestation under control and dormant.

But thankfully Mrs Alverston seemed to catch on.

'Oh yes, yes – I'm sure she was.'

That was something, at least.

'Could she be staying with friends perhaps?' Arianwyn offered, thinking back to the gaggle of girls that permanently trailed after Gimma when they had been at school together.

Mrs Alverston looked as though she might be considering this for a second but then said, 'Well, naturally I have called on them already.'

Of course, Arianwyn thought. This was the last resort bookshop!

'Is there anywhere else she might have gone?' Salle asked, coming to stand beside Mrs Alverston. 'How about the Civil Witchcraft Authority offices?'

Mrs Alverston turned and looked at Salle as though she was surprised to find her there. 'I suppose I hadn't really considered that . . .'

'I could ask my grandmother when she gets back, as she might have seen Gimma perhaps, or heard something,' Arianwyn said reassuringly.

'Or we could ask Miss Newam?' Salle suggested, thinking of the head of the Magical Research Department they knew from the C.W.A.

'Hmm.' Arianwyn didn't relish the thought of seeing Miss Newam, even if there was a sort of truce between the two of them. During her time in Lull, Miss Newam had inadvertently discovered that someone – possibly someone from the Council of Elders – had deliberately spread hex in the Great

Wood. Since then, she and Arianwyn had set aside their differences and worked together, but Arianwyn really did not like her, try as she might.

'Or Colin?' Salle added eagerly.

'Would you mind? That would be so very helpful.' Mrs Alverston turned back to Arianwyn, her eyes wide with hope.

'Of course,' Arianwyn said.

'If you do hear anything, you'll let me know immediately, of course?' Mrs Alverston took a small ivory card from her handbag and handed it to Arianwyn. The address for the Alverstons' Highbridge home was printed on the other side in crisp black letters. 'I'd be ever so grateful.' She pulled the fur stole tighter around her shoulders and then turned and headed towards the door and out of the bookshop.

'Crikey!' Salle sighed. 'You can see who Gimma takes after, can't you?'

'I think she was just worried, that's all,' Arianwyn said.

'No excuse to be so rude, though. You should have heard her before you came back, bossing me about as if I was a servant just like ... well, just like Gimma.'

'I'd better get a message to my grandmother,' Arianwyn said, searching through the piles of books for the shop telephone.

'Won't it wait till she gets back?' Salle asked.

'The hex, Salle!' Arianwyn said.

'But Mrs Alverston said Gimma had the charms on when she saw her last. So she should be fine, right?'

'It doesn't mean the charms are still working. They don't last for ever, Salle, and the hex is so strong.' Arianwyn turned to face her friend. 'Look, I know you and Gimma have never seen eye to eye but she could be in serious trouble. And if she doesn't replace her charms so could other people.'

Salle chewed her lip and blushed a little. 'Sorry, Wyn, is there anything I can do to help?'

'Go and use the phone upstairs and see if you can get through to Colin or Miss Newam. I'll try Grand-mother on the shop phone.'

Salle dashed off to the apartment upstairs as Arianwyn dialled the number for the C.W.A.

Chapter 4
A NIGHT AT THE THEATRE

Arianwyn leapt from the taxi on to the pavement outside the Ethel Claymore Theatre. The bright lights made it feel like midday but the city around the theatre was dark, lost to the night. Grandmother followed her from the taxi and smiled. 'Well, this is very thrilling indeed, coming to see young Salle in her first play!'

Excitement and pride bubbled up inside Arianwyn. She'd been worrying about Gimma since Mrs Alverston's visit the day before and this was just the distraction she needed. 'She said to go to the stage door and ask for her there,' Arianwyn said, hurrying down the narrow alleyway beside the theatre. It was far less glamorous than she had imagined. She had pictured crowds of fans clamouring for autographs, but perhaps that happened after the performance? For now the alleyway was littered with crates. Stage-hands hurried this way and that or stood chatting in small groups.

'I'm so pleased I can come and see the play before I head back to Lull,' Arianwyn added, as they approached a very ordinary-looking door at the end of the alley, sidestepping sack barrows piled high with discarded bits of scenery.

'Do you really have to go back so soon? You've only just arrived!'

Arianwyn would've liked to spend more time in the city too, but the mayor had been insistent. 'It's the rain, its causing some flooding on the water meadows and the mayor thinks the qered should be moved elsewhere.' She knew she needed to help the huge, horse-like spirit creatures; it was her job, after all.

She pushed the door open and they passed through and into a long corridor that was decorated in rather dingy brown paint. Another door at the end of the corridor was labelled 'Dressing Room'.

A long list of names was pinned to it.

'Oh, look!' Arianwyn smiled, spotting Salle's name. She knocked.

Immediately a chorus of voices shouted: 'COME IN!'

Pushing open the door Arianwyn was hit with a riot of sound and colour and light. Bright lights surrounded huge mirrors that seemed to fill one whole wall of the room. The other was hidden under layers of costumes in all manner of colours and styles and shapes. People dashed across the small room, some pulling on costumes, others straightening hats and wigs, and yet more applying make-up to someone beside them whilst also doing their own. It looked like utter chaos.

'Wyn!'

Arianwyn heard Salle before she saw her. But then the crowd parted for just a moment and there was Salle, and somebody else Arianwyn wasn't expecting.

'Colin?' Arianwyn hurried forwards, but just a metre or so from her friends she tripped over a discarded velvet cape and stumbled. The floor loomed up at her and at the very last moment hands reached out and grabbed her, carefully pulling her upright just as both Salle and Grandma cried out in dismay.

Arianwyn looked up, brushing her curls from her face. 'Thank you, Colin,' she said, regaining her balance and taking a deep breath. They stood staring at each other for the longest moment until they both seemed to become aware that they were holding on to each other and everyone in the dressing room seemed to be looking right at them. They both blushed and looked away before quietly mumbling, 'Sorry.' And, 'Thanks.'

'Well, hello everyone!' Grandma called from

31

behind Arianwyn. 'I must say this is all very exciting indeed. Thank you so much for the tickets, Salle. I can't remember the last time I came to the theatre. It's so very kind of you.' She gave Salle a quick hug.

'I didn't think you were coming?' Arianwyn said to Colin. 'Haven't you been twice already?' Her voice sounded sharp though she hadn't meant it to and her face still felt warm.

'It *is* a really good play.' Colin smiled. 'And Salle's fantastic!'

Salle laughed and swatted Colin on the arm, then turned away to fiddle with a brush on the dressing table in front of her.

'I'm sure she is!' Grandma agreed.

Grandmother wandered off a little way to look at the rail of costumes. Salle leant towards Arianwyn. 'Have you heard any more about Gimma?' she asked in a hushed voice. 'Colin said there was no news from the C.W.A.'

Arianwyn shook her head. 'No, nothing. I'm really worried.' She looked at Colin. 'The charms I made for her only last a few days, a week at most. If she doesn't get a new one soon . . .'

'I know,' Colin said, taking a deep breath. 'It's really scary.'

'There's something else, but . . . I don't have time to look into it. I have to go back to Lull the day after tomorrow.' Arianwyn touched the strange photograph in her pocket. She'd kept it there since finding it. Once or twice she'd thought about showing her grandmother but she clearly had plenty on her plate at the moment. She wanted to know what her friends thought about it and whether they thought it linked to Gimma at all.

'What have you found?' Colin asked, but Arianwyn shook her head slightly.

A quick look passed between the three friends that they all knew meant: *not now, not here!*

'Well, I can't wait to see the play,' Arianwyn said, quickly changing the subject as Grandmother approached the threesome.

'You might not be seeing it tonight, I'm afraid,' a girl with wiry black hair that might have been a wig said from the seat next to Salle's section of the dressing table.

'Why? What's going on?' Colin asked.

'There's been a problem with the lighting for the stage,' the wiry-haired girl said mournfully.

'I heard it were snotlings chewed through the wires or something like that,' another voice called from behind the rack of costumes.

'Snotlings?' Arianwyn asked. *Not again*, she thought, her heart sinking a little. Sometimes it felt like snotlings had a personal grudge against her!

'Oh, Wyn. You could sort it out, couldn't you?' Salle's pleading eyes looked up at her and Grandma – and so did the eyes of every other young performer in the dressing room.

'I can't see any snotlings on the stage anywhere!'
Arianwyn called into the dark theatre, just a little
frustrated.

'Well, there don't appear to be any more snotlings
in the auditorium either,' Grandma called from the
back of the theatre. 'Apart from these two.' She held
two stunned snotlings by their ankles, lit up in the
glow of Grandma's light orb. 'They'd started to build
a nest under this last row of seats!'

Stagehands and the gaggle of young performers
who had been in the dressing room with Salle
waited nearby holding torches, lanterns or candles. A
faint light wobbled at the edge of the stage, occasionally revealing a glimpse of scenery, painted trees
and hills and an ocean that was too blue to be real. A
pretend pile of rocks stood in front of Arianwyn.

'But there's still no time to get the wiring fixed
for tonight's show.' A tall and very slender man in a
dark velvet suit hurried forwards clasping a clipboard
to his chest like a shield. 'And these lights will never
do, not at all – why, you can barely see the set, let
alone the cast!'

'This is Mr Malcom, he's the director,' Salle said to
Arianwyn quickly.

'Do we have any more candles?' Mr Malcom
called back off the stage.

'We've used all we have, Mr Malcom,' a voice replied.

The director sighed and sat on the pretend rock. 'Botheration! The doors open in fifteen minutes and if we have to refund the tickets we won't be able to pay anyone and . . . we might have to close the play early.'

There were gasps of shock from the cast and crew. Arianwyn glanced at Salle, who looked like she might be about to cry.

'Can't you do something, Wyn?' Salle asked quietly, nudging her in the ribs.

Arianwyn looked as her grandmother made her way back towards the stage, the snotlings now banished. Her light orb still hovered beside her head.

An idea began to unfurl in Arianwyn's mind. 'We could make some light orbs – that might help with the candles and everything else?'

'Yes!' Salle cried, grabbing Arianwyn's arm and jumping up and down on the spot.

Mr Malcom glanced round, his eyes wide and a little watery. 'Oh, would – could you?' he breathed, clutching the clipboard ever tighter.

Arianwyn nodded and Mr Malcom gasped with delight. He gestured with a flourish to the centre of the stage and took a large step backwards. The chatter and babble of the stagehands and actors died away at once. And Arianwyn felt suddenly nervous. Even though light orb spells were the easiest to work, it would be a challenge to create them large enough to light the theatre. She knelt on the boards of the stage and stared to sketch Oru, the light glyph.

She let her senses reach out for a pocket of magic. There was a seam of magic far down, below the cellars and foundations of the theatre, deep within the earth. It connected with the glyph and flowed slowly towards Arianwyn. As the orb of light began to form, she shaped it, pulled it and turned it until the small light orb was like a huge lantern. Satisfied, she spread her arms wide and the light orb floated up into the high arch above the stage.

By this point, Grandma had joined her and in a few minutes there were five large light orbs high over the stage casting a bright, magical light over everything.

'Perfection!' Mr Malcom called and he hurried forwards to shake Arianwyn and Grandma's hands as they were treated to their very own round of applause.

'Thank you, Wyn. I think you should take a bow!' Salle laughed.

But Arianwyn just blushed bright red and smiled.

When the doors of the auditorium opened, the cast and stagehands scattered like rats in a barn. The huge red curtain was drawn quickly across the stage and Arianwyn and Grandmother were pointed down a flight of steps that took them back to the other side, to the auditorium and their seats.

'See you all in a bit!' Salle called brightly as she hurried away.

Colin, Arianwyn and Grandma were walking to their seats, fighting against the flow of incoming theatregoers, when someone called, 'Elder Stronelli! What a surprise to see you here.'

Walking towards them were two women, displaying their silver-and-gold stars that marked them as members of the Council of Elders, like Grandma. Arianwyn had no reason to suspect it was one of these two witches that might somehow be involved or responsible for threatening Gimma and planting the hex in the Great Wood, placing Lull and her friends and indeed all of Hylund in great danger, but the thought crossed her mind all the same. After all, the council was made up of fifteen elder witches from all across Hylund. The traitor had likely used a glamour charm to disguise themselves, so finding the culprit was never going to be easy. It really could be any one of the council.

As they exchanged pleasant chit-chat and council gossip with her grandmother, Arianwyn noticed how the two witches kept glancing towards her, as if they knew something.

'My granddaughter's friend is in the play,'

Grandma said proudly.

'Ah, how very exciting,' the taller of the two elders remarked.

The shorter witch, her hair in intricate braids, smiled at Arianwyn slightly. She felt a shiver run down her spine.

'Have either of you seen Gimma Alverston recently?' Arianwyn blurted. She was surprised to hear the words come out of her mouth and felt Grandma's grip tighten on her wrist.

'No, I haven't seen Miss Alverston since . . . well . . . when would it have been, Ellynor?' She turned to her colleague.

'It must've been several weeks now,' the other witch replied lightly, as though they were just discussing the weather or the price of bread. 'Why?'

Grandma quickly stepped slightly in front of Arianwyn, cutting her short as she was about to reply. 'A family disagreement, it would appear. The girl's mother was looking for her yesterday. I'm sure it will have all blown over by now.'

The theatre bell's bright but urgent call cut through the noise in the auditorium. 'Well, we had best find our seats,' the elder witch said. 'So delightful to see you again, Miss Gribble, Elder Stronelli.'

And with that the two elders moved past Arianwyn, Colin and Grandmother and off to their seats. 'What did you do that for?' Arianwyn asked as they settled down. 'Do you think they—'

'Now is not the time, Arianwyn,' Grandmother warned.

The hidden orchestra began to play and the huge red curtain swished back. Arianwyn and Grandmother's light spells cast their magical glow across the stage. The audience gasped.

And then very quietly Grandmother said, 'But I don't trust either one of them.'

Chapter 5
The PHOTOGRAPH

'*S*alle, you were amazing!' Arianwyn called as Salle stepped through the stage door. 'Will you sign my programme?'

Salle blushed and then beamed with delight as she signed her name in big curly handwriting across the front of the programme.

'Yes, Salle. You really were marvellous,' Grandma said. 'Not that I'm in the least bit surprised.'

Arianwyn, Grandma and Colin clapped with delight whilst Salle took several curtseys, two bows and one twirl to much cheering and laughing.

'Now it's getting late, my dears. We all ought to be getting home,' Grandmother said.

'It's my day off tomorrow, shall we do something?' Salle asked as they were gently guided towards the main road to find taxis to ferry them all home. Colin to his parents' house in Longferry, a district in the east of Kingsport, Salle to her boarding house just a few streets away. And Grandmother and Arianwyn back to the bookshop.

'I have to go and visit my dad in the afternoon. Do you fancy meeting me at the sanatorium at twelve?' Arianwyn suggested. 'We can go for lunch and then you can come and see my dad? I'm sure he'd love to meet you at last!'

'Super!' Salle beamed.

'I'll see if I can get away for a longer lunch break,' Colin added.

'That's all settled then.' Grandma ushered Salle and Colin into a taxi and Arianwyn watched as they sped off into the night. She could see them laughing and giggling through the window and it made her feel strange in her stomach, though she didn't know why.

At lunch the next day, Arianwyn, Salle and Colin were wedged into a booth in a small café just around the corner from St Morag's. Three steaming mugs of hot chocolate sat on the table before them along with a plate of toasted sandwiches. 'So what's going on then?' Colin asked.

Arianwyn slipped the photograph out of her pocket and – glancing quickly around them – slid it on to the table. 'I found this in my dad's things. He'd told me about a Urisian witch in one of his letters. Do you see it, on his arms?' she asked, peering at her friends as they in turn peered closely at the photograph. 'And Dad said a witch from the council had been to see him, asking him about the Uris. Don't you think that's a bit fishy?'

'What *is* that?' Colin asked as he leant in for a better look.

'Are those—' Salle began and then stopped. 'But they look like. No, it can't be!' She gave a small nervous laugh.

'Hex?' Colin asked hoarsely.

'I think so,' Arianwyn replied. 'Almost like the markings on Gimma's arms, don't you think?'

They fell silent as they all stared at the photograph.

'Has Miss Newam found out anything more about the hex in the Great Wood?' Arianwyn asked, turning to Colin.

He shrugged. 'Not really. The hex matches samples stored in the C.W.A. labs but we knew that much already. And so many people have access to the building. But she'll want to know about this, I'm sure.'

Arianwyn handed over the picture. 'Then you'd best show her,' she said.

Once they'd eaten, the three friends crossed the road to St Morag's — early visiting hours were nearly over so they raced inside, signing their names in the visitors' book. As Arianwyn leant over the ledger, she spotted an entry for a few days earlier. There on the page was the name 'Elder Tully'. Tully . . . she had been one of the witches at the theatre, one of the High Elder's closest assistants. And the date was the same day Arianwyn had visited for the first time. It had to have been Elder Tully who quizzed her father — it was too much of a coincidence otherwise.

Arianwyn pointed it out to Salle and Colin. 'What do you think?' she whispered.

'She came outside of official visiting hours,' Salle noted grimly. They all exchanged a glance. Perhaps Grandmother was right to be suspicious. And judging by what Dad had said last time, the elder had been asking about the Urisian witch. Arianwyn felt cold.

'Do you think it could be the same witch who threatened Gimma and spread the hex?' Colin asked.

'It does seem likely,' Arianwyn replied softly.

A few minutes later they were all standing in Sergeant Gribble's chilly and cheerless bedroom.

Sergeant Gribble was sitting up in bed. He gave them all an appraising glance as though he was preparing a rather disappointing group of cadets for a parade. 'And who do we have here?' he asked.

'Oh, this is Salle Bowen. My friend from Lull,' Arianwyn explained.

'Of course. Salle. I've heard a lot about you in Arianwyn's letters. The actress, yes?'

Salle blushed and nodded.

'And this is my other friend, Colin Twine. Colin works for the C.W.A.'

Sergeant Gribble stared hard at Colin.

'How d'you do . . . sir.' Colin reached out a hand in greeting but Sergeant Gribble didn't take it.

Instead, he turned back to Arianwyn. 'I've just seen my doctor and he says I'll be out of here in time for Yule! Isn't that great?'

'That's wonderful.' Arianwyn hugged her father.

'So you'll be coming to Lull for the festivities then? How exciting.' Salle beamed.

But Sergeant Gribble didn't reply straight away. He sat up a little straighter. 'Well, I'm not sure about that yet. Perhaps we can celebrate here in Kingsport like we always used to?'

Arianwyn couldn't remember the last Yule she had spent with her father. She vaguely recalled a rushed celebration just before or after Yule about five or six years ago as her father had passed through Kingsport on his way to somewhere else. A hurried meal, hastily wrapped gifts. Nobody had enjoyed it then. She was looking forward to a proper family celebration this year, and she had pictured it in Lull, surrounded by everyone she loved. She saw that her father's comments had surprised Salle and Colin as well. She cleared her throat nervously. 'But . . . Dad, I have to go back to Lull tomorrow. There are things I have to do – and they're going to need me there over Yule. I can't leave Lull without a witch for long.'

'But I'll need some help while I'm here. Surely they can spare you for a bit? Blasted C.W.A.' He glared at Colin as though this were entirely his fault.

When Arianwyn replied it was with a small voice. 'I don't think they can, Dad . . . I'm sorry. I have to get back to help move the qered from the meadow because of the flooding – and I'll be so behind with the rest of my work too.'

Everything was silent but for the sound of a bed being wheeled somewhere and the hurried footsteps of a nurse. 'Well, I suppose if that's how it is, then that's how it is,' her father said eventually with a small smile that made Arianwyn feel suddenly guilty.

'I could come and check in on you, though,' Salle offered, 'once Wyn's gone.'

'But I wouldn't want to be a bother to you, Salle,' Sergeant Gribble said.

'I really don't mind.' Salle smiled at Arianwyn. She was trying to help.

'Thank you, Salle.' Arianwyn squeezed her friend's hand and smiled.

'And you, me and Elder Stronelli can all travel

back to Lull together when the play closes in a couple of weeks.' Salle beamed, already pleased with her plan.

'Oh, I could travel back with you then as well,' Colin said, only to be met with another sour look from Sergeant Gribble.

'You're spending Yule in Lull as well, are you?' he asked.

'Yes . . . sir!' Colin replied, almost standing to attention. 'My parents are going to visit my aunt in Newbold for the holidays and there's not really room there for all of us.'

'Aunt Grace and Uncle Mat invited Colin to stay with us,' Salle said, her cheeks going quite pink.

'Lovely.' Arianwyn's dad groaned.

'Stop being such a grump, Dad!' Arianwyn laughed, but deep down she had a feeling this was not going to go smoothly at all.

Why was her father being like that? Was it his injuries or was something else bothering him? Perhaps a rest and getting out of this gloomy hospital would help things to improve.

Chapter 6
MRS ALVERSTON

The next day, early in the morning, Arian-wyn was packed and dressed and reluctantly ready to return to Lull. She waited just inside the front door of the bookshop, her bags at her side, her coat pulled tight around as icy rain fell for the third day in a row.

She was sorry to leave so soon, but pleased her father was getting better. Although Salle was going to pop in when she had time, he clearly didn't need anyone to be checking up on him every day and was itching to leave the hospital. Arianwyn couldn't blame him.

'I packed up some food for you for the journey,' Grandma said, appearing with a small parcel wrapped in brown paper and a yellow thermos flask.

She was wearing a long dressing gown with a thick woollen scarf around her neck. 'Hot chocolate!' she said, giving the thermos a gentle shake. Arianwyn forced a smile. 'Oh, cheer up,' Grandma said gently. 'We'll all be on our way to Lull soon for Yule.'

Arianwyn felt torn. She wanted to do her work, and she missed Lull. But she felt terrible rushing away, leaving her father in the hospital, no matter how well he was. And then there was Gimma.

Grandmother pulled her into a tight hug that Arianwyn hoped would never end. Then she planted a kiss on the top of her springy curls and whispered, 'All will be well.'

But Arianwyn knew that Grandmother was just as worried about Gimma's disappearance as she was and the mystery that now quite clearly linked an elder witch to Gimma, the hex and her father's encounter with the Urisian witch who bore the same strange hex-like markings on his skin.

From behind her she heard the sound of a car pulling alongside the kerb. 'Your taxi's here,' Grandmother said quietly, still holding her tight. 'I'm sorry I can't come and see you off but there's a council meeting this morning and I'm going to raise Gimma's disappearance again with a few friends who I trust.'

'Thank you, Grandma.'

Within a few minutes all Arianwyn's bags were gathered up and secured in the taxi and Arianwyn was smiling at her grandmother through the rain-speckled window. She waved as the taxi pulled away from the kerb, until the bookshop and Grandmother were out of sight. Then she sat back in her seat and took a deep breath, trying to chase the sadness away with thoughts of Yule and being home in Lull. She bit her lip and fiddled with the catch on her suitcase.

'Kingsport central station, isn't it, miss?' the driver called brightly across his shoulder as he sped along the quiet streets.

'Yes pl . . .' She paused as another thought rushed into her head. In her coat pocket she felt for the small ivory card that Mrs Alverston had given her just a few days ago. 'Actually, could we make a very quick detour to Highbridge, please?'

The Alverston house stood white and gleaming in a short row of similarly grand-looking and entirely intimidating houses. Its ebony-black front door waited at the top of a short flight of white marble steps. Perfectly clipped bushes guarded either side of the front door like fat green sentries. Arianwyn checked the card and the number on the brilliant brass plaque beside the door: number 14.

'I'll just be a few minutes,' Arianwyn reassured the driver as she climbed out of the car and splashed through puddles towards the imposing house.

She had fished out a package of charms that she had made for Gimma from her luggage. If Gimma turned up at home, she'd need them – there was no point in Arianwyn bringing them to Lull.

She pushed on the bell and took a step back from the door. She could hear the chimes echoing inside the house as she adjusted her coat, suddenly realizing she had buttoned it up wrong and it was all wonky and a bit twisted as a result. She was just trying to re-button it when she heard a dry voice ask, 'May I help you . . . miss?'

The 'miss' was said almost with a sneer – as though the speaker was more used to saying 'madam' or 'Countess'.

Arianwyn looked up at the tall man framed in the doorway. He was dressed in a fine dark suit, his hands encased in pristine white gloves. He was looking down his long shiny nose at her, one eyebrow arched. 'Oh, hi,' Arianwyn said. 'I'm Arianwyn Gribble. I'd like to see Mrs Alverston, please . . . thank you.'

'And are you expected, *Miss* Gribble?' he sniffed.

'Not exactly, no.' Arianwyn fumbled with an explanation. Why was she really there, after all? 'I . . . have a parcel for Mrs Alverston,' she said, quickly holding out the small box of charms.

'Who is it, Lucas?' The unmistakable voice of Mrs Alverston sounded from somewhere beyond the door.

'A young witch, madam,' Lucas replied.

'Well then, do show her in, of course.'

Lucas stepped to one side and Arianwyn caught her first glimpse of the space beyond: a vast hallway with a gleaming black-and-white marble chequer-board floor. Mrs Alverston stood in the middle of the hall, as elegantly dressed as when she had visited the bookshop. She clutched a glossy magazine in one hand.

'Arianwyn – what on earth are you doing here?' she asked, moving forwards quickly. Then she seemed to think twice and purposefully slowed, smiled, and asked, 'How are you? What a pleasure to see you.'

Arianwyn stepped into the hallway and walked cautiously towards Mrs Alverston. 'I thought I should come to see you. I have to go back to Lull today.'

'So soon?' Mrs Alverston fiddled with the magazine. Arianwyn thought she looked tired. It was probably the worry about Gimma.

'And I'm sorry, but I've not been able to find out anything more. Nobody has seen Gimma. But I thought I should leave these charms for her for when she does come home or in case you hear from her.' Arianwyn offered the parcel to Mrs Alverston, who eyed it with a great deal of suspicion.

'That's very kind of you, but actually Gimma is back.' Mrs Alverston smiled a half-smile.

Arianwyn felt a lightness come over her then, a

relief. 'That's good. Is she here? Can I see her?'

Mrs Alverston's eyes flicked to Lucas and then back to Arianwyn. She slowly placed her magazine on the table that stood just behind her and held nothing but a huge vase of exotic flowers. 'Lucas, don't you have things to attend to elsewhere?' It didn't sound much like a question and Lucas responded by moving slowly across the hall and then disappeared through an archway, his echoing footsteps fading.

Arianwyn and Mrs Alverston were now quite alone in the vast hallway. And yet Arianwyn couldn't shake off the feeling that they were being watched. Perhaps it was just Lucas lurking behind a curtain or door somewhere. Mrs Alverston leant in close and said quietly and quickly, 'Gimma turned up yesterday, as it happens. It was all just a bit of a silly misunderstanding and everything is fine now. But . . . I . . .'

The feeling of relief was suddenly replaced with a stomach-wobbling sense of worry. 'But what?' Arianwyn asked softly.

Mrs Alverston's expression suddenly stiffened. She moved forward and placed an arm around Arianwyn's shoulders and gently but firmly turned her back towards the door, which was still wide open. They moved together quickly, Mrs Alverston chatting brightly as they went: 'You won't want to get caught in the morning traffic, Miss Gribble. It can be awfully horrid this time of day. My husband is always complaining about Kingsport traffic. What a lovely scarf you are wearing, wherever is it from? What a gorgeous shade of red!' Her fears and worries from a moment ago were apparently forgotten. She gave a high nervous laugh as they reached the door. 'Thank you, Miss Gribble, for all your assistance. I shall pass your best wishes on to Gimma when she comes down for breakfast, of course.'

'You're sure everything is all right, Mrs Alverston?' Arianwyn asked. She was quite certain something was not right at all.

Mrs Alverston gave another smaller laugh and blushed. 'Gimma is home now, and that's all I care about. Gimma is my only concern.' Her eyes widened a little now. She ushered Arianwyn through the open door, paused and looked down at the box in Arianwyn's hand. 'I'm not sure we will be in need of your . . . trinkets now.' She looked out to the taxi waiting by the kerb. 'I'll wish you a safe journey back to Lull.' The door swung shut.

Arianwyn walked slowly down the steps, slightly stunned. She had reached the pavement when she heard a noise off to her left. The squeaking of a gate. She turned, expecting to see a member of staff from the Alverston household emerging from the steps that no doubt led down to the kitchens and cellars. A pale face looked up at her. 'Arianwyn . . .'

'Gimma!'

Gimma didn't move any further forwards. Arianwyn couldn't see any signs of a charm around her neck — but perhaps it was just hidden under her clothes. Though if there was a charm, it was fading: Arianwyn was certain of it. She could feel the rough brush of dark magic and she knew this came from the hex that lurked within Gimma.

'Are you OK?' Arianwyn asked.

Gimma nodded slowly. But something in her eyes suggested fear. 'But stay there.'

'Oh, Gimma,' Arianwyn breathed as she fumbled with the package of charms. 'Where have you been?'

Gimma's too-dark eyes flicked to the front door, then away again. 'I ran away,' she said calmly. 'I thought it was the best thing to do. I thought it was best for everyone.'

Arianwyn knew that feeling. She had often thought of running away.

'Well, it's good that you came back,' Arianwyn said. 'We were all so worried about you.' She stepped forward to hand over the parcel of charms.

'I didn't want to come back, though . . . it was the Council of Elders that found me. Now I think I'm in more trouble than ever.' Her pale hand wrapped tightly around the black swirls of iron on the gate.

'You're not in any trouble, Gimma,' Arianwyn reassured her.

'Then why has the council sent someone to keep an eye on me then?' she asked.

'What?'

'There's an elder in the house right now, apparently for my own protection. I don't trust them any more. I don't trust anyone now . . . except for you, Arianwyn. What should I do?'

Arianwyn could feel her heart thudding in her chest, suspicions flying round in her head. 'Is it Elder Tully?' she asked softly.

'It's someone different each day,' Gimma said quietly, '. . . just like before.'

Arianwyn frowned. Of course. She remembered Gimma telling her how the witch that had wanted her to obtain the *Book of Quiet Glyphs* had worn a different face every time, using a dangerous glamour spell to change her identity. Whoever the traitor was, were they once again posing as several different members of the council?

For a second she thought about reaching out and grabbing Gimma's hand and saying, *Come back to Lull with me, you'll be safe there.*

But would she really be? She hadn't been safe there in the autumn, had she? The hex had spread through Gimma until she was almost lost entirely. At least this far away from the Great Wood and the worst of the spread – and now with Arianwyn's box of new charms – Gimma would be able to keep the hex at bay. And here she had her family to look after her: Arianwyn was sure of that, if nothing else.

It was her best chance.

Gimma looked as though she might cry. 'What if my parents are in danger as well because of me? Because of *this*?' Gimma pulled back the sleeve on her dress to reveal the thick ridges and swirls of hex that marked her skin – it looked almost as bad as the first time Arianwyn had seen it.

'You need to change your charm, Gimma,' she said, handing over the box at last, 'right now. And don't let them drain right down. They'll keep you and your family safe from the hex until we can work out something . . . more permanent. I'm trying, I promise.'

Gimma looked as though she were considering it all, working it all through. Eventually she nodded. 'OK.'

Arianwyn breathed a sigh of relief.

The taxi driver was still waiting by the side of the road, the engine rumbling gently. 'We'd best be on our way, miss, or you'll be too late for your train,' he called across.

'I have to go,' Arianwyn said to Gimma. 'I'll ask my grandmother to watch out for you. I'll write to her from the train, I promise.' She hurried back to the taxi and climbed into her seat.

As the taxi pulled away, she looked back at Gimma's pale face through the iron twists of the gate. She was holding the box of charms tightly to her chest. Then Arianwyn lifted her eyes to the Alverston house. She thought she saw the movement of a curtain in a high window, but she wasn't sure. And then the car was speeding away, heading for the central station in the heart of Kingsport.

Chapter 7
The 11.30 TO STANBURY HILL

'Tickets please! Any tickets for Little Felsham or Bunton Loxley?'

The train guard, a small wiry man with a grey moustache, wandered through the carriage glaring at people in a rather accusing manner that made Arianwyn instinctively reach for her tickets even though he had checked them twice already. She had been on the train since nine thirty and it was now nearly midday. And she still had most of the day ahead full of travel.

She heard the *snip-click* of the guard's ticket punch and she turned to the glyph notebook. A gift from Salle and Colin, the small leather notebook had the glyph of silence embossed on the front. Inside, she had started to record the other quiet glyphs she had discovered and notes on each of them. So far she only had three contained in its pages.

The first was the shadow glyph, a glyph she had known for as long as she could remember, a glyph she had once feared as a herald of trouble and darkness but which had ultimately saved her and Lull from a terrifying night ghast. The second was the glyph of silence, the last glyph retrieved from the original *Book of Quiet Glyphs* which was lost when the feyling city of Erraldur was overrun by dark spirit creatures.

But Estar, her feyling friend, had discovered that Arianwyn held all of the quiet glyphs within herself and so the slow process of discovery had begun. So far, she'd only managed to draw out one further glyph with Estar's help – a curling, twisty glyph that Estar had helped her to find, buried within herself – though using it was proving more than a little tricky, despite weeks of trying. The glyph remained a mystery. Slippery and fast like an eel.

She felt anxious about returning and continuing her work with Estar.

The process so far had been painfully slow. She'd tried to see more new glyphs too – but there was no way to force the process, Estar had said several times. He had been at her side throughout, helping, encouraging and occasionally pushing her. But it was no use: she wasn't making any progress at all.

'Useless!' she grumbled to herself, glaring at the

notebook before shoving it back into her satchel.

'Excuse me, but is anyone sitting here, please?'

Arianwyn looked up quickly at an elderly lady with a gentle, warm face and soft curling white hair. She was peering through silver-framed spectacles and clutched a small travelling bag tightly to her chest.

'No it's free,' Arianwyn replied. 'Help yourself.'

'Oh, I was certain I was going to have to stand all the way back,' the lady chatted as she settled into the seat and started to extract items from her bag: a bundle of knitting, three books, a thermos, a pack of playing cards and a cake tin. She smiled at Arianwyn and then said, 'You're a witch!'

Arianwyn nodded and smiled.

'Me too!' The other woman beamed, pulling aside her bright pink scarf and pointing at her own silver star, just like a newly qualified witch. 'Hettie Cummings. Pleasure to make your acquaintance.' She leant forwards, extending her hand.

'I'm Arianwyn Gribble.' Arianwyn shook the older witch's hand.

'So where are you off to? You're not from round here, are you? I've not seen you before. Mint imperial?' She had now plucked a small metal tin from her bag and was offering this to Arianwyn.

'Thank you.' Arianwyn reached for a sweet and quickly popped it into her mouth. Hettie did the same and Arianwyn assumed this would mean she wouldn't be chatting for a while but Hettie just continued with the sweet in her mouth, which made it slightly difficult to hear exactly what she was saying. 'So where did you say you were from?'

Arianwyn smiled. 'I'm from Kingsport—'

'Oh, Kingsport – fancy that!' Hettie cooed. 'I live in Stanbury Hill, have you been there?'

Arianwyn had a vague recollection of visiting there once on a school trip, or perhaps it had been one of the few holidays with her father.

Her father. The thought of him stuck in hospital suddenly made her feel terribly sad and worried again.

Hettie, oblivious, had continued to chatter away. 'It's my day off and I've just been to visit a friend of mine, Elder Colby, d'you know her?' Arianwyn shook her head. 'She lives in Bunton Loxley, next to the library on Merry Street, d'you know it? Not a patch on Stanbury Hill, of course.' As she spoke she took up her knitting needles and began to work, the needles going almost as fast as her talking. 'And my, but the wonderful shops we have in Stanbury Hill, I'd say they are better than some of the finest in Kingsport! Just look at this cardigan I picked up last week at the department store, Glostermans. It's a designer label, I'm certain of it.' As she spoke she tried to show Arianwyn the label in her cardigan without actually taking it off, so she looked like she was trying to fold herself up inside the woollen garment. 'D'you see?' she asked, her voice muffled by her own arm and several layers of wool.

'It's a lovely cardigan,' Arianwyn said. 'Looks very . . . cosy.'

Arianwyn tried to guess what it was Hettie was knitting and decided it was some sort of bed cover or possibly a jumper for an octopus. There seemed to be acres of it cascading over the older witch's lap and the floor of the train carriage.

'Where did you say you were going again?' Hettie asked.

'I'm on my way to Lull. That's where I'm stationed.'

'Lull? Lull? Lull?' Hettie said quickly, her brow knitted in concentration. 'Nope, never heard of it.' She smiled even wider than before. 'And are you spending the Yule holidays there?'

Arianwyn nodded.

'And will your parents be joining you?' Hettie asked.

Arianwyn looked out of the train window at the rushing-past world that seemed to be all river and fields and trees. 'My dad will be coming,' she said softly, 'but my mum, well – she died when I was little.'

The clicking knitting needles fell silent and Hettie blinked up at Arianwyn. 'I am sorry, my flower – that's terrible.' She reached forward and patted Arianwyn on the knee. 'Was she a witch as well?'

'Yes.' Arianwyn nodded, her throat unexpectedly tight.

'I've got two children, and neither one of them showed the slightest inclination towards being a witch. But my grandson, Jack – now, he is going to make a fine witch in a year or so.' The knitting doubled in speed for a few moments and Arianwyn thought Hettie had finally said all she wanted to say when she suddenly reached forwards again with the tin of mint imperials. 'Sweetie?' she asked.

And at that very moment Hettie lurched forwards in her seat and the tin of mint imperials flew from her hand, the sweets all falling into Arianwyn's lap as most of the passengers gave a gasp or cry of shock. She heard the screech of brakes as the train came to a dead stop.

'Crumbs, whatever do you suppose that was?' Hettie asked as she sat back in her seat.

Arianwyn turned and pressed her face to the glass of the window – hoping somehow to see past the long snaking curve of the train. She could see they had just pulled on to a bridge when they had stopped, so perhaps there was something wrong with the tracks on there.

'I'm sure it'll just be sheep or cows on the track, flower, nothing to worry about,' Hettie said warmly, scooping up the fallen mint imperials from Arian-wyn's seat and the floor.

Arianwyn settled back in her seat and pulled out

the notebook again, but nothing made sense, not the glyphs or her notes. She reached for the package of sandwiches her grandmother had given her and was just unwrapping them when there was a commotion in the doorway of the carriage. Two train guards, the moustached man and a younger man, stood having a rushed conversation. 'But I saw her in here earlier, Mr Andrews. I'm sure of it,' Arianwyn heard. They both scanned the carriage and when the younger guard saw Arianwyn his eyes lit up and he pointed with excitement and hissed excitedly, 'Yes! There she is, told you, Mr Andrews.' And he pointed straight at Hettie. 'She's the witch from Stanbury Hill.'

Every pair of eyes in the carriage turned to Hettie, who went almost as pink as her cardigan.

The train guards moved over to stand beside Hettie. She folded her knitting in her lap and looked up at them both. 'Can I help you gentlemen?'

'Could you come along with us please, Mrs . . . er?'

'Cummings, flower. Hettie Cummings.' She smiled.

'Mrs Cummings, would you come with us please?' the moustached train guard said in a loud and officious voice.

Arianwyn stood up; she was just a bit taller than the train guard, which made him stop and give her a second glance. 'What's going on?' she asked. 'What do you want with Mrs Cummings? She hasn't done anything wrong.'

'I never said she had!' the train guard barked. 'Now please take your seat . . .' He fell silent as his eyes caught on Arianwyn's silver star badge. He nudged the younger man whose eyes widened at once. 'On second thoughts,' he said, pointing at Arianwyn, 'you'd best come with us as well. You can leave your bits and pieces here.' And with that he marched out of the carriage.

Hettie gave Arianwyn a questioning look as they followed the two guards.

The next carriage was filled with more people who stared curiously at Arianwyn and Hettie as they hurried through after the train guards. The carriage beyond that one was the buffet car, where a few people looked up from their lunches as the party dashed on. Finally they found themselves in what seemed to be the mail car, full of sacks and piles of parcels all neatly tied with string and sat in boxes and crates. There was also luggage stowed overhead and piled by the door. The guards stopped and turned to look at Hettie and Arianwyn. 'You are both witches, yes?' the moustached guard, Mr Andrews, asked.

'Yes,' they replied in unison.

The younger guard took the opportunity to speak now in a hurry, his face bright red. He was clearly thrilled that his day-to-day job of being a train guard had suddenly taken on a very new and exciting element. 'There's something odd on the bridge and we don't know what it is or if it's safe to continue—'

'Yes, thank you, Marcel!' Mr Andrews snapped. 'This might well be confidential information you are divulging, I suppose you are aware of that?'

Marcel blushed and mumbled an apology. 'Sorry, Mr Andrews.'

Mr Andrews continued the story. 'As Marcel has said, we need someone to check what it is and if it's safe to continue – the driver has stopped until someone *qualified* can make that decision.'

'Us?' Arianwyn asked.

Mr Andrews nodded. 'You are the only witches on board.' He didn't sound entirely thrilled about that.

'Well, come on then, flower, let the dog see the rabbit and all that!' Hettie smiled and winked at Arianwyn.

A few moments later, having clambered rather inelegantly out of the mail car, Arianwyn and Hettie were following the two guards once more as they walked very carefully between the engine – which was still steaming and hissing – and the low wall of the bridge. A light drizzle was falling, but aside from that the view was quite stunning. A fast-flowing river rushed far below the arches of the bridge while the banks either side were covered in thick pine forest. The sky was grey and stormy.

As they cleared the engine they could see ahead for the first time: the tracks going straight on and on.

But about a hundred metres ahead of the engine, suspended over the tracks, hovered a shimmering, fizzing mass of magic.

A sudden strange feeling came over Arianwyn's knees. She reached out to steady herself on the side of the bridge.

It was a pocket of magic, that was clear. And it wasn't that unusual. But it was strange that it was visible – and not just to Arianwyn and Hettie, but clearly to Marcel and Mr Andrews as well.

It fizzed and popped, and the air crackled around them all.

'Do you know what that is?' Mr Andrews asked, pointing at it.

Arianwyn looked at Hettie, who nodded and swallowed hard. She had sensed it too.

'Well?' Mr Andrews asked.

'It's a pocket of magic – a seam of magical energy,' Arianwyn said slowly. She paused as her senses now picked up something else, something different, something that surrounded the magic, combined with it . . . no . . .

Polluted it.

Chapter 8
WHAT AN AFTERNOON

Somehow, the seam of magic had become entangled with hex. 'Wait here!' Arianwyn warned the two guards. She began to walk forwards, stepping carefully over each thick, wooden railway sleeper.

The seam of magic flickered and flapped in the air like a loose hair ribbon or a scarf caught in a breeze. Its magical energy seemed to roll towards her in waves, tickling against her skin. The other sensation, the hex, was rough and urgent and was trying to drown the pure pulse of natural magic. It was like hearing two different pieces of music playing at the same time.

'What's happened to it?' asked Hettie. 'Is that seam of magic infected with *hex*?'

'That's what it looks like.' Arianwyn paused and sniffed the air, her nose full of the rancid reek of dark magic.

'Oh dear,' Hettie sighed beside her. 'What do we do now?' She stuffed her hands deep into the pockets of her pink cardigan and puffed out her cheeks, making a sound a bit like a horse.

'D'you need any help, miss?' Marcel called from his position near the engine.

'No, it's . . . fine,' Arianwyn lied, her voice clear and bright to mask the untruth. She caught the look Hettie gave her. 'We don't need to frighten them,' she added quietly.

'Right-o,' Hettie agreed, though she looked terrified herself.

Arianwyn carried on forwards, but slower this time – trying to piece it all together: what she could see, what her senses were telling her. She heard Hettie following behind her, muttering to herself about glyphs and what sounded like a recipe for beef stew. What would it mean if hex was now infecting natural magic? She had never heard of anything like this before. Her palms were sweaty with fear, even in the cool drizzle.

'What would have happened if we'd just gone through that on the train?' Hettie asked, knotting her hands together.

'Well, you know, normally nothing, since nobody would have noticed unless they were a witch. But if this seam of magic truly has been infected by the hex then who knows what might have happened,' Arianwyn said.

She peered over the edge of the bridge at the tree-covered hills and the river rushing past far below, searching for answers. She looked up next at the grey sky and finally back to the seam of magic, which had now turned from purple to a bright green. Little flecks of bright light flashed from it and then tumbled across the ground like blossom gusted by a spring breeze.

A breeze!

That was just what they needed!

Wind could move the seam of magic away.

'Any thoughts, ladies?' Mr Andrews had come up behind them and stood on the tracks surveying the view before them, his eyes wide in wonder and fear.

'We need to move it,' Arianwyn said.

Pretending to be more confident than she felt, she turned towards the seam of magic. Everything on the far side of the bridge was viewed through its flickering green light, like it was underwater. She heard Hettie's crunching footsteps behind her. 'OK,' Arianwyn said. 'So we need to summon Briå together and use it to move the seam from the bridge.'

She wasn't sure why *she* had taken charge of the situation – but despite being the senior witch, Hettie didn't seem to be coming up with any ideas.

'Ready?' Arianwyn asked and after a nod from Hettie she raised a shaking hand and began to sketch the air glyph into the gap of open air between herself and the seam of magic.

As Arianwyn and Hettie finished the quick sketch of the glyph together, the seam flashed, more sparks of energy flying all around.

It was now or never. Arianwyn moved her hands and at once felt the breath of a faint breeze on her skin. A magical breeze whispered across her face, moving her hair. The two witches twisted their hands in unison, the spelled breeze increasing at their command. The seam of magic rippled like a snake moving through water. And that's when Arianwyn realized her mistake: the glyph was pulling on the nearest seam of magic to create the spell. And the nearest seam of magic was, of course, the one immediately in front of them, riddled with hex.

Instead of moving west off the bridge and out over the river, the seam of magic fluctuated, as though it was shaking something off. Then it began to move straight towards Arianwyn and Hettie, flickering and fluttering.

'Snotlings!' Arianwyn muttered as she stumbled back.

'Er – is it meant to be doing that?' Mr Andrews shouted. 'LOOK OUT!' But in their rush to move away, Arianwyn and Hettie collided and Arianwyn tripped and fell against the hard metal of the railway track. She threw out her hands to save herself, the grit and stones scraping at her palms. Hettie had fallen back against the wall of the bridge and sat there panting, her eyes fixed on the seam of magic, which was moving quickly towards them . . . and then past them, and on towards the train!

'No!' Arianwyn cried as she scrabbled to her feet.

'What do we do?' Hettie called, following Arianwyn, a little slower, as she hurried after the seam of magic.

Marcel and Mr Andrews dived clear as the seam picked up speed, hurtling towards the gleaming blue and gold engine. Arianwyn watched in horror as the seam was swallowed up by the train. There was a loud hiss, and seconds later billows of bright green steam pumped out of the engine's chimney along with a burst of bright, fizzing sparks that crackled in the air.

Then everything fell silent.

Was that it? Arianwyn glanced at Hettie, who began to smile in relief, certain of their success. But a few moments later a shrill scream broke the silence. It was coming from one of the carriages.

They raced back and climbed quickly into the train the way they had come, back into the mail car, but its tidy stacks of parcels, letters and luggage were a distant memory. Everything had toppled over and lay scattered across the floor. Some of the trunks and cases were bulging, before exploding open, ejecting their contents into the carriage like strange seed heads going pop!

'Oh, jinxing-jiggery!' Arianwyn groaned as letters swirled around her like a paper blizzard.

There was another cry followed by a shout followed by a scream in one of the other carriages, and without thinking Arianwyn scrambled over the tumble of trunks and hurried through the door into the dining car.

She ducked just in time as a plate smashed into the carriage wall beside her. People watched in surprised silence as a finely dressed woman wrestled with a tablecloth on the floor of the dining car. Worryingly, the tablecloth appeared to be winning. Arianwyn dodged another two side plates and a spinning fork and hurried forwards. She summoned a stunning orb and hurled it straight at the possessed tablecloth. There was a soft *thwump* and the woman who had been so valiantly wrestling with it gave a small cry of shock and delight when it gave up the fight and slipped to the floor, an ordinary tablecloth once again and nothing more.

'Oh, thank you!' the lady cried, stamping on the twist of fabric for good measure.

But just as Arianwyn thought she was making progress a chorus of cries came from beyond the next door.

The next carriage was in even more disarray. But now that the seam of magic was in sight, hovering in the middle of the carriage, the passengers backed up to the walls, keeping as much space between themselves and the magic as they could. But the seam wasn't moving now; it had come to a stop.

'Quickly,' Arianwyn said, turning to Mr Andrews. 'We need to get the train across the bridge as soon as possible.'

He gaped at her, unsure.

'Hurry!' she said.

There was no sense in trying to move the seam again, as that had clearly made things worse. But she hoped now that the seam would stay put as the train moved on and cleared the bridge. There was a sudden *click-pop* sound as a case burst open and a whirlwind of socks, shirts and underwear filled the carriage like a blizzard, making it impossible to see. Arianwyn didn't dare try to stun the luggage in fear of hitting a fellow passenger. 'Open a window, quickly – anybody!'

She heard the slide of a wooden frame and then the clothes were suddenly funnelling out through the open window and across the bridge, lost to the world.

As the last sock vanished the carriage suddenly lurched, once, twice, and then she could see out through the window that the train was indeed moving at last.

Everyone held their breath and watched as the seam of magic slipped slowly through the end of the carriage and back outside. It shifted just above the train tracks for a few moments and then it twisted, tumbled in the air and rolled out over the bridge and into the open air above the river. The train moved off over the other side of the bridge and then Arianwyn could see nothing more.

'I'd better let the stationmaster at Bunton Loxley know about all of this,' Mr Andrews said, straightening his tie and jacket.

'Can you ask him to notify the C.W.A. as well, please?' Arianwyn asked as she rested against the carriage wall.

Mr Andrews nodded as the train gathered speed.

The passengers gave a collective sigh of relief and excited chatter and nervous laughter filled the carriage. Arianwyn flopped down into a seat beside Hettie just as the final suitcase popped open, showering everyone with a selection of fine dresses, hats and various silk underclothes.

'What an afternoon!' Arianwyn sighed.

'Sweetie?' Hettie asked, offering the tin of mint imperials once again.

Êmparris – *The Glyph of Silence*

Êmparris is the feyling word that
means silence – or more specifically to
sink into or be surrounded by silence.
The glyph generally produces a small
spell sphere that appears translucent
to the point of being nearly invisible.
It is easy to increase the size of the
sphere and it is the spell orb that
either absorbs all the sounds near to
it, or – if you are inside the sphere –
stops any sound from travelling
outside of it.

The spell sphere can travel through
physical objects such as walls and
floors and does not appear to have any
influence or damaging effects on these
or electrical equipment.

THE NEW BOOK OF QUIET GLYPHS BY ARIANWYN GRIBBLE

Chapter 9
CINNAMON MUFFINS

*I*t was dark when Arianwyn finally reached Lull, and the rain was falling heavier than ever. She had transferred from the train to Beryl, Lull's town bus, for the last hour or so of the journey.

Mr Thorn kindly drove her straight to the door of the Spellorium and then helped her inside with her luggage, even though there really wasn't that much of it. 'Nice to have you back again, miss. How's our Salle getting along in the big city?' Mr Thorn asked, his little white moustache wobbling as he spoke, his cheeks bright from the cold night air.

'She's really well, Mr Thorn, and the play is fantastic,' Arianwyn said as she bent to scoop up a pile of slightly damp letters and notes from the doormat.

'Well, I'd best be off. Mrs Thorn'll be waiting

up. Goodnight, Miss Gribble. Good to have you back.' Mr Thorn waved as he headed out of the Spellorium. The door closed behind him, the bell charms ringing gently as they tapped against the window.

Arianwyn leafed through the papers from the doormat. She recognized the bold handwriting of the mayor's secretary, Miss Prynce: a list of jobs she would need to attend to after being away. And there was a note from Estar too: his strange handwriting filling a small square of paper.

My dear friend,

I hope your father is well and you are home safe and sound. I have decided to go back to Edda for a while to help with things there. I'll be back soon so we can continue working on the quiet glyphs, though.

Your friend, Estar

Edda was the ancient place the feylings used in times of trouble, an old village in the Great Wood they had fled to after the loss of their city, Erraldur. Arianwyn felt a moment of guilty relief knowing she wouldn't be working on the quiet glyphs until Estar returned – but this was quickly followed by sadness. She already missed Salle, Grandmother, Colin and her dad so much and now Estar had returned to Edda. She felt selfish and silly, but wished the days would hurry past until Yule and they would all be together again.

She flicked on the Spellorium lights. Everything was just as it had been when she left a few days ago. She sighed as she heard the church bells ring out midnight. She was tempted to collect Bob, her moon hare, from the Blue Ox – just so she wouldn't be alone. But it was too late and everyone would already be tucked up in bed, fast asleep. She stifled another yawn and headed for the stairs and the small apartment and her own bed.

The next morning Arianwyn woke to the sound of rain pattering against the windows of the apartment. Usually, there was something comforting and cosy about the sound of the rain when she was snuggled up under the covers. But she knew it had been raining pretty much since she had left just under a week ago. This wasn't good news. She glanced at the stack of notes on the small table beside her bed. For a town that had coped for years without a witch, they had quickly become dependent on her in the not-quite-a-year she had been living in Lull. But her first duty really should be to deal with moving the qered herd from the meadow to somewhere safer and drier.

They had obviously grown attached to Lull, she

thought, or they would have already gone off some-where else. They must feel safe. That at least gave her a feeling of hope.

There was also the need to officially report the encounter with the seam of magic and hex. She had written down as much as she could remember of the details ready to complete a report and call the C.W.A. as soon as the offices opened at nine o'clock.

'Well, I can't lie here all day,' she mumbled to herself, throwing the eiderdown and blankets off. She jumped out of bed and padded quickly across the cool floorboards towards the bathroom.

A few minutes later she emerged, washed and dressed. She was rummaging through the wardrobe in search of her standard issue rain mac when she heard a gentle tap on the door downstairs followed by the unmistakably musical voice of Aunt Grace. 'Hello? Wyn, are you there?'

Hurrying down the twisting metal staircase and into the Spellorium, she saw Salle's Aunt Grace framed in the window of the door, her umbrella partly hiding her face which broke into a broad welcoming smile as she saw Arianwyn. It made her even more beautiful than she was already. Arianwyn smiled back as she raced to open the door. At once Bob scampered into the Spellorium and dashed around Arianwyn's legs in fast tight circles, making small yipping sounds of excitement. 'It's not too early, is it?' Aunt Grace said as she stepped inside. 'I was worried I'd wake you up … Oh, are you on your way out?' she asked, seeing Arianwyn was already wrapped up for the wet morning.

'I was just coming to see you,' Arianwyn said with a smile.

Aunt Grace carried a small woven basket over one arm; a red-and-white checked cloth covered the contents, but Arianwyn could already smell the delicious wafting aroma of cinnamon. Aunt Grace's famous breakfast muffins! 'I knew you'd be hungry!' Aunt Grace smiled as she walked to the counter and placed the basket there. Then she turned and pulled Arianwyn into a quick, tight hug. 'How was Salle?' she asked.

'Wonderful,' Arianwyn replied. 'She's having the best time and the play is amazing.' She beamed and dug into the basket of muffins.

'And how is your father?'

'He's fine,' Arianwyn said quickly. 'He'll be coming for Yule.' She started to pull a fluffy piece of muffin free, her stomach rumbling hungrily.

'Well, I can't wait to meet him,' Aunt Grace replied. 'Bob has certainly missed you.' She looked down at Bob, who had now curled up on top of Arianwyn's feet and fallen fast asleep. 'Though there's been some rather odd behaviour.'

'Odd? How?' Arianwyn asked, gazing down at the moon hare. Was Bob sick?

'Oh, probably just something and nothing. But

every time we've been for a walk Bob seems to want to go off into the Great Wood. I was worried we might have to get a lead.'

Arianwyn leant forward and let her fingers rub the length of Bob's silky white ears, one after the other. Bob opened a single bright blue eye and gazed up at her. 'You don't want to run away, do you, Bob?' she asked as the moon hare started to wash its feet. It looked at her as though she was quite stupid.

'Well, I'd better let you get on with your work. Why don't you come across for some dinner later?' Aunt Grace called as she headed back out into Kettle Lane. 'Cheerio!'

'Bye!' Arianwyn called and turned back to the counter and the pile of notes from Miss Prynce. 'Right-o then, Bob, let's see what we've got to deal with here and then we'd best go and look at the qered.' Arianwyn rifled through the papers as she bit down into the warm cinnamon breakfast muffin.

As she passed through the South Gate a short while later, Arianwyn was amazed to see how the meadow between Lull and the Great Wood had been transformed by the continuous rain.

Instead of the open space of dry brown grasses that had been there when she left, it now looked like a huge puddle. The expanse of water mirrored the grey clouds that hung over Lull. Across the water, where the land sloped upwards a little towards the edge of the Great Wood, the herd of qered moved about. They were huge horse-like spirit creatures with long flowing manes and tails. One of the young qered moved towards the water but gave a loud snort and then trotted quickly away, its head shaking this way and that. Trapped between the water and the wood, there was not much meadow left for the qered, whose numbers had increased again, it seemed. Arianwyn counted at least ten now.

'They really don't like the water, do they?' Arianwyn said to Bob, who simply sneezed in agreement and huddled closer to her legs to stay under the cover of her umbrella.

'I had thought they might have just returned to the Great Wood.'

Arianwyn jumped, hearing the mayor's voice behind her. 'Oh, hello, Mayor Belcher,' she said, turning.

The mayor stood under his own umbrella, swathed in a purple rain mac, proudly wearing his mayoral sash and medal over it all, of course. 'Welcome home, Arianwyn,' he said. 'Thank you for returning so quickly. Though I'd expected you back earlier yesterday. I gather the return journey was quite interesting?'

Arianwyn nodded.

'And now you are back, we have lots and lots to

do.' He gestured to the qered. 'What do you suggest for moving them?'

Arianwyn truthfully had no idea. She scratched at her curls and looked back across the meadow at the qered. There were more younglings now; at least half the herd were babies. She hoped if one moved, the others would simply follow.

'Exactly where are we going to move them to?' she asked the mayor.

'Ah, well – Farmer Eames has kindly offered to house them for as long as is needed on his farm. The land to the west is slightly higher there and hasn't been affected by the flooding.'

Bridge Farm was not only the other side of Lull but the other side of the river. So the only way to get the qered there was to take them right through the very centre of the town. This was not going to be as easy as anyone had thought.

Chapter 10
RELOCATION

'*G*etting the qered to follow me is going to be half the battle, but they're really not going to like going through town either,' Arianwyn explained to Mayor Belcher as they stood watching the spirit creatures across the meadow. 'They're not as shy of humans as they were when they first came to Lull, but even so they won't be used to large crowds of people, motorcars, buildings . . .'

'Can't we get Mrs Johansson, the vet, to knock them out and move them that way, in the back of a trailer or lorry?'

Arianwyn turned and glared at the mayor. 'Absolutely not, Mayor Belcher. They're spirit creatures and they have to be treated with respect.' She couldn't believe he had even suggested it. 'What we need is something to tempt them away from the meadow . . .' She pulled out her copy of *A Witch Alone: A Manual for the Newly Qualified Witch*, and searched through the creature glossary, hoping it might yield something that would help.

'You mean like food, perhaps?' Mayor Belcher asked.

'Precisely!' Arianwyn said, finding the entry on the qered. 'I think we need to go and pay a visit to the greengrocer, Mayor Belcher.'

A short while later they stood with two large baskets of fresh fruits and vegetables from the greengrocer's: apples, oranges and lemons from Grunnea, bunches of fresh celeric, brambleberries and huge onions.

'Please explain what we are doing, Arianwyn,' Mayor Belcher grumbled.

'Qered are herbivores, so this yummy food might be able to tempt them away from the meadow, through the town and on to Bridge Farm. They've probably been living off mushy meadow grass for the last couple of weeks. This should look lovely to them . . . I hope.'

'That'll be half a crown please, Mayor Belcher,' Mr Gumby the greengrocer said with a smile.

'That seems awfully expensive to me,' the mayor complained, struggling to extract his wallet from under his purple rain mac.

'Well, our deliveries have been patchy due to the bad weather. Had to put prices up, I'm afraid.' Mr Gumby blushed a little and smiled at Arianwyn.

Once they had paid for the fruit and vegetables they made their way back to the meadow.

'I'll go and start to tempt them towards the South Gate,' Arianwyn explained. 'I'll need you to try and keep the path through Lull calm and quiet.'

'Calm and quiet. Yes, of course,' the mayor said. He placed his basket by the South Gate and hurried back into town, calling over his shoulder, 'I'll get Constable Perkins on to it at once!'

Arianwyn waded across the flooded meadow, the water sloshing around her ankles, the squelchy grass and mud churning slightly under her boots. Bob bounded beside her, unbothered by the water. The qered watched her approach but didn't move or dash away as she feared they might.

'Hello,' Arianwyn said calmly as she waded out of the water and on to the slightly higher and drier ground at the edge of the Great Wood.

She reached into the basket over her arm and offered the nearest qered to her a large juicy-looking apple. 'Would you like one of these?' She reached out her hand until her arm was stretched out straight and just a few centimetres from the qered's huge scaled nose. She saw its nostrils flare out as it sniffed at the apple. Then it gently brought its head down and took the apple between its huge teeth.

She expected that to be followed by a crunching sound as it devoured the fruit, but the huge spirit creature turned and offered the fruit to one of the younger qered that waited nearby. The youngling munched into the apple at once.

'So far so good!' Arianwyn said to Bob, who was eyeing a brambleberry very carefully.

The larger qered tuned back to Arianwyn, its eyes blinking. It seemed to be asking, 'What next?'

Slowly, Arianwyn picked up another apple and offered this. The qered took it and offered it to the other youngling that had come forward and was watching Arianwyn curiously. 'I'm here to help you,' she said. 'But you need to follow me out of the meadow.'

The adult qered turned back again, and this time Arianwyn lifted the basket over her arm and took a few careful steps backwards. Then waited.

The larger qered turned and looked at the whole herd, then took a few careful steps forwards, towards Arianwyn and the food.

This just might work! she thought.

A few minutes later, Arianwyn was standing right in the middle of the huge puddle. The larger adult qered had followed her, but the rest of the herd waited on the higher ground, close to the edge of the Great Wood. Was she really going to have to tempt them across the town one by one? That would take for ever!

'How are you getting on, Miss Gribble?' Mayor Belcher's shout fractured the peace in the meadow.

Arianwyn winced, praying this wouldn't startle the qered, but it seemed unbothered by the noise and continued watching the basket of fruit and vegetables. So far it had eaten one apple and a large crunchy onion. And it had happily followed Arianwyn this far.

She turned quickly and held a finger to her lips. The mayor waved back and waited beside the gate.

'Come on then, let's get out of this puddle, shall we?' Arianwyn said and started to back away again, a little quicker this time, a stick of celeric held in her hand.

But the qered didn't move.

'Oh, come on,' Arianwyn said, shaking the stick of celeric as though that might make it more enticing.

But the qered only turned and looked back across the flooded meadow at the others.

Arianwyn wasn't sure what to do next. She was just about to get another apple from her basket (perhaps they were its favourite?) when the qered gave a loud call. Its deep resonating cry echoed back in a higher pitch by the others. The call seemed to fill every molecule of space around the meadow. It reverberated off the high walls of Lull. It was beautiful and strange.

Then the herd started to move slowly across the meadow, into the water and towards Arianwyn. 'Oh, yeees!' Arianwyn said just as the lead qered turned and snaffled the celeric stick out of her hand.

They kept up this strange, slow-moving procession until all the qered were across the meadow and heading along Meadow Street.

Constable Perkins was further along the street, quietly ushering people to stand back as the qered approached. People watched in fascination as Arianwyn tempted the leading qered with her basket of fruit – now replaced by the second basket the mayor had left at the gates – and every now and then it would stop and call to the others who would then trot along to catch up. At which point it would share out the offerings from Arianwyn before they could move on again.

Arianwyn had started to move further each time before she offered the fruit in the hope of speeding up the process, and it seemed to be working, sort of. She caught sight of the curious gazes of townspeople as she moved further along Meadow Street, heard the hushed questions and occasionally Mayor Belcher's quiet reassurance that 'Miss Gribble has everything under control!'

However as they emerged into the town square things took a turn for the worse. It was market day and the square was all bustle and noise. Arianwyn could see Constable Perkins and Mayor Belcher hurrying about attempting to shush everyone and convince them not to panic or make too much noise and startle the qered.

A strange silence fell across the square as Arianwyn approached. People froze like statues as she coaxed the qered carefully and slowly through the market. The spirit creatures seemed very interested in the market stalls, especially when they passed one loaded with fruit and vegetables. The younger qered snapped up several apples as they passed, Arianwyn offering apologetic looks to the terrified stallholder as they moved away.

As they reached the far side of the market square, just beside the Blue Ox, a car rumbled around the corner. There was a loud bang as the engine backfired.

Arianwyn jumped, fruit and vegetables spilling from her basket.

The qered called frantically, searching about for each other.

And then they bolted.

Arianwyn tumbled to one side as the larger adult qered charged past her, swiftly followed by the others.

They raced along North Gate Street as townspeople shrieked and jumped out of their way. She heard worried cries and frantic screams. A screech of brakes and something that sounded like rubbish bins tumbling over the cobbles.

'Jinxing-jiggery!' Arianwyn spat as Bob made the best of the opportunity to gobble up the tumbled brambleberries.

Mayor Belcher and Constable Perkins hurried over and helped Arianwyn to her feet. Snatching up the basket and some of the fallen fruit, Arianwyn raced along the street and out through the North Gate.

The qered waited anxiously the other side of the gate, near the few houses that stood outside the walls of the town. Two children stood amazed, staring up at them. Thank goodness they'd run in the right direction, Arianwyn thought.

'Well, at least they didn't go far,' Constable Perkins said as they hurried across the bridge.

As Arianwyn approached them, the larger adult qered turned and blinked at her. Then gave a bright cheerful call. It was different from the sounds from before: lighter, happier. She felt the rush of magic brush against her skin, and for a fleeting moment she knew for certain that the qered knew she was trying to help and that they would follow her wherever she wished to take them.

'Come on then, let's get you to Farmer Eames,' Arianwyn said as she started to lead the qered slowly along Old Town Road and away from Lull.

By the time Arianwyn returned to the Spellorium it was well after lunch. She was soaked through, as was

Bob, and hungry again. As they neared the Spellorium they saw Miss Delafield's bright green car parked outside. Her supervisor, who lived nearby in Flaxsham, leant against the bonnet, fiddling with her driving gloves.

'Oh, Miss Delafield. I wasn't expecting you today . . . was I?'

Miss Delafield looked a little startled, then crestfallen and said, 'Yes, dear. I'm here for your annual inspection!'

'Today?' Arianwyn gasped. Through the window in the door she could see the pile of disorganized notes on the counter, and the dusty shelves. A number of unopened delivery boxes were stacked near the small storeroom door.

'Yes, sorry, I thought I'd told you about it when we spoke, dear.'

If she had, Arianwyn couldn't remember.

'Is it not a good time, shall I come back another day?' Miss Delafield asked.

'Oh no,' Arianwyn said, unlocking the door. 'Go bananas! Give me five minutes to get changed and then I'll put the kettle on!'

'Smashing!' Miss Delafield smiled. 'That's the spirit!'

An hour later, Arianwyn was dry and dressed in a clean uniform and anxiously sorting through her pile of notes on the counter, updating the Spellorium's ledger as Miss Delafield wandered about with a clipboard. Every now and then she would mumble quietly to herself and quickly scribble something down before moving on again.

Arianwyn didn't think the mumbling or scribbling sounded very positive. Even so she had been chatting on merrily, hoping to keep Miss Delafield distracted from the slight sense of turmoil in the Spellorium. 'And then the seam of magic just wafted out across the bridge at last and the train moved off. I wrote it all down here, Miss Delafield.'

But Miss Delafield didn't reply. She seemed entirely focused on a large chunk of amber on the shelf in front of her. 'Miss Delafield?' Arianwyn called gently.

Her supervisor gave a little jump, her eyes fluttering as though she had just awoken from a dream. 'Did you say something, dear?'

'Are you OK? You seem a little . . . distracted.'

Miss Delafield gave a deep sigh. 'Truth be told, dear, no. I'm not OK in the least.' She dropped the clipboard on to the shelf she was examining.

Arianwyn moved around the counter and towards Miss Delafield. 'What's the matter? Are you unwell? Why don't you come and sit down here?' Arianwyn gestured at the little chair beside the pot-bellied stove. Without waiting for a reply she led Miss Delafield towards it.

'Oh, heavens, dear, I'm honestly in tip-top condition, healthwise.'

'But then, what is it?' Arianwyn asked. 'You're worrying me.' She didn't let go of Miss Delafield's hand and now she gripped it tighter.

'Well, you see, dear.' Miss Delafield took a deep breath. 'I heard from the C.W.A. And . . . I'm being reassigned.' She said it as though it was just an everyday sort of thing. Nothing important at all. 'I'll be leaving Flaxsham within the next week or so.'

Now it was Arianwyn who had to sit down.

Chapter 11
YULE PREPARATIONS

'You're leaving?' Arianwyn gasped. 'But you can't leave, Miss Delafield.' Arianwyn gripped her supervisor's hand ever tighter, as a wave of worry and fear crashed against her.

What would she do without Miss Delafield? She could feel tears in her eyes and saw the watery shimmer in Miss Delafield's too. 'Well, what can I tell you, dear? I most certainly am leaving. I've been reposted and that's that.' She sniffed and looked away.

'But how? Why? Who would do this?' Arianwyn asked, one question tumbling into the next like stones rolling down a hill.

Miss Delafield reached into her satchel and pulled out a crumpled letter. 'This arrived two days ago. From the Director of the C.W.A. Though it's the

Council of Elders' work, I'm sure of it.' Miss Delafield was suddenly on her feet and marching across the Spellorium. 'They've wanted rid of me for a while and now they can see that by forcing me into a new district I'll just resign or throw in the towel because of that.'

'But you can't really think that?' Arianwyn gaped. She felt suddenly uncomfortable, as though something was squeezing her. What if this was connected to the hex and Gimma somehow? It felt like whoever it was, her unknown enemy was trying to weaken her and her friends by pulling them apart. 'You have to speak to my grandmother. Perhaps she can help somehow?' she suggested.

But Miss Delafield only shook her head. 'I don't think it will do any good, dear.'

'But you aren't just going to give up?' That didn't sound like the Miss Delafield Arianwyn had come to know, respect and even love.

'Of course not, dear,' Miss Delafield said, spinning round quickly. 'What a strange notion!' Her cheeks displayed two perfect pink circles like a china doll. 'But I can't outright refuse – where would that put us?' She folded her arms over her chest and fixed Arianwyn with a stare of such determination it made her look away briefly. 'I'll fight this every inch of the way – of that you can be sure – but I'm not going to turn my back on my duty as a witch.' She paused, taking a deep breath and straightening her back.

'Honour the magic, serve the kingdom, honour the King, serve the magic. That is our solemn duty, dear.'

'But—'

'Our *solemn* and sacred duty,' Miss Delafield added carefully. There was no arguing, that much was clear.

'And where is it they're posting you to?' Arianwyn asked.

'Handley Boscom, on the east coast somewhere. Hagley Bottom, we used to call it!' Miss Delafield laughed.

'And . . . who will replace you as district supervisor?' Arianwyn asked, suddenly unsure now was the time to ask that question.

'Oh, I have no idea. You can bet it will be someone well in with the council clan, though. Oh, of course I don't include your grandmother in that,' Miss Delafield added quickly.

The Spellorium fell silent. Arianwyn looked at Miss Delafield, and Miss Delafield looked at Arianwyn. 'Perhaps it *is* time to think about moving on to something new,' Miss Delafield said quietly, staring out of the window into Kettle Lane. 'I've probably been here too long because of Effie . . .'

Her sister! thought Arianwyn. Effie had been the witch in Lull many years ago, the last before herself. 'I'll miss you,' she said, even though what she really wanted to do was to throw her arms around Miss Delafield and never let go.

'Anyway, dear, enough of all this gloom and

doom. We still have Yule to look forward to, if nothing else.'

'Perhaps Mayor Belcher will say something to the council for you, I mean about you leaving . . . or not leaving.'

'That's very good of you, dear, but I will not hold my breath – the mayor and I have hardly ever seen eye to eye.'

Arianwyn gasped. 'Oh, I forgot! I have to go and see Mayor Belcher about some Yule *festival* or something. I'm sorry . . . do you mind if I dash out for a while?'

'Don't let me keep you then, dear. They take Yule very seriously here in Lull, mark my words!'

'But what about the inspection?' Arianwyn asked.

Miss Delafield crossed back to where she had abandoned her clipboard and quickly ticked all the boxes on the form, signing it at the bottom. 'There,' she said, smiling triumphantly. 'That should see the C.W.A. off your back for a while.'

'Oh, Miss Gribble, there you are!' Miss Prynce scuttled around her desk as Arianwyn entered the town hall. 'Mayor Belcher has been expecting you for a while now.' She pursed her lips and stared at Arianwyn.

'Sorry. I was trying to catch up on the jobs you

recorded for me and then Miss Delafield came for—'

'I haven't really got time for chit-chat. Some of us have work to do. The mayor is waiting for you in his parlour.' Miss Prynce pointed up the huge staircase and then went back behind her desk and rifled through the papers and folders that permanently cluttered it.

Arianwyn smiled and hurried up the stairs. The door to the mayor's parlour was ajar and she could see Mayor Belcher framed by the windows that looked down into the town square. Arianwyn knocked gently and stepped inside. 'I'm sorry I'm late, Mayor Belcher,' she said.

The mayor turned and beamed broadly at her. 'Ah, Miss Gribble. Recovered from this morning's escapade, I trust?'

'Just about! Mayor Belcher, have you heard that Miss Delafield is being—'

'Relocated? Yes, I had heard from friends in Flaxsham.' The mayor walked back to his desk and flicked through a blue card folder.

'Well . . . is there anything you can do to . . . stop it?' Arianwyn asked.

The mayor sighed. 'I'm afraid as Miss Delafield is stationed in Flaxsham it is quite outside of my juris-diction, as Mayor of Lull.' Arianwyn was about to protest further when he added quietly, 'However, I have written several letters making my displeasure clear to those who have made this erroneous decision.' He must have noticed the surprised look on Arianwyn's face, for he added, 'We are as fond of Miss Delafield as you are, I can assure you, Miss Gribble.'

'Thank you, Mayor Belcher,' Arianwyn said, suddenly ashamed to have doubted him so much.

'I am so grateful for your helping to move the qered, Miss Gribble. But now we must turn our attention to Yule.' The mayor rubbed his hands together. 'And what a Yule it will be!' Suddenly Mayor Belcher stepped forwards and grasped Arianwyn by the hands. 'The first Yule in forty years since we have had a witch! You do realize what this means, of course? We have always kept the old Yule traditions here, you know,' he said with a broad smile. 'But *this* year!' He did a little dance on the rug and clapped his hands.

'Oh.' Arianwyn wasn't at all sure what the mayor meant.

He started to list things, counting them off on his fingers as he strode around the room. 'The traditional Yule feast, complete with all the usual scrumptious Yule food, of course. The nomination of the Winterthorn Queen, from one of the young ladies of Lull, who then gets to pick her Yule Lord. The Yule blessing wands. The kiln of wishes and sorrows. Gathering in the Yule logs from the Great Wood, naturally—'

'Um, what's that?' Arianwyn asked quickly. 'About

the Great Wood?' Should she have been writing this all down?

The mayor's head whipped around. 'We all go to collect the Yule logs from the Great Wood. It is a tradition that goes back for hundreds and hundreds of years. Possibly even further.' He beamed.

'But that's surely not a very good idea *this year*?' Arianwyn said carefully, hoping he would pick up on the obvious reasons why without her having to explain.

'But we have *always* gathered the Yule logs from the Great Wood, Miss Gribble. There are no two ways about it.' He stared at her.

'But it's not safe, Mayor Belcher.'

'Oh, nonsense, nonsense! We shan't go far into the wood and we will have you to look after us, of course. What could possibly go wrong?'

Where to start? Arianwyn thought. But the mayor took her silence as a sign to carry on with his list.

'Dances in the town hall, canticles in the town square, exchanging gifts – and then, when the river freezes over . . . the *frost fair*! But the most exciting bit, the thing that kicks off all the celebrations, is the summoning of the frost phoenix.' Mayor Belcher smiled knowingly.

'I'm sorry . . . the what?' Arianwyn asked. 'Who summons the . . . What is it?'

'The frost phoenix, Miss Gribble. *You* will summon the *frost phoenix*, of course. Isn't that delightful?'

Arianwyn found herself nodding even though she had no idea what it would involve. 'How . . . exciting,' she said, giving the mayor a thumbs-up and smiling as broadly as she could. It didn't make her feel any more confident, though.

This all sounded like a lot of hard work.

When Arianwyn reached home again after her meeting with the mayor, she found Estar waiting on the doorstep. He smiled up at her, his yellow eyes shining warmly.

'It's good to see you,' Arianwyn said and reached forward to embrace her feyling friend. 'How are things in Edda?'

'Things are coming along slowly but surely. It is taking some longer to adjust than others. There are those amongst the feylings who believe we should return to Erraldur, but most are happy to make Edda our permanent home now,' he said. 'But I thought it was time to come back and see to those glyphs.' His high voice was bright and cheerful, but the prospect of tackling the quiet glyphs again made Arianwyn's heart sink. She felt guilty.

'Come on in then,' she said, unlocking the door.

Upstairs in the Spellorium's apartment, she busied herself with the tea things and then, whilst the kettle boiled, she found blankets in the wardrobe near her bed and made up Estar's makeshift sleeping arrangements in the squishy old armchair that stood beside the stove. 'You'll stay for a few days?' she asked.

Estar nodded.

But even as she occupied herself with these little domestic chores, Arianwyn's mind filled with doubts and more doubts about all the work and mysteries that were building around her.

Chapter 12
A BRIEF SPELL

*M*agic fizzed around Arianwyn.

She took a deep breath and tried to relax her shoulders. The feeling was as familiar as a comfy pullover or her favourite chair: the prickle and tingle of energy against her skin, the swirl of magic around her that seemed to brighten everything, even on this dank, grey and rainy morning.

She raised her right hand and slowly began to sketch the newest glyph once more – the third she had found. She knew it off by heart now. She'd sketched it hundreds of times in the past weeks. But so far it hadn't done anything. However, now there was another sensation too. Something tangled or undone, like an unpicked seam. The sensation wasn't unpleasant, but it niggled at her, a puzzle begging to be solved.

The new quiet glyph hung before her, an arm's length away. This was her third attempt in a row at summoning it this morning.

She felt the energy begin to dissipate and, as her eyes flicked back to the glyph, she could see it was shimmering and beginning to fade.

'Concentrate!' cautioned Estar. 'Or you'll lose it – *again*!'

'I *am* concentrating,' Arianwyn replied quickly. Why was Estar being so disagreeable? *Come on*, she urged herself – but the pull of magic was beginning to fade again.

'Arianwyn!' Estar cautioned.

The glyph flickered once, twice, and then vanished completely, leaving only a small cloud of yellowish smoke behind. It hung in the air, still and unmoving.

'Oh, Estar! You put me off,' Arianwyn said, turning to face the feyling.

He raised a thick black eyebrow and tutted loudly. 'I did no such thing, thank you. As always, I was simply trying to help.'

'I'm not doing it on purpose.' Arianwyn stooped to pick up her notebook to look at the sketches of the glyph she had drawn. She had several different versions in her notebook. Perhaps she had drawn the staves in the wrong place, or not curled the spiral enough? 'You look,' she said, handing the notebook to Estar. 'Which one of these is right?'

Estar didn't take it. 'Perhaps you should take a break for a bit?' he said, shifting where he rested against a tree, a thick flowery blanket wrapped around him, protecting him from the chill air. 'If it's too much.'

'No. I need to try again or this is going to take for ever!'

Arianwyn sighed and looked away towards Lull. She would need to head to the Spellorium soon and start her day's work. If she didn't figure out this glyph, she'd be back here early tomorrow, and the next day and the next, with nothing to show for it except for a cold most likely. Right at that moment she felt that it was all a colossal waste of time. She hoped another glyph might make itself known and perhaps they could focus on that for a while?

But that was probably wishful thinking at best.

The little yellow cloud seemed to stare back, taunting her.

'The glyphs have kept themselves well hidden for thousands of years. I don't think you'll be able to just suddenly make them appear just because you want them to. You have to be patient! It's no good rushing at them like a child hurrying to play. This is serious.'

'I am being patient, Estar – and serious,' Arianwyn snapped, frustrated. 'I do know how important the quiet glyphs are. But you said they were inside me, so . . . I thought this would be easier?' She stared at the page again. Estar was being remarkably unhelpful. Didn't he know how much she was trying to cope with and sort out?

'Why should it be easy?' he replied, pulling the blanket tighter about himself and sniffing. 'The glyphs are very powerful. A gift of magic. If it was easy anyone would be able to summon them.' He glanced away.

'If only!' Arianwyn replied, her voice sharp. 'I've seen the same glyph every night for a week in my dreams, but each night it looks slightly different. I don't even know if I'm drawing the right thing now.'

Estar sighed. 'Take a deep breath and start ag—'

'Oh, Estar, will you stop being so . . . *calm* all the boggin' time!' Arianwyn growled and kicked at a damp tree root.

'There's no need to take it out on the tree,' Estar said, still as calm as ever. It was really quite infuriating. 'I think you might be trying too hard,' he added quietly. 'It's not just seeing the glyphs, it's understanding their . . . intention as well. That's the—'

'MISS GRIBBLE!' The booming voice of Mayor Belcher cut through whatever Estar was about to say next.

Arianwyn turned. 'Boil it!' she grumbled; this was all she needed. She had been seeing rather too much of the mayor lately for her liking.

'Oh, what does he want?' Estar asked, a sly smile on his blue face, his lamp-like eyes full of mischief before he speedily closed them, pretending to be fast asleep.

'Hello, Mayor Belcher,' Arianwyn said brightly. 'How can I help you?' Though she already knew quite well why the mayor was there.

'Just how much longer will you be *practising* for? We are behind with the preparations for the Yule festival, you know.' He stared at the little yellow cloud. 'What's that?'

'Nothing,' Arianwyn fibbed. 'Look, I'm sorry, Mayor Belcher, but the thing is—'

'You can't spend all day playing in the woods, Miss Gribble. We need you doing your work for the Yule festivities, you know.'

'I'm hardly playing.' Why was everyone suddenly having a go at her?

'Please do not neglect your other duties, Miss Gribble. Half the town seems to be waiting outside the Spellorium, you know, for their Yule charms. Charms that only you, as Lull's witch, can provide.'

'Arianwyn . . .' Estar's voice was higher than usual; he sounded worried.

'Oh, what now?' she groaned, spinning round to see what was wrong.

He sat in his same spot, but her notebook was now open in his lap. His brow creased as a slender blue hand rested on the pages, all marked with her sketches of the new glyph.

'This glyph, I've just realized what it is.'

'And?' Arianwyn asked.

'That symbol is genara.'

'And precisely what does that mean?' the mayor sighed.

'It means discord, mischief, disharmony.' Estar's brows arched.

'You mean this glyph is what is making us quarrel? *Now* you tell me!' Arianwyn complained, realizing with some relief that it was the spell that was causing the ill feeling between her and Estar.

'Well, can you undo it, Miss Gribble, or not?' The mayor gestured to the small yellow cloud. It even *looked* mean, now that Arianwyn thought about it. Mean little cloud!

Arianwyn took a deep breath and tried to draw the glyph backwards, the easiest and quickest way to undo a spell, usually.

'I don't think that's going to work,' Estar said carefully.

'Well, how about suggesting something that will!' Arianwyn snapped. Then added, 'Sorry – it's the spell.'

Estar nodded. 'The glyph hasn't presented itself the same way twice, so it won't undo like that, I don't think. It would be wise for us all to move away from the clearing as soon as possible.'

'You can't just leave it like that, surely?' Mayor Belcher grumbled. 'Does it pose any threat to the town? This is very irresponsible of you, Miss Gribble!'

'It will go, *eventually*,' Estar replied, glancing at Arianwyn. The edge was back in his voice as well.

He clearly thought this was Arianwyn's fault too, and now he wasn't being subtle about it.

'But what if it drifts towards town?' the mayor asked Estar.

'I don't think it will.'

'But you're not sure?'

'Of course there is a risk—'

'That's simply not good enou—'

'Wait – stop it!' Arianwyn said, striding between the mayor and Estar, her hands held out as though she had to keep them apart. 'Don't you see – it's the glyph,' she said. 'We should move away from the cloud.'

'Well really, Miss Gribble, you don't need to snap!' the mayor huffed and, turning on his heels, hurried away from the clearing. He cast one quick and rather hurt glance over his shoulder at Arianwyn and Estar.

Arianwyn sighed and started gathering up her things as quickly as she could and moved away from the little cloud too. She had only gone about a metre when she turned back to see where Estar was.

He was facing the other way, off into the woods.

'Are you coming?' Arianwyn asked. 'I'm getting wet.'

Estar was quiet for a moment and then shook his head. 'No, I think I'm going to go back to Edda.'

'What? Estar, why? I didn't mean to snap – it was just the spell.' Arianwyn tried to laugh it off, but she felt suddenly uncomfortable.

Estar sighed. 'I don't think it was *all* down to the spell,' he said quietly, without looking at her.

The thought that it wasn't stabbed Arianwyn through the heart. 'I'm sorry,' she mumbled. But it seemed inadequate.

'It's not just you. But you are distracted. And so am I. I can't stop thinking about the others back in Edda. I feel bad having to leave them all the time.' He gave a half-smile. 'It's not easy rebuilding a whole town somewhere new, you know. So, I shall leave you to focus on your Yule preparations, go home for a few days and we can resume our work later,' Estar finished quietly. He didn't look up at Arianwyn, only pulled the flowery blanket closer about himself and turned to face into the depths of the wood. The yellow cloud was as still as stone, floating in the air where it had formed.

Arianwyn hadn't even considered that Estar must feel as torn as she did. She had only been thinking about her own work and the demands on her time – but Estar had other duties too. She knew he was important to the feylings and their founding of the new settlement.

'Well . . . bye then, I guess,' Arianwyn said, at last.

Without turning back, Estar started to walk away. 'Goodbye, Arianwyn,' he said quietly as the trees of the Great Wood swallowed him up.

Chapter 13
WINTERTHORN & MISELBERRIES

'I need my Yule charm, Miss Gribble, and Mayor Belcher said that you would have it all under control.' Mrs Myddleton loomed across the counter and glared at Arianwyn.

'I, er . . .' she stammered. She had no idea what a Yule charm actually involved.

'I've come for mine as well, please. I need three: one for the farmhouse and the others for the barns.' Mrs Caulls from Low Gate Farm puffed up to the counter. She was bundled up with several ratty-looking scarves and a woollen hat that Arianwyn was certain had once been a tea cosy.

'Perhaps you could call back tomorrow? I'll see if I can get them ready for you then,' Arianwyn said.

There were concerned mutterings from the

customers assembled in the shop.

'Erm, have you *all* come for Yule charms?' Arianwyn asked, already afraid of the answer.

There was lots of collective nodding.

'Well, not me; I wanted a charm as a Yule gift for my wife.' A gentleman who Arianwyn thought worked in the library twisted his cap in his hands.

Arianwyn scratched at her curls and sighed. She looked briefly at Bob who was busy nosing a dustball across the floor and offered no help at all.

'Look, can't you just reactivate this old one at least?' Mrs Caulls said, slapping a bedraggled collection of sticks and leaves down on to the counter.

Arianwyn stared at it for a few seconds, unsure exactly what it was she was looking at . . . Was it a bird's nest or a flower arrangement? Or something between the two?

'Oh, *that's* the charm?'

'Well, what did you think it was?' Mrs Caulls laughed. 'A flower bouquet?' There was an eruption of giggles from some of the waiting queue that still snaked out of the door and partway along Kettle Lane despite the continuously falling rain. Arianwyn had worked solidly since opening time, but there seemed to be more customers than ever – and now they were asking for Yule charms.

Arianwyn could feel her cheeks flush. Charms were her thing, her speciality. But she'd never encountered a charm like this before.

As she lifted the jumble of whatever-it-was up, a few leaves cascaded to the counter. It looked like a simple wreath. 'Ah-ha!' Arianwyn smiled.

'Have you worked it out?' Mrs Caulls asked.

'These are old charms, ancient in fact,' Arianwyn explained. 'Before the glass orbs and containers were introduced, all the charms witches made would have been woven like this from plants or scraps of fabric, a bit like my door charm.' She gestured to the bell charm that hung on the door of the Spellorium, an old Grunnean heirloom that had been in her grandmother's family for hundreds of years.

She looked back at the wreath charm before her. She carefully started to pull some of the components from it. 'What are you doing that for?' Mrs Myddleton asked.

'I need to see exactly how it's made so I can copy it.' Arianwyn lifted the pieces of the wreath and studied them carefully.

There were definitely winterthorn leaves woven in, and sprigs of miselberries too. There were also some dried canvor flowers and the rest didn't look too complicated or out of the ordinary. She had a stock of the bright green deja stone that was also part of the charm but she wasn't sure she would have enough if everyone suddenly decided they wanted one . . . which it looked like they did.

Would she be able to get everything she needed from the Great Wood? And was it safe? She needed time to figure it all out. 'OK, I can probably sort out a few for tomorrow but the rest of you will have to come back again if you want a wreath charm.'

There were groans of displeasure. 'I'm sorry,' Arianwyn mumbled as half the customers in the Spellorium filed back out on to Kettle Lane. She could hear the pop of umbrellas being put up against the rain.

'Can I keep hold of this?' she asked Mrs Caulls.

'Well, what do you think *I'm* going to do with it?' Mrs Caulls sniffed, grabbed her bag and stormed towards the door. 'Wear it?'

An hour later, Arianwyn was making her way back to Lull from the Great Wood, Bob hopping at her side. She carried two large baskets, one full of winterthorn leaves and the other with miselberries – enough to make the promised few charm wreaths ready for the next day and plenty more besides. She had depleted most of the bushes and trees on the edge of the Great Wood.

She'd also checked the place where she had practised with Estar the day before, wondering about the little yellow cloud, but to her relief it had finally disappeared.

She felt a small pang of regret when she thought about her feyling friend. She wished she'd managed to be as patient with him as he'd been with her.

Her hands were full so she couldn't carry an umbrella and she was completely soaked through – mostly from the falling rain but also from wading out through the flooded meadow. This was her last dry uniform, as well. The others were all hung over the bath back at the Spellorium. She hoped they might be dry soon or she'd have to go to work in her pyjamas!

She turned to check where Bob had got to, realizing that the moon hare was no longer at her side. In the middle of the flooded meadow the moon hare sat staring into the dark line of trees, seemingly oblivious to the rain.

'Are you coming, Bob?' she called, but Bob didn't move. Its long white ears were alert, its nose twitching. The moon hare stretched forwards as though searching for something in the ferns and brambles at the edge of the Great Wood.

'Bob?' Arianwyn called again and the moon hare turned to look at her with a quizzical expression on its face.

'Are you coming? I'm soaked through!'

Bob looked back to the Great Wood once more and then turned slowly and moved to catch up with Arianwyn, but she noticed that it kept turning to glance back. What had Bob seen? she wondered. She hoped it wasn't anything dangerous. There was no hint of dark magic nearby, no stench of hex. The mean little cloud had vanished. That was good. But something had caught the moon hare's attention, that much was sure.

The small bridge by the South Gate was now partly underwater, the flooded meadow merging with the small pond it usually spanned. Arianwyn leapt over the deeper parts of water, splashing as she landed. And as she glanced up she saw Aunt Grace coming through the gate, huddled under her umbrella, wearing a sturdy pair of wellington boots. She waved and hurried forwards. 'I've just had a telephone call from Salle,' she called with excitement. 'They're all coming home the day after tomorrow.' Aunt Grace beamed and the news filled Arianwyn with a burst of excitement and hope.

'That's great news!'

'I'll make up rooms for your grandmother and father at the Blue Ox as well, for you won't all be able to squeeze into the Spellorium, I don't suppose.' Aunt Grace smiled.

'Thank you,' Arianwyn said as they turned and walked back into Lull, Bob still trailing slowly at her side and looking back to the wood every now and again.

'You're welcome to stay with us as well,' Aunt Grace said, covering her with the brolly and wrapping an arm around Arianwyn's wet shoulders. 'No sense you being alone. I'm sure we can squeeze an extra bed into Salle's room.'

'That would be lovely,' Arianwyn said, her mind already full of how wonderful Yule would be this year with all her new friends and her father home.

She could feel a huge smile spreading across her face, a feeling of love and contentment warming her from within.

Chapter 14
STEAM & SMOKE

*M*r Thorn pulled Beryl into a wide loop in front of Flaxsham train station. Beryl's windscreen wipers swished back and forth, sending the icy rain flowing across the window. 'Rotten weather,' Mr Thorn sighed. 'Not seen rain like this for years.'

Arianwyn and Aunt Grace pitched forwards in their seats as Mr Thorn slammed on the brakes. A terrific screech filled the air as Beryl skidded a little too close to several parked taxis. Aunt Grace gave a small cry of alarm and looked at Arianwyn. They both knew Mr Thorn was the the clumsiest driver in the world, though he somehow never actually managed to have an accident, thankfully.

The bus came to a safe stop, just.

Passengers hurried towards the station, carrying cases and travelling bags – heading to other places to spend the Yule holidays. Arianwyn grabbed her umbrella and jumped out of the bus and straight into a huge puddle. The water splashed a gentleman hurrying past with a gleaming leather suitcase and fine wool coat. He cast Arianwyn an unimpressed look as he strode away whilst Arianwyn called 'Sorry!' to his back.

Aunt Grace followed more carefully, sidestepping the puddle as she pulled up her umbrella. Mr Thorn waved and called, 'I'll be back in five minutes, just have to go and pick up the order from the market.'

Arianwyn and Aunt Grace linked arms and hurried towards the station, excited to be reunited with their loved ones. They zigzagged through the people coming and going, leaping over more icy puddles and trying not to splash anyone else or be splashed. Huddled near the door were a small group of people singing Yule songs: 'Winter, winter, frost and snow!' they sang.

If only! thought Arianwyn. At the moment it was more like winter, winter, rain and rain.

As they reached the high arched door of the station another tide of people surged forwards and hurried to the waiting cars and taxis. The train had arrived! Couples embraced, children rushed into the waiting arms of grandparents or aunts and uncles. For a moment Arianwyn and Aunt Grace were held frozen between the two tides of people.

And then suddenly someone barrelled into Arianwyn, nearly knocking her down the steps. 'WYN! AUNT GRACE!'

It was Salle.

As Arianwyn half stumbled down the steps, she felt herself being pulled into a tight hug along with Aunt Grace.

'Oh, it's so lovely to see you!' Aunt Grace said and promptly burst into tears. 'I've missed you *so* much!'

'It's only been six weeks!' Salle laughed as Aunt Grace wiped at her eyes with a clean handkerchief and laughed as well. 'I know, but still.' She squeezed her into a tight hug. 'My girl! I missed you every second of every day.'

Arianwyn waited until they pulled apart from each other. 'Where's everyone else?' she asked, peering into the oncoming crowd.

'They're all still on the platform waiting for the luggage or something, come on!' And Salle grabbed Arianwyn's hand and Arianwyn grabbed Aunt Grace's and they started to move slowly through the mob of people and into the busy station.

'I'm so pleased you're back, Salle. I need your help,' Arianwyn said as they passed the ticket office with its maroon wooden panels and bright brass grilles at the ticket windows.

'Oh, how come?' Salle asked.

'It's all these Yule traditions. I'm not used to how

you celebrate in Lull – it's a bit different to how my grandmother always does it and not as elaborate as things in Kingsport . . . and you'll have to tell me all about the . . . frost festival—'

'The frost *fair*!' Aunt Grace corrected. 'My mother used to tell me they had one every year in Lull. But now we only have one if it's cold enough for the river to freeze over.'

'I remember one from when I was about eight or nine,' Salle said. 'It was so much fun, skating and games on the ice.' Her eyes lit up with excitement and expectation.

'Well, don't get your hopes up, I don't think it's ever going to stop raining!' Arianwyn said sadly. 'Oh, and apparently Mayor Belcher wants me to summon an ice phoenix or something but I can't find out anything about, well, *anything*. Will you help?' she asked as they emerged at last on to the platform which seemed to have even more people on it. It was crammed from the waiting room, with its cheery fire, right up to the platform edge where a huge train waited, occasionally shrouding everything in clouds of steam and smoke. Arianwyn had never seen the station so busy.

'Yes, of course, there's bound to be something in the library or town archives.'

'Thanks, Salle!' Arianwyn felt relieved to have Salle back at last. And then, as the crowd shifted ahead of them, Arianwyn saw her grandmother. The tall elegant woman cast her gaze this way and that across the packed platform, her favourite yellow scarf draped over her shoulders. Her eyes, fixed on Arianwyn's, lit up and the broadest smile spread across her face. She raised a hand as Salle, Arianwyn and Aunt Grace battled towards her through the crowd.

In a few moments they were all huddled together on the platform: Arianwyn, Salle, Aunt Grace, Grandmother, Sergeant Gribble and Colin. Occasional gusts of rain-filled wind swirled across the platform mixed with the steam and smoke from the train engine.

There were hugs all round. Arianwyn threw herself into her grandmother's waiting arms first and then turned to hug her father. His bandages were gone, though he still looked pale and tired. He stood stiffly and said, 'Steady on, old girl, it's only been a week!'

Arianwyn felt a little bruised by his comment and didn't know how to look at anyone for a moment. Salle quickly introduced Aunt Grace to Arianwyn's father. 'Well, shall we get back?' Aunt Grace asked. 'You must all be tired from the long trip, and Mr Thorn should be back from his errands by now.'

'Of course, but where on earth has our luggage got to, do you suppose?' Grandma asked.

'Perhaps you should go and have a look, Twine?' Sergeant Gribble said suddenly, his voice gruff and a little dismissive.

Colin blushed. 'Er – yes, of course, Mr Gribble . . . sir!' he mumbled and hurried off into the crowd.

'Dad! Don't bark at Colin like that!' Arianwyn said quickly.

Another passenger bumped into her father and he winced. He was clearly in pain. Perhaps that was why he was so grumpy.

'Is your arm still hurting?' Arianwyn asked.

It was Sergeant Gribble's turn to blush now. 'No, just tired is all – and will you look at the state of this!' He gestured at the platform. 'No organization at all. This is utter chaos!' he grumbled.

'How was the journey?' Aunt Grace asked, clearly trying to change the subject.

'Oh, well, you know . . .' Grandma smiled. 'Long!'

'Never-ending!' Sergeant Gribble snapped.

Aunt Grace jumped a bit. There was a difficult silence, cut short as Arianwyn's father mumbled an apology to Aunt Grace.

'Shall we go and see where Colin has got to?' Salle suggested, tugging on Arianwyn's coat sleeve.

'Good idea, and we can go and find somewhere to sit for a moment,' Aunt Grace said calmly.

As Arianwyn and Salle pushed their way through the crowd once more, Arianwyn said, 'Sorry my dad is such a grump. Was he like this all the way?'

'It's just the jolting of the train, and he's tired, I think. We tried to persuade him to do the journey over a few days, but he refused. I think Colin has borne the brunt of it, though.'

'Poor Colin!' Arianwyn moaned. 'Can you see him anywhere?'

Salle turned and, standing on tiptoe, searched the wall of coats and scarves and umbrellas. Another cloud of engine smoke swirled across the platform, enveloping everyone for a few seconds. It made Arianwyn cough and blink, her eyes suddenly watery. The wall of people blurred for a second and then Arianwyn saw a pair of too-dark eyes fixed on her and a curtain of pale, almost white hair.

It couldn't be . . . ?

'Gimma?' Arianwyn breathed. She froze and Salle stumbled into her.

'Oh, Wyn – what's the matter now?'

Another rolling cloud of steam and smoke and rain billowed over the platform, swallowing up the pale figure along with the rest of the crowd.

'Wyn, are you OK? You've gone as white as a sheet!' Salle said, taking Arianwyn's gloved hand.

'I thought I just saw . . .' She paused; it already seemed absurd.

'What? Who?' Salle asked.

'. . . Gimma . . .' Saying the name aloud made it seem even more ridiculous.

The smoke swirled away and Salle spun quickly to look in the direction Arianwyn had indicated. 'But Gimma wouldn't be coming back to Lull surely, would she? She hates it!' Salle said.

Arianwyn shook her head. It did seem a strange idea – particularly after their conversation in High-bridge. And Mayor Belcher would have certainly mentioned if Gimma – his very favourite niece – was coming to visit, she was quite sure.

'She'll be at swanky parties with her parents, no doubt, and eating at the finest restaurants and getting the biggest pile of Yule gifts anyone has ever seen,' Salle crowed.

Arianwyn nodded slowly. She must have been mistaken. It must have been someone who looked like Gimma, that was all. The station was so busy and, what with the smoke and rain . . . She'd confused what she saw, that was all; it was a trick of the light, smoke in her eyes.

But even so she still felt confused and a little upset by it, like icy fingers had brushed the backs of her arms. 'I'm here!' a voice suddenly called from behind them, making them both jump.

Turning, the girls were confronted with a huge pile of cases, two trunks and several bags and what was unmistakably Sergeant Gribble's army kitbag. Colin's face peeked out from behind it all. 'I managed to find a trolley,' he said, beaming. 'I just hope we've got everything.'

They manoeuvred the luggage carefully back to where Grandmother, Sergeant Gribble and Aunt Grace were seated on the hard wooden benches along the station wall. 'Well, that certainly took long enough!' Sergeant Gribble barked as they came forward with the trolley.

'Sorry,' Colin mumbled, looking down at the floor, the smile abruptly falling from his face.

'Don't be such a grump now, Oliver,' Grandmother said sharply. 'It's a frightfully busy day and I think Colin has done a fine job finding all our things. Thank you, Colin,' she added brightly.

Sergeant Gribble mumbled something which may have been an apology or a thanks, Arianwyn couldn't tell. She shot Colin an apologetic look and he smiled quickly back in reply.

Sergeant Gribble marched off back through the ticket office and everyone else followed, Salle and Arianwyn helping to push and steer the trolley through the throng of people until they were back outside and beside Beryl who gleamed brightly on the dark winter's day. 'So lovely to see you again, Madam Stronelli.' Mr Thorn tipped his cap as Grandmother clambered on to the bus with a cheery 'Hello!' then he saluted Sergeant Gribble who said 'Good afternoon' and hurried up the steps of the bus and out of the rain.

Aunt Grace climbed in next as Arianwyn and Salle helped Colin with loading the luggage into the back of the bus.

'Right-o, let's get home, shall we?' Mr Thorn called.

'How did you get on with the trip to the market,

Mr Thorn?' Aunt Grace asked.

'Market was cancelled because of the rain, so I've not been able to get as much as we hoped, I'm afraid. But I don't think we'll starve!'

As Beryl negotiated the busy streets of Flaxsham, Arianwyn couldn't help but think about what had happened on the platform. She kept seeing those dark eyes watching her as the steam rolled past.

But it couldn't have been Gimma, could it? Well, they'd soon know once they got back to Lull, that much was sure.

Chapter 15
The FROZEN HOUSE

Arianwyn's father's mood did seem to improve a little on the bus ride back to Lull. He chatted warmly with Mr Thorn, who it turned out had also been a soldier in his youth.

'Fought alongside the Veersland Seventh Platoon in the Battle of Igretzia,' Mr Thorn called over the hum and occasional roar of Beryl's engine.

Arianwyn and Aunt Grace shared out the picnic lunch that Aunt Grace had packed, though the thermos of soup proved tricky to manage as Beryl negotiated some of the bumpier parts of the road. 'How delicious!' Grandmother declared happily. Arianwyn sat with Colin and Salle, the three of them happily eating sandwiches and chatting quietly. 'Did you show Miss Newam the . . . *you-know-what?*' Arianwyn asked and looked quickly over at her father and grandmother, but they were both occupied chatting with Mr Thorn and Aunt Grace.

Colin reached inside his jacket and handed Arianwyn back the photograph of her father and his platoon with the strange Urisian sorcerer. 'She was really interested in the photograph and she said she was going to do more research and let us know when she finds anything out,' he said quietly as the bus rattled along. 'She took a copy.'

'Oh, let's talk about something else!' Salle said, clapping her hands together. 'I'm so excited that you're both going to be in Lull for Yule. We are going to have so much fun!'

Arianwyn glanced out at the world rushing past the windows of the bus and smiled. Squeezed into the seat beside her friends with her dad and grandmother just a few seats away, everything felt right for the first time in a long while.

Beryl rattled through the West Gate and headed up towards the town square. 'Your rooms are all ready,' Aunt Grace said warmly, 'so you can all rest up for a bit if you'd like.' She placed a hand on Sergeant Gribble's shoulder but he shrugged her off.

'I'm quite all right, thank you. What I need is a

brisk walk – I've been cooped up for too long, that's all.' He wasn't quite as gruff as he had been earlier and Arianwyn was thankful. She was sure Aunt Grace, for all her niceness and warmth, would not have stood for it for long.

Beryl stopped outside the Blue Ox with a screech of brakes and everyone rocked slightly in their seats. 'Lull town square. Final destination!' Mr Thorn called.

In a few minutes everyone had climbed off the bus and stood outside the Blue Ox, as Mr Thorn unloaded the luggage, as well as provisions he had collected from Flaxsham. Uncle Mat hurried out and caught Salle up in the tightest of hugs. It made Arianwyn feel as though she was missing something. Why had her father not done the same to her at the station? She was sure he was as happy to see her as Uncle Mat was to see Salle, she thought. He just had a different way of expressing himself, that was all. Wasn't it?

She looked across at her father who was taking in the town square.

'Well, see you later for dinner, Arianwyn?' Aunt Grace said brightly as she and Uncle Mat walked into the Blue Ox, their arms wrapped tightly around Salle.

Arianwyn turned to look at her father, Grandmother and Colin who were still sorting through the pile of luggage with Mr Thorn's help.

'I'm going to have a rest, I think,' Grandmother added, hefting her travel bags and smiling. 'See you for dinner.'

'I'm going to drop my bags in and take a walk,' Sergeant Gribble said to Arianwyn.

'A walk does sound like a nice idea . . .' Colin said uncertainly, but as Sergeant Gribble shot him a look he mumbled, 'But maybe I'll go in and read my book and have a cup of tea. See you later, Arianwyn.' And he hurried off towards the inn after Grandmother, carrying as many bags and cases as was humanly possible.

'Dad, please stop being so mean to poor Colin!' Arianwyn said at last. She felt like a bottle of fizzy pop that had been shaken up too much.

'Pardon?' Sergeant Gribble said.

But before Arianwyn could repeat herself, Salle came running from the Blue Ox, waving a note. 'Wyn! There's been an urgent call from Mr Curry on Maple Terrace.' She flapped the piece of paper in Arianwyn's face.

'What is it?' Arianwyn asked, taking the note. She peered down at the writing, even as the rain drenched the paper, making it close to illegible.

'Something about the doors and windows,' Salle said, trying to look at the piece of paper upside down.

'Well, I'd best go and investigate,' Arianwyn said to her father. 'See you later on. Enjoy your walk.'

'Wait, should I . . . should I come with you?' her father asked. 'Is it safe to go on your own?'

Did he think she wasn't allowed to go on her own? That she couldn't cope?

'No need, I'm sure it'll all be fine.' Did he look worried? Arianwyn turned and was hurrying across the town square when she heard fast footsteps sloshing through puddles behind her. For a moment she hoped it was her father, but as she turned to glance over her shoulder she saw it was Salle, hurrying after her. 'Wyn, wait. I'll come with you.' She smiled and linked her arm with Arianwyn's, and the two girls raced across the town square.

Arianwyn knocked on the door of Mr Curry's house. 'Hello?' she called. 'It's Arianwyn, Mr Curry . . . are you there?'

She waited for a few minutes but there was no answer. She glanced uncertainly at Salle. Was this someone's idea of a joke? 'Is this the right address?' Arianwyn asked.

Salle nodded and knocked again, louder than before. 'HELLO!'

Then they heard the sound of a window opening high above them. They both stepped back and looked up just as a shower of fine powdery ice fell from the opened window on to Arianwyn and Salle.

Arianwyn frowned in confusion – where had all the ice come from? 'Hello, Miss Gribble! Is that you?' A man's head poked out and peered down at them.

'Hello, Mr Curry.' Salle waved.

'Could you let us in please?' Arianwyn pointed at the door. 'We got a call to say you were having problems with something?'

'Well, that's the bother, you see,' Mr Curry said, adjusting his thick spectacles and blinking at the girls once more. 'I can't get out of the house . . . the doors and most of the windows are frozen shut.'

Arianwyn glanced at Salle and then looked more closely at the door. What she had thought was faded wood wasn't that at all, but a trace of fine, feathery ice all across the painted wood. It ran around the door frame and over the edge of the door too, which was strange as there was no ice anywhere else nearby. The rain was still falling steadily. Arianwyn pressed her hand against the wood and sure enough it felt frozen.

'It's not locked,' Mr Curry added. 'You could always try pushing from your side perhaps?' He blinked down at them again.

Together, Arianwyn and Salle shoved on the door. First with their hands, then bracing against the door with their backs and shoulders. But the door wouldn't budge. It was well and truly frozen solid.

'Can you try a spell?' Salle suggested after another failed attempt at shoving the door open.

Arianwyn nodded and started to sketch Årdra against the frozen wood. She could feel a seam of magic running somewhere nearby, in the air above perhaps. But there was other magic close by as well, most likely whatever had caused the house to freeze. She had to concentrate to pull the magic towards the glyph which she could see shimmering against the wood of the door. But it was like standing on tiptoes and grabbing something that was still a centimetre out of your reach and just as she finally felt the magic pour towards her, the glyph she had sketched faded from the door and her magic flowed away, like silk tumbling out of her hands.

'Jinxing-jiggery!' Arianwyn muttered.

'Everything OK down there?' Mr Curry called. 'Only I'm getting really quite chilly now!' His voice juddered with cold.

'It's all fine, Mr C!' Salle called brightly. 'Try again,' she said to Arianwyn quietly.

This time it worked and the second glyph flashed as the magic connected with it. Under Arianwyn's touch the door began to warm, the feathery white ice fading from the wood, and after a few seconds there was a soft click and the door swung open. 'We're in!' Salle called up to Mr Curry.

They heard the sound of the window closing and Mr Curry sighing, 'Thank heavens!'

But as the door swung open they saw the full extent of the problem. The frozen front door was only the beginning.

Beyond the door was the hallway, a staircase heading off and up into the house to the left. The walls were painted a warm yellow, there was a patchwork of tiles on the floor and several doors leading off into other rooms. Arianwyn caught a glimpse of the kitchen. But everything was frosted over, pale under a fine layer of ice. 'My word,' she breathed, taking a step inside. Salle followed her. But as they stepped through the door and on to the tiles they realized their mistake: the hallway was one big sheet of ice. They both immediately slipped straight to the floor even as they tried to grip hold of each other for support.

They landed with an 'Ooof!' and 'Ouch!', and a tangle of legs and arms. Then they started laughing just as Mr Curry reached the bottom of the stairs.

'Oh, dear me.' He smiled.

'Be careful, Mr Curry. The floor is . . . slippery,' Salle said, and immediately burst into another fit of giggles even as she tried to get to her feet.

'Do you know what caused this?' Arianwyn asked, as Salle hauled her upright. They both steadied themselves against the cold wall.

'Saw something in the kitchen yesterday, but didn't think much of it,' Mr Curry explained, pointing down the hall.

'We'll take a look, but I think you'd best find somewhere else to stay, Mr Curry, until we can get the house thawed out.'

'Oh, right.' Mr Curry's brow creased and he tapped his hand against the banister rail.

'It'll be OK,' Salle said brightly. 'Have you got someone you can stay with? If not, I can speak to Aunt Grace—'

'No, it's all right,' Mr Curry said, rubbing his hands together for warmth. 'I can stay with my brother and his family for a bit, I'm sure.'

'I might just take a look in the kitchen,' Arianwyn said.

'Shall I help you sort some things to take with you?' Salle asked Mr Curry.

As Mr Curry and Salle went upstairs to pack some clothes, Arianwyn walked very carefully down the hallway and into the kitchen. The floor in there was just like the ice rink in Amble Square Gardens where Grandmother had taken her skating as a child, and Arianwyn slipped as she looked around the kitchen, trying to work out what had caused this strange, magical indoor frost.

She looked into the sink where the once-dripping tap was now frozen over into a miniature icicle. She tried to open the pantry door but it was – of course – frozen shut.

And then, as she was heading back to the hallway, Arianwyn saw something glistening in the gap between the dresser and the stone wall. She leant forwards and peered closer.

The space was full of ice crystals. They tangled together, overlapping and criss-crossing rather like a very untidy and frozen web.

'What is *that*?' Arianwyn asked the empty frosty kitchen.

But she couldn't get close enough to see deep into the space.

'Have you found something?' Salle asked, slipping across the floor towards her.

Arianwyn nodded. 'There's something odd down the side of the dresser here.' She pointed to the icy crystal web.

Salle peered closer and then leapt back as something darted hurriedly near their feet. Salle shrieked in surprise. Another one followed, shooting across the floor.

'What are they?' Salle asked, stumbling backwards in shock.

Another whatever-it-was zipped straight towards Arianwyn. It was fast – but Arianwyn was quick as well and she reached out, grasping the creature in her hand.

The cold stung her at once but she didn't let go. The small creature wriggled in her grip.

It was no bigger than an egg cup, its skin frosty blue with mottled ice-white patches here and there. It had huge eyes and a large beak-like nose. It made an angry hissing sound and then suddenly it was too cold to keep a grip of. The coldness burnt and stung her hand and fingers. Arianwyn cried out in pain and dropped the thing to the floor where it quickly scuttled off, vanishing under the kitchen sink.

'Boil it!' Arianwyn spat.

'Whatever are they?' Salle asked.

Arianwyn had no idea; she turned and shrugged at Salle as Mr Curry shuffled forwards into the kitchen and said, 'Looked like a nithering to me!'

'A what?' Arianwyn asked.

'Oh,' Salle groaned. 'Ice imps!'

Genara – *The Glyph of Discord*

This was the first glyph that I discovered within myself through working with Estar. He says the glyphs we use match closely to the old feyling language. Many of the books destroyed in the demon library in Erraldur contained the written form, but these are now all lost. Estar recognized this one, luckily. He says it links with the feyling phrase for 'discord' or 'upset' – and once I managed to summon it . . . well, it certainly does seem to amplify any discord already present.
I'm not sure I can see what use there will be for this glyph . . .

THE NEW BOOK OF QUIET GLYPHS BY ARIANWYN GRIBBLE

Chapter 16

FIRE GAZING

'*A*nithering? Are you sure, dear?' Miss Delafield asked down the phone. 'Oh my, oh my!'

'That's not very reassuring,' Arianwyn sighed.

'Oh, sorry, dear. It's just – well, once you've got one or two of those little blighters then you've usually got a much wider problem.'

'Meaning?'

'It's unlikely to be an isolated incident, dear. You'll need to tell everyone to be on the lookout and you need to try and stop the spread sooner rather than later.'

'Oh, I can't boggin' believe it,' Arianwyn groaned. She gazed off down the corridor in the Blue Ox, through the curtained archway that led back into the main room of the inn. The tables had been arranged to form one huge dining table, draped in white tablecloths and already laden with steaming dishes of buttered carrots and bright green peas topped with a sprig of mint. Aunt Grace and Uncle Mat, Salle and Colin were moving about quickly, placing plates and cutlery and glasses on to the table. Music was playing from the wireless that Uncle Mat had moved from their sitting room.

'Are you still there, dear?' Miss Delafield asked sharply.

'Yes, sorry – what did you say, Miss Delafield?'

'I said there's a notice you'll need to put up to help people identify the ice imps; there are three types, and the nitherings are – I'm afraid to say – the worst sort. They won't leave under any circumstance until the temperature is cold enough outside, usually not until the first snowfall at least . . . and sometimes not even then.'

'SNOW?' Arianwyn groaned. 'I don't think it's ever going to be cold enough for snow.'

'I know, dear. But look, there should be an example of the notice in the back of the ledger. Take it to the local printers and get them to make it up as soon as possible, dear. This is *very* important. You'll need to get notices up around town as soon as you can.'

'OK. And how can you get rid of them then?'

'Well, you can't actually get rid of them, dear. Sorry,' Miss Delafield said.

'They're not spirit creatures?' Arianwyn asked, her voice nearly a wail.

'Afraid so,' Miss Delafield said quietly. 'You'll just have to wait them out!'

'Wyn, we're nearly ready!' Aunt Grace called brightly, hurrying past with a huge pie. A warm wafting pastry aroma drifted behind her.

'Just get the notices up, dear, and we can worry about everything else in due course.'

'All right,' Arianwyn said, hoping there would be time to resolve the problem before Miss Delafield left or before the nitherings spread any further.

Dinner was delicious, and everyone was in good cheer. Even Sergeant Gribble's mood seemed to have improved after his walk and a rest. He joked with everyone and more than once put a comforting arm around Arianwyn, pulling her into a tight hug, once or twice planting a gentle kiss amongst her curls.

She caught her grandmother watching, a warm smile on her face.

Talk turned to Yule and various family traditions.

'We all used to sleep downstairs together in front of the fire at Yule,' Colin said. 'Of course, that might have been because it was too expensive to heat the whole house, but I still rather liked it.' He smiled.

'Aunt Grace always makes the biggest Yule cake,'

Salle explained. 'And everyone has to take a turn to stir the mixture and make a wish. And once or twice the wishes even came true!' There was a ripple of good-natured laughter and Salle protested, 'But they did!'

'When I was growing up in Grunnea we had all sorts of different Yule traditions,' Grandmother said. 'We would lay a feast out and the food had to remain on the table for three days and three nights to share with any passing spirits.'

'Did anything ever get eaten?' Colin asked. He held a spoonful of pudding in front of his mouth, gazing at Grandmother in wonder.

'*Once!*' Grandmother said quietly, her eyes sparkling. The room erupted into sounds of amazement.

'But the best thing was fire gazing,' Grandmother added.

'What's that?' Salle asked, leaning across the table.

'It's an old Grunnean tradition,' Grandmother said. 'We always used to do this during Yule. But I haven't done it in years and years.'

'But whatever is it?' Aunt Grace asked. 'I've never heard of it.'

'It's seeing into the future!' Colin said quietly.

Grandmother laughed. 'Well, no. Not exactly, Colin,' she said, trying to play down the buzz of excitement that had zipped around the dinner table like an electric current. 'Or only occasionally – and then a very short way into the future. Generally, the flames show you something you should be aware of, or something within yourself you need to know. And it doesn't always work.'

There were murmurs of disappointment until Colin added, 'But you do know how to do it, don't you?' His eyes were huge.

Grandmother blushed. 'Perhaps . . .'

'Oh, please, Madam Stronelli!' Salle pleaded.

Grandmother's bright laugh sang out through the Blue Ox. 'Very well, who wants to know their future?'

'ME!' Salle said immediately, her arm shooting into the air like an eager student. 'Pick me!'

Moments later, Grandmother and Salle knelt on a small rug before the embers of the dying fire, a few flames flickering into the darkness.

'Take my hand, Salle,' Grandmother said, and they linked hands. 'Now close your eyes and try to keep your mind clear.'

Salle nodded and closed her eyes.

Everyone else clustered around Salle and Grandmother in a semicircle. Hushed, excited chatter filled the room.

'Quiet, please,' Grandmother said, raising a hand and the chattering stopped like songbirds scared by a woodhawk. Next, she reached forwards and, using the poker for the fire, sketched Aluna, the glyph best for those skilled in divination, into the ashes that spilt out on to the hearth in front of the fireplace.

The flames flickered gently at the back of the fire, flashed for a moment, and then returned to their gentle dance, casting shadows about the room.

Arianwyn shifted so that she could see more closely, trying to guess how the spell worked.

Grandmother's eyes were closed but her eyelids flickered like somebody dreaming. And her mouth moved as if she were muttering something, though there were no words.

'How does it work, Wyn?' Uncle Mat asked quietly.

'I have no idea,' Arianwyn whispered. 'I never knew she could do this.'

After several minutes of this Grandmother let out a small gasp and her eyes flew open. The poker fell to the stones of the fireplace with a loud clang that made everyone gasp and jump before the room filled with nervous laughter.

'Did it work?' Salle asked. 'What did you see? Will I be a great actress?'

Arianwyn moved forwards to help her grand-mother back to her feet. She looked suddenly pale and her hands were shaking.

'What is it?' Arianwyn asked, reaching out towards Grandmother, whose fingers were trembling over her lips. 'Grandma, what did you see?'

Grandmother's eyelids flickered, like someone waking from a dream.

'Oh, nothing, nothing at all. I'm afraid it didn't work.'

Salle's shoulders drooped and she sighed, 'Oh, never mind.'

But something made Arianwyn worry that her grandmother was lying. She had looked terrified just a moment before.

'I think we have all had enough excitement for one evening!' Aunt Grace said, clapping her hands together. 'I'm sure it must be bedtime.'

Arianwyn kissed her father and grandmother goodnight, clinging on to her grandmother's hands for a while longer, as though that might reveal something of what her grandmother felt or had seen in the fire. 'Goodnight,' Grandma said gently. 'See you in the morning.'

Arianwyn lingered for a few moments more and then followed Salle to bed. But although she was tired, her mind raced and kept flitting back to the memory of her grandmother's face as she had peered into the flames. What had she seen there in the flames that had scared her so much?

'Salle? Are you awake?' Arianwyn asked and waited. But the only reply was Salle's gentle rhythmic breathing. She was fast asleep.

Slipping from her bed, Arianwyn padded out of the room and headed back downstairs.

The fire was nearly out, just the last couple of flames dancing in the embers, the room already cooling a little. Would it be enough? Arianwyn knelt by the hearth, as she had seen her grandmother do.

She lifted the poker and sketched Aluna into the ash before her. Then closed her eyes and waited. She had no idea if she was doing the right thing. Even if it was some skill she had inherited from her grandmother, she'd never even attempted this spell before – what were the chances it would work?

After some time, she sighed and opened her eyes. This was useless. Her knees hurt from kneeling on the cold floor. She lay the poker to one side and started to get back to her feet when she saw something moving in the shadows and light that danced across the bricks at the back of the fireplace.

'What's that?' Arianwyn asked the empty room, and leant in closer for a better look.

Amidst the last flickering flames and the occasional twirls of smoke, she could see what looked like two figures. And she was sure one of them was her grandmother. Peering closer still, feeling the heat from the flames on her cheeks, she could see her grandmother's familiar yellow scarf caught in a strong gust of wind, flapping in the air around her. The vision shifted and then dark eyes were glaring at

Arianwyn, a too-white face and grey twists of hair. It was a look so full of anger that it made her stumble back with fright – and yet there was something familiar in that look. 'Gimma?' she breathed.

The flames flickered again, and now the figures were gone and the yellow scarf fluttered to the ground, which was white with snow.

As the vision faded, Arianwyn watched the snow-white ground turn back to the grey ash of the fire as the flames died at last. A chill crept in around her at once and she couldn't shake the feeling of the dark eyes staring at her from the back of the hearth, even though all she could see now was bricks and ash.

What did it all mean?

Chapter 17
TRADITION

'Are you OK, Wyn? You're very quiet this morning,' Salle said brightly as Uncle Mat handed them both bowls of steaming, creamy porridge.

Arianwyn glanced over at the fireplace which was ablaze again, Bob stretched out on the rug before it, basking in the warmth. She still felt the chill from the previous night creep about her. She looked at her grandmother who was gently sipping on a cup of tea and reading the newspaper. Had they shared the same vision? Grandma glanced up and smiled across at Arianwyn.

'Wyn?' Salle prompted, and Arianwyn realized she hadn't replied.

'I'm fine,' Arianwyn lied. 'Just not really looking

forward to today's trip into the Great Wood.' Today was the trip to gather Yule logs, and Arianwyn was particularly worried about it given the hex infestation. She still had to sort the nithering notices around town too, *and* make up the rest of the outstanding Yule charms. How was she going to fit it all in?

But it was the memory of the half-seen vision in the dying flames that weighed on her mind the most.

Uncle Mat hurried back through from the kitchen carrying a teapot wrapped in a knitted rainbow tea cosy. 'Best eat your porridge up quickly, Wyn: the Parkinsons have been waiting out in the town square for half an hour already.' He inclined his head towards the large clock that hung over the mantel. It was after nine.

'Oh, jinxing-jiggery!' Arianwyn said, scooping another two mouthfuls of steaming porridge into her mouth. It warmed her stomach so thoroughly that for a fleeting moment she forgot the worry of the night before.

'When will you be back?' her father asked, folding his newspaper and standing slowly from his seat. He tucked the paper under his arm.

'Um, not sure,' Arianwyn said, pulling on her coat. 'We're off for the cutting ceremony, for the Yule logs.'

'In the forest? Is that safe?'

'It's the Great Wood,' Arianwyn said slowly. 'And I'm not sure really but it's part of my job. I can't just let the Parkinsons go on their own.'

'Well, I don't think you should go,' her father said, quickly and firmly. He slapped the newspaper down on the table.

'Sorry, what?' Arianwyn asked, wrapping her long red scarf three times around her neck.

'I don't think it's reasonable of them to ask you, a young girl, to go and protect them. Can't your Miss Delafield come over?'

'Dad – Miss Delafield has her own work to do. She can't do mine for me. And it *is* my job!' Arianwyn noticed the sideways looks she was getting from Colin and Salle. She half laughed, hoping her father was joking, teasing her . . . or maybe playing a game? Though it didn't feel terribly funny.

He looked cross. 'Be back before it gets dark then,' he said gruffly and brought his hand up to brush stray curls from her face.

'I'm really late now!' Arianwyn said, hurrying outside into the town square as Salle called, 'But you've not finished your breakfast yet . . . Wyn!'

Across from the Blue Ox, by the steps of the town hall, stood a huge horse and a large wooden cart, painted red with curling yellow letters on the side:

She hurried towards the cart, leaping over the ever-expanding puddles, Bob at her side. A cheery-looking couple waited beside the cart, wrapped in slick oilskins. Mrs Parkinson also wore a flowery rain hood. They smiled shyly as Arianwyn approached. Bob edged close to the huge carthorse, making excited yipping sounds before rolling on the cobbles of the town square and showing off a snow-white belly.

'Good morning, Mr Parkinson, Mrs Parkinson. I think Bob likes your horse!' Arianwyn said, stepping forwards and shaking their hands. Mr Parkinson blushed a little but smiled warmly, while Mrs Parkinson actually started to curtsey.

'Such an honour to meet you at last, miss,' Mrs Parkinson said.

Arianwyn blushed. 'Thank you.' She smiled quickly. 'Look, I'm not sure this is a very good idea—' Arianwyn began to explain, but she was cut short.

'Ahem – now then,' Mayor Belcher boomed as he came down the town hall steps. He was wearing some cropped trousers in a mustard tweed, bright green wellingtons and his purple rain mac, which was flapping behind him. He was quite a sight. Arianwyn was sure she heard Mr Parkinson gasp, 'Crikey!'

Mayor Belcher clapped his hands together as he approached the Parkinsons' horse and cart. 'We have a small group of townspeople who have volunteered to accompany you on your trip today.'

'But, Mayor Belcher — that's really not a good idea—' Arianwyn protested.

He held up his striped, mittened hands. 'I understand your concerns, Miss Gribble, and they are duly noted. But this is tradition! And it is important to the whole town that we are able to retrieve the Yule logs from the Great Wood. I thought this would make the work quicker and would result in less time actually spent in the Great Wood. Many hands and all that. Everyone has agreed to follow your instructions at all times. And I will join you also.' The mayor folded his hands across his ample belly and looked at Arianwyn carefully.

'At the first sign of trouble—'

'Yes, I know. We will return straight away.' The mayor bowed low. 'We are at your command, Arianwyn. Ah, and here come our brave volunteers.' Mayor Belcher gestured to the town square as a group of about ten men and women walked towards them. She recognized a few faces: Mrs Attinger the postmistress, Mr Bandolli from the café, as well as Dr Cadbury and Constable Perkins. And then from the Blue Ox she saw Salle and Colin hurrying across the square with a large picnic basket between them. 'Wait for us!' Salle called. 'We've got the lunch.'

'No. No way. You two are not coming,' Arianwyn said, walking towards them, determined to send them back.

Colin looked crestfallen. 'Oh, come on Wyn. I was looking forward to taking part in the cutting.'

'Yes, I've told Colin all about it,' Salle said as they temporarily rested the huge wicker basket on the cobbles of the town square.

'But it's not . . . safe,' Arianwyn said quietly. 'I've told the mayor we shouldn't really be going at all.'

'What's the hold-up, Miss Gribble?' Mayor Belcher called impatiently from where they all waited beside the cart. Elouise the carthorse snorted in the wet morning air, clouds of steam rising from her huge nostrils.

'Salle and Colin want to come along.'

'We've got a yummy lunch from Aunt Grace!' Salle called quickly.

Arianwyn spun round and fixed Salle with what she hoped was a stern look, though Salle didn't react in any way.

'Well, hurry along then!' the mayor called as he was heaved into the back of the cart by most of the others who had already climbed aboard.

Hefting the wicker basket between them, Salle and Colin rushed past Arianwyn towards the waiting horse and cart. Arianwyn sighed. It looked like they were all going, whether she liked it or not.

A few minutes later, the cart rattled out across the

bridge near the South Gate. The rain had swelled the grassy puddle, leaving the ground so flooded that the meadow between Lull and the Great Wood looked like a giant lake that stretched all the way from where the Torr River used to be visible. Lull now looked like a little island floating in a sea, ringed by a forest.

'My word,' Arianwyn sighed.

'Oh, this isn't anything much at all, Miss Gribble,' Mrs Parkinson sang as she flicked Elouise's reins. The wheels of the carriage trundled through the flood-water. 'Ten years ago, the water came right up to the gates and flooded part of the town.'

'Do you think it will get as bad this year?' Colin asked, peering up at the grey sky.

'I shouldn't think so. Rain'll stop in a day or two, I'd say,' Mrs Parkinson replied cheerfully. 'And it won't be so damp in the Great Wood anyway once we're a ways in. On you go, Elouise, there's a girl.'

And Mrs Parkinson had been right: once they had passed under the cover of the trees of the Great Wood, the ground became dry and firm, and Elouise was able to move quicker. Her bridle jingled as they moved on under the dripping canopy. Arianwyn, Salle and Colin hopped down from the cart and followed behind, Mr and Mrs Parkinson chatting with the rest of the cutting party cheerfully from their seats.

Soon the cart rumbled into a clearing and Mr Parkinson called, 'This is the best spot.' There was a wide clearing, the old trees forming a natural circle. Arianwyn could see that two of the trees had died, one already half toppled over into the clearing.

'So do we just start cutting?' Colin asked, picking up a small axe.

'Gracious, no!' Mayor Belcher said. 'We can't just start cutting – not until Miss Gribble has asked permission from the spirits that live in these trees.'

Arianwyn turned in surprise. The mayor seemed to know all about spirits all of a sudden – perhaps because it was to do with Yule.

The mayor gestured towards the two dead trees. 'After you, Miss Gribble.'

Arianwyn stepped forwards until she was standing before the first fallen tree.

'Gentle spirits, we thank you for protecting these trees and for their gift this Yule.'

She reached forwards, sketched Erte – the earth glyph – against the rough dry bark of the dead tree stump and waited.

She could feel a breeze move through the wood. It was followed by the rustle of leaves about her feet and then several faint lights began to emerge from within the trunk. Rising out through the bark and drifting up into the air above the fallen tree, the lights caught on the breeze and then drifted away, like dandelion seeds.

She heard the oohs and aahs of the group watching near the cart and Elouise gave a gentle snort as several spirits drifted towards her. And there in the swirl of the spirit light, Arianwyn saw a shape. But not just any shape!

It was such a surprise that she gave little squeak of excitement.

There in the blur of lights from the tree spirits hung a new quiet glyph!

Arianwyn scrabbled quickly in her satchel to retrieve her notebook and a pencil. But it was buried in the bottom under an apple, a spare scarf and other clutter. In frustration she cast the bag aside and grabbed a twig. There in the soft earth of the Great Wood she quickly sketched the shape, noting the soft lines and curves of the new quiet glyph.

'What's that?' Mrs Parkinson asked, coming to stand beside Arianwyn and staring at the glyph, hastily drawn into the ground.

Arianwyn turned. 'Nothing – just . . . part of the spell. You carry on with the cutting now!' She blushed a little and grabbed up her bag. She felt elated. It was as though the spirits had given her a gift all of her own, enabling her to see another of the glyphs she held somewhere inside herself. She found the notebook and started to sketch the glyph from the ground on to a blank page, lost in the shapes and lines for a moment.

Mrs Parkinson clapped her hands together and said, 'Right, m'dears. Let's get to work! Logs won't chop themselves, you know!'

They were soon all employed with different tasks, helping to saw the huge old trunks into the Yule logs or collecting fallen twigs and branches for kindling. Mayor Belcher — who was getting in the way far more than he was actually helping — was sent to collect more miselberry sprigs and winterthorn branches around the edge of the clearing. 'Stay nearby and call if you need anything!' Arianwyn had cautioned as he walked reluctantly away from the main group.

She too patrolled the edge of the trees, checking for signs of hex or dark spirit creatures lured by the human activity in the wood. There could well still be skalks and night ghasts and who knew what else in the Great Wood, just waiting for someone to wander off.

After a couple of hours the cart was loaded with a good pile of wood. Salle and Colin were handing out sandwiches and small metal cups of vegetable soup for the cutting party's lunch. Everyone was just tucking into the picnic when there was a loud scream from beyond the clearing. Followed by: 'MISS GRIBBLE!'

It was, unmistakably, Mayor Belcher.

Chapter 18
RESEARCH

'Oh, snotlings!' Arianwyn spat. Casting aside her sandwich, she ran off out of the clearing, leaping over the neatly stacked pile of logs that had already been gathered and heading in the direction of the mayor's frantic shouting.

She didn't have to run far to see the mayor half collapsed and backed up against the trunk of a huge oak tree. His bunches of miselberry lay discarded on the ground around him. 'Miss Gribble!' he shouted again. 'It's going to attack me!'

Arianwyn still couldn't see what 'it' was. She had slowed to a walk, now that the mayor was in sight. A crackling stunning orb flickered and sparked in her open palm.

'Oh my goodness!' the mayor moaned.

As Arianwyn drew closer she could see at last what was standing in front of the mayor. She felt relief wash over her as the silver antlers of a stagget caught the afternoon light.

It was a female, quite small, and she was watching the mayor as though fascinated by him. 'It's all right, Mayor Belcher. She's not dangerous.'

Arianwyn scanned the stagget for signs of hex. The last stagget she had seen had been one ravaged with hex in the Great Wood, a male that had attacked Miss Newam and Colin and their feyling friend, Tas. Arianwyn had banished it, an illegal spell for which she had nearly lost Colin's friendship.

The memory of it came back, hot and urgent.

'What does it want?' Mayor Belcher asked, glancing across at Arianwyn.

She didn't answer, but moved forward carefully. She was almost sure that it would spook at any second and run back into the wood.

'It wants the miselberry.' A high-pitched voice sounded from behind Arianwyn, making her jump.

She turned to see Estar standing in amongst the brown and orange ferns. 'Staggets enjoy eating miselberry leaves, surely you knew that, Arianwyn?' He smiled.

'Oh, Estar!' she sighed. 'It's so good to see you!' It really was; she had felt so bad about the way they'd left things last time, even if part of it had been caused by a spell. She dropped to her knees and wrapped her arms around her small blue feyling friend, their disagreement forgotten, she hoped.

'Miss Gribble!' Mayor Belcher called again.

Arianwyn turned back to the mayor. 'Just give it some of the miselberry leaves,' she said.

The mayor reached out a shaking hand of pale green miselberry towards the stagget. She eyed the bunch of greenery for a few moments and then slowly, carefully, reached for it and gently bit off a mouthful. She chewed for a few moments before stretching forward again and taking another delicate bite.

Then, silently, the stagget turned and moved slowly off into the woods once more, casting a brief look back at Arianwyn and Estar as she went.

'Oh, not you again!' the mayor sighed when he saw Estar following Arianwyn back from the cover of the ferns.

Estar bowed low, a single slender hand held across his chest. 'Mayor Belcher.'

Arianwyn helped the mayor to his feet, and as he dusted himself off he said, 'I found something odd over here, Miss Gribble. What do you make of it?'

Arianwyn and Estar followed him a little further along a dirt track to another much smaller clearing. There were signs of a campfire and the earth in the clearing was all flattened. 'Someone has been here,' the mayor said, gesturing to the blackened remains of the fire.

'And recently,' Estar said as he picked up a piece of charred wood and sniffed it.

'But who?' Arianwyn asked. 'Everyone knows that the woods are out of bounds.'

'Well, it looks to me as though someone has been making a camp here nevertheless.'

'Not more feylings on their way to Edda?' Arianwyn asked, looking at Estar.

He shook his head. 'We have had no more new feylings arrive for many weeks now,' he said sadly.

'I'm sorry,' Arianwyn said.

'Well, many of us were lucky and we should be thankful for that,' Estar said.

'How are things at Edda?' Arianwyn asked as they turned and followed the mayor back to the others.

'Complicated, but well enough under the circumstances.'

'And how is Virean?' Arianwyn asked, thinking of the white feyling she had met and the connection that clearly existed between the she-feyling and Estar.

'She is quite well.'

Arianwyn saw the slight blush under his blue skin. 'Thank you so much for coming back,' she said gently. 'I know you must be in demand in Edda at the moment.'

'Not at all.' Estar smiled and asked, 'And the glyphs?'

'One new one,' Arianwyn said. 'Came just now –

when I wasn't even thinking about them.'

'How surprising,' Estar said, though he didn't sound surprised at all. 'Excellent, you'll have to tell me all about it.' Then he clapped his hands together and said, 'So how do you humans celebrate Yule?' His yellow lamp-like eyes twinkled in the gloom of the Great Wood.

'Oh, don't ask,' Arianwyn moaned, and then in a whisper asked, 'What do you know about frost phoenixes?'

'I brought everything that was in the library about the old frost fairs.' Salle smiled as she placed a small collection of what appeared to be little more than pamphlets in front of Arianwyn. Then she quickly pulled off her coat and wellingtons and joined the others before the small fire.

They had returned from the Great Wood and the cutting ceremony soaked through. And now Arianwyn, Colin and Estar sat on the floor of the Spellorium wrapped in towels and blankets, sipping on hot chocolate. A collection of socks hung damply over a wooden airing frame before the small pot-bellied stove.

Arianwyn leafed through the first of the pamphlets. It was mostly full of old photographs of women in very old-fashioned clothes skating on the wide section of the River Torr that skirted the edge of Lull.

'Any luck, Colin?' Arianwyn asked over her shoulder.

Colin and Estar were searching through some of the old ledgers that dated back to the time when Miss Delafield's sister had been Lull's resident witch.

'Effie would have been the last witch to have presided over a frost fair here,' Colin said. 'There must be something we can use!'

'Oh, look, is this her?' Salle flipped around one of the small booklets she had brought back from the library. The photograph showed a young witch with tumbling blonde curls. She stood on the bridge that crossed the River Torr near the East Gate while others walked or skated below on the frozen river.

'Yes, that's Effie. She looks a little like Miss Delafield, don't you think?' Arianwyn asked, peering closer at the photograph.

Effie's mouth was open, as if she was in the middle of saying something – or casting a spell perhaps? There was a bright flashing blur of light across the top half of the photograph.

'Is that the frost phoenix?' Arianwyn asked, her fingers resting against the picture. 'How did Effie summon it?'

'Ah, here we are. I've found something,' Colin called, his voice full of excitement. But his enthusiasm was only very brief for then . . . 'Oh dear.'

'Oh dear what?' Arianwyn asked.

'Well, put it like this,' Estar chipped in, leaning over Colin's shoulder to look at what he'd found. 'How are you at singing?'

'*Singing?*'

'There's a song to summon the frost phoenix – the only way to summon it, it would appear,' Estar said with a slight sniff.

'I can't sing!' Arianwyn squeaked in shock. She looked at Estar and Colin and then Salle as though one of them would offer an answer.

'Oh dear – not even a teeny bit?' Salle asked.

'Not well enough to be singing in front of the whole of Lull!' Arianwyn collapsed into the small armchair beside the pot-bellied stove which was full of bright orange embers.

The Spellorium fell silent.

'Do you have the music in those pieces of paper?' Salle asked.

Estar and Colin quickly searched through the books and letters until Colin gave a triumphant 'Ah-ha!' and held out a small slip of paper that was marked with musical notes and words. At the top was a picture of a most marvellous-looking bird in full flight, a long tail trailing behind and snowflakes dotted around it.

'Look, Wyn – it's not very long,' Salle said, smiling. 'Want to give it a quick go?'

'No, Salle – not even a little bit.'

Salle laughed quietly. 'Who'd have thought after

everything *you've* faced you'd be scared to stand up and sing a silly old song?'

Arianwyn knew she had meant the words to be light and fun but they hit her straight in the chest. Salle must have noticed as she quickly stepped forwards and, taking Arianwyn's hand, said, 'Well, how about if we sing it together then? Look, it's only a few lines really. It'd be over in less than a minute. Would that work, do you think?' She looked at Estar and Colin.

'I don't see why not.' Estar shrugged. 'I imagine the song is mostly symbolic; as long as Arianwyn completes the spell correctly beforehand there is no reason to assume that this frost phoenix won't appear as everyone seems to think it might. How thrilling!'

Arianwyn smiled at Salle. 'Oh, all right – as long as you promise to stop boggin' well going on about it!'

Salle beamed and did a little dance across the Spellorium while Estar and Colin laughed and clapped.

Chapter 19

The WINTERTHORN QUEEN & THE YULE LORD

*E*arly the next morning Arianwyn hurried down into the Blue Ox to find her grandmother drinking tea quietly and alone. 'Everyone has already gone,' Grandmother said. 'What have you got to look forward to today?'

'The mayor is handing out the Yule logs this morning in the town square. Apparently, I have to be on hand too.'

'Well, why not sit and join me for a drink before you go?' She reached for the teapot as Arianwyn sat down and snatched up a piece of warm toast from her grandmother's plate, the butter oozing gently down its sides.

They sat in companionable silence for a few minutes, Grandmother flicking through some post that had arrived for her.

Arianwyn was just about to ask her grandmother what she had seen in the flames of the fire but at the last moment she changed her mind, scared to know the answer, and asked instead, 'Have you heard how Gimma is getting on?'

'I did make enquiries before I left Kingsport, but nobody seems to know who it was that was stationed at the Alverston house. And now the council is in recess for the holidays and apparently Constance, the High Elder, is off travelling somewhere. I doubt we will find out more until the New Year.'

'Where has the High Elder gone?' Arianwyn asked.

'On some sort of tour of the kingdom apparently.' Grandmother sipped her tea and carried on reading her letters. 'Don't worry, Gimma is better off with her family. Safe in Kingsport, away from the hex.'

Arianwyn hoped that was true.

The town square was packed with people, many hidden underneath umbrellas, all crowding around the Parkinsons' cart as the mayor handed out the Yule logs. 'Yule blessings to you all,' he called cheerfully as he handed a large chunk of wood to a family.

The town band played some bright Yule tunes as the rain continued to fall. Arianwyn made her way to the cart with Grandmother and Miss Delafield close behind. As soon as Mayor Belcher saw her he stopped handing out the logs and clapped his hands together – glaring at the band until they fell silent.

'Ladies and Gentlemen. I am pleased to say that Miss Gribble has consented to help us with some of the traditional Yule festivities this year. Tomorrow we will assemble on the East Gate bridge for the summoning of the frost phoenix.'

The sound of excited cheers filled the town square.

'And I am also pleased to say it is time to announce who will be this year's Winterthorn Queen.' More enthusiastic cheers rose from the crowd. Arianwyn felt a hand on her shoulder and turned to see her father behind her, as Mayor Belcher started what sounded like one of his legendary and lengthy speeches.

'What's all this about then?' Arianwyn's dad asked, gesturing to the cart and Mayor Belcher.

'He's just been handing out the Yule logs, and now he's going to announce who is the Winterthorn Queen!' Arianwyn said.

'Oh, we can't miss that, can we?' Sergeant Gribble smiled.

Arianwyn gave a small laugh as the mayor cleared his throat after a pause and continued, 'So, without further ado, I am very pleased to announce that the town council has named . . . Salle Bowen our

Winterthorn Queen for this Yule!'

The town square burst into a roar of cheers and clapping.

Arianwyn turned, searching for Salle in the crowd. She saw a flash of a faded red coat and then Salle was hurrying forwards as everyone continued to applaud.

Mayor Belcher helped her up on to the back of the cart and placed a crown that was woven with winterthorn, ivy and red and green ribbons on her head. The crowd shouted again, there was a round of applause and several loud whoops of delight, the loudest being from Aunt Grace and Uncle Mat.

Arianwyn thought she might burst with excitement. She was so pleased for Salle.

The mayor signalled for calm, and after another minute of noise, the market square fell silent again.

'And now, Salle, as Winterthorn Queen, you have the great pleasure of choosing your Yule Lord from all of our fine young men in Lull.' The mayor gestured to the crowd.

There were several long seconds of quiet.

Arianwyn wondered who Salle would pick. Perhaps Jonas Attinger? He had asked her to a dance a few months ago, Arianwyn recalled.

She watched as Salle whispered into the mayor's ear.

The mayor's eyebrows arched a little in surprise as he declared, 'And Salle's Yule Lord will be . . . Colin Twine!'

There was another bright chorus of cheering and rounds of applause. Colin was suddenly there and clambering up on to the back of the cart and standing beside Salle, completely red-faced, as she placed another, smaller crown on his head. Then they turned and faced the crowd again. The band started playing its bright tune and everyone cheered once more.

Arianwyn smiled as she watched her two friends taking a bow. Then she saw their hands linked together and it made her feel strange – rather like she had when she had found out that Colin had been to see Salle's play twice. She suddenly didn't want to be in the town square. She turned to leave.

'Where are you going?' her father asked, reaching out to catch her by the elbow.

'I just remembered I have some errands to run,' Arianwyn mumbled quietly.

'But I thought you had to be on hand for this – isn't it part of your duties?' He laughed.

She felt a flash of annoyance. Was he making fun of her work now? He hadn't been so quick to recognize her duties before when she'd had work to do – but suddenly, now that it suited him, he was trying to guilt her into staying. 'Not now, Dad,' Arianwyn snapped, and slipped away into the crowd.

Arianwyn hurried along Kettle Lane. There were only a few people wandering into the shops along the street and everyone was too busy with their own holiday preparations to notice Arianwyn hurrying off somewhere as usual.

As the Spellorium came into sight she saw Miss Delafield's motorcar parked out the front. Her supervisor leant against the bonnet, studying her driving gloves. 'Oh, there you are, dear,' she said. But the usual brightness in her voice was gone. 'I went to see you at the Blue Ox and I hadn't a hope of finding you among the crowds in the marketplace. So I thought I'd wait here.'

Arianwyn unlocked the door and they both went inside. 'Tea?' she asked.

Miss Delafield shook her head. 'I'm afraid I've got some news.' She twisted her hands together. 'Gimma Alverston has gone missing.'

'Again?'

'So it would seem,' Miss Delafield replied gravely.

Thoughts and worries stormed through Arianwyn's mind. What had happened? She wondered if she'd done the right thing in leaving Gimma behind in Kingsport, after all.

Chapter 20
The FROST PHOENIX

The next day, everyone gathered outside the town walls to witness the summoning of the frost phoenix.

The bridge that spanned the River Torr by the East Gate was full of people, with more hanging over the town walls and pressed in around the gate. The meadows were now too flooded for anyone to watch from there, even in long wellies. Arianwyn had imagined a Yule full of snow and frost, not rain and wind and flooding. The only frost so far had been due to the ice imps and that really didn't count! But still, the mood was festive: the air rang with the sounds of bright expectation, greetings and laughter, all rising high up into the grey sky above Lull.

Salle rushed forwards from the crowd, dressed in a

long green robe, with her Winterthorn crown in her hands. 'There you are – what happened to you yesterday? Your dad said you had some errands to run.' She looked as though she didn't quite believe this.

Arianwyn nodded. 'I had the charms to finish and there's been another outbreak of nitherings.' This was all true, even if it wasn't the real reason Arianwyn had left.

'Well, we missed you,' Salle said. '*I* missed you.' She reached out and took Arianwyn's hand, squeezing tightly. Did she suspect Arianwyn had felt odd about Colin being chosen as Salle's Yule Lord? 'Ready?' Salle asked.

Arianwyn suddenly felt like a fool for being jealous of Salle. She was her friend and she was pleased for her above everything else. 'I'm nervous!' she admitted as the two girls made their way along the path.

People called out excitedly as they passed:

'Good luck, Miss Gribble!'

'All the best, Arianwyn.'

'We're so excited!'

Arianwyn forced herself to smile but her nerves had twisted her guts into absolute knots and she felt sick. She couldn't remember any of the words to the blasted song. She'd never felt more nervous in her life – she felt utterly ridiculous.

'It'll be fine, Wyn,' Salle said, giving her a quick

hug as they reached the centre of the bridge. 'It's just a silly song.'

'That's right. It's just a boggin' song!' she muttered.

'Ah, there you are at last!' Mayor Belcher loomed out of the crowd towards them, almost but not quite shoving aside anyone who stood in his way. 'I was beginning to worry you'd forgotten about the ceremony.' Arianwyn raised her eyebrows at Salle, who smiled back, her eyes twinkling, full of their usual mischief.

'Yule blessings, Mayor Belcher.' Salle smiled and handed the mayor a small parcel. 'All the way from Kingsport.' She winked at Arianwyn and mouthed, 'Miss Newam!'

The mayor quickly stuffed the parcel into his raincoat pocket, blushing a little, though his cheeks may have been red because of the cold. He turned and gestured to a spot by the wall of the bridge. A small wooden platform had been placed next to the stone wall and was swagged with voluminous purple materials that matched the mayor's ever-present sash, everything now slightly damp and droopy. Winterthorn and miselberries had been woven around the purple material as well. And on the platform stood a gleaming microphone.

'Is that really necessary?' Arianwyn asked, her knot of worry tightening even more.

'Goodness yes, Miss Gribble, of course. We want

everyone to hear your beautiful voices! Besides, it will lend the ceremony a certain . . .' He waved his hand in the air and smiled. 'You know! Don't you think, Miss Bowen?'

'Oh, absolutely.' Salle avoided Arianwyn's burning gaze.

'*Traitor!*' Arianwyn mumbled under her breath as Mayor Belcher led them towards the stand and the microphone.

Miss Prynce, the mayor's secretary, stood close by, holding a clipboard. She was dressed in a bright yellow rain mac and matching hat. 'Yule blessings, Arianwyn, Salle.' She handed the mayor a slip of paper.

'Oh, snotlings, he's making a speech as well – *again!*' Salle said through gritted teeth.

But then the mayor glanced around and gestured to someone dressed in a long red-and-green tunic, wearing a funny hat with three corners that Arianwyn thought she had once seen in a museum in Kingsport. The unfortunate wearer of this outfit was Constable Perkins, Lull's police officer. And he looked far from pleased to have been roped into the festivities.

'Hello,' he said quietly as he approached the small platform.

He raised his right arm and Arianwyn could see he was carrying a large handbell, rather like the one they had used at her old school at the start and end of the day. Constable Perkins gave the bell three loud rings and the chatter on and around the bridge died away as everyone turned, faces full of expectation, to the platform.

'O yey, o yey. O yey! I command that the peace of our lord, the King, be well kept by night and day and that all manner of spirit and mischief-maker be welcome this day in Lull, whether they come late or early at the reverence of the Winterthorn Queen and Yule Lord' – he turned and bowed to Salle and Colin, who had just stepped forward from the crowd, all swathed in his Yule Lord costume – 'till the feasting days be passed. God save the King!'

'God save the King!' everyone cheered loudly.

Mayor Belcher and Constable Perkins swapped places. The mayor coughed gently and then tapped the microphone with a gloved finger.

'Ahem, good day ladies, gentlemen and children. Citizens of Lull, and dear friends.'

Arianwyn gazed out over the edge of the bridge wall. The riverbank was packed with people where the land rose up slightly and wasn't flooded, almost like a small island. She could see Grandmother with her dad, and Estar bundled up in several blankets and scarves standing with them. Nearby, Colin and Miss Delafield stood with Uncle Mat and Aunt Grace. They all waved enthusiastically.

The mayor continued his speech. 'After years without a witch of our own we have been unable to follow our traditions and celebrate Yule properly. But this year I am delighted to say that Miss Gribble – with able assistance from Miss Bowen . . .'

Aunt Grace, Uncle Mat, Colin and Miss Delafield gave a loud echoing whoop.

'. . . has consented to lead our Yule celebrations in the traditional way by summoning the frost phoenix. Merry Yule to you all!'

'MERRY YULE!' the assembled crowd called back, along with a loud clatter of applause.

Mayor Belcher stepped down from the platform and tucked the speech away in his coat. Then he gestured to the platform.

Salle stepped forward first, taking Arianwyn's hand in her own and squeezing tightly. Arianwyn followed, though her legs felt like lumps of iron. As they stood on the platform, the microphone between them, Arianwyn glanced down into the river below. It moved slowly, its waters heavy, full and dark, dark blue. She was almost tempted to throw herself in.

'Ready?' Salle whispered.

Arianwyn took one last deep shaking breath and nodded. She stood as straight as she could and smiled down at the crowds on the riverbank and then up at the people hanging over the high walls of Lull, grateful that all she mostly saw were the tops of umbrellas.

She reached forward and started to sketch Briå into the air before her. Once that glyph was

181

complete she began to draw Oru, the light glyph, over the top of Briå.

She didn't have to reach far for the pocket of magic: a rich seam ran in the blue waters of the river, right beneath the bridge.

The magic surged upwards, naturally drawn towards the glyphs like electricity searching for the earth. The two connected glyphs fizzed and fused together, burning bold and bright for all to see, high above the river.

'Now?' Salle asked.

'Now!' Arianwyn nodded and the two girls stepped closer to the microphone and began the song.

'Bird of ice and air and light,
Summoned here this Yuletide bright.
Awaken winter, bring the frost,
Return to us what once was lost.

Bird of snow and sleep and sorrow,
Fleeting, gone again tomorrow.
Pathways glisten in your wake,
To ice and snow tomorrow wake.

Bird of silent song and yearning,
Your ice–fire heart so deeply burning,
Bring us winter this Yuletide bright.
Come to the call of the good and the right!'

Their voices died out, replaced by the sound of the water moving under the bridge and the drumming of rain on the sea of umbrellas around them. The occasional call of a bird could be heard, or someone coughing in the crowd.

After what felt like for ever, Arianwyn heard a muttering behind her: 'I don't suppose she knows what she's doing, poor love.' She felt her cheeks redden as Salle glanced at her.

'Did it work?' Salle hissed.

The crowd were all staring up at the sky, but the clouds were still grey, the rain still falling.

'I have no idea,' Arianwyn replied, staring around herself. 'Doesn't look like it, does it?' she mumbled. Could the day get more humiliating?

'Look!' a voice called, somewhere from the crowd high up on the walls of Lull. 'Look – there it is!'

Arianwyn turned, almost falling from the platform. There, high in the air to the west of Lull, something was moving, something white, almost like a piece of cloud shifting on its own.

It was moving towards them.

It was fast and graceful and seemed to shimmer somehow in the weak winter light, as though it were lit from within, or as though it were made of crystal or ice. 'Is that it?' Salle asked.

'I think so.'

'It had better be,' Mayor Belcher said gruffly, and then flashed a quick smile at the watching crowd.

And then a haunting song filled the air above them, echoing like a peal of far-off bells.

As the frost phoenix drew closer, people began to cheer and call and clap. Arianwyn could see the spirit creature clearer now, and she could also feel its immense power. Its wings were gigantic and, she guessed, easily spanned the width of the river. They were pure snow-white edged with brilliant ice-blue and they sparkled like diamonds, like ice!

Its long tail feathers fluttered out behind it as it flew towards Lull, following the line of the River Torr. It dipped down and its graceful claws disturbed the surface of the river, which rippled and then froze instantly, an icy pattern swirling out in every direction. There were loud gasps from the crowd.

Then from high above again came a second call to match the first. There was a gasp from the watching crowd as a second frost phoenix spun overhead before it spiralled down to join the first.

'Oh my goodness,' Salle gasped, clutching Arianwyn's arm.

'I know.' Arianwyn giggled with delight and surprise, heart thrumming in her chest.

The two frost phoenixes spiralled together, flying high once more. They seemed to take in the watching crowd, turning this way and that to show off every feather, every breathtaking angle. The crowd cheered louder than ever as the two birds tumbled downwards, heading towards the bridge.

At the last second their wings spread wide and both creatures landed on the edge of the bridge wall, folding their shimmering wings behind them. The phoenixes' eyes were sparkling blue-green like the now-frozen river water.

They studied the crowd which had fallen silent once more and then both birds leant forwards and bowed low before Salle and Arianwyn, who stood open-mouthed in wonder, unable to move.

As they did, the largest snowflake Arianwyn had ever seen, about the size of a small plate, fell through the air and tumbled into her open hands. Then another landed on the dark blue of her coat. It was joined by another and then another.

The rain had stopped, and the air was now filled with a bright, crisp winter chill. And snow, lots and lots of snow!

'It's snowing!' Salle said, her voice full of expectation and excitement.

Chapter 21
The FEAST

The two frost phoenixes sat for a while on the bridge as townspeople moved forwards to gaze in wonder at the amazing birds. The mayor made sure that he was first to be photographed with the spirit creatures along with Arianwyn, and Colin and Salle, both wearing their crowns. 'I expect the *Flaxsham Chronicle* might well include an article with the photograph,' he said, puffing himself up and adopting his most regal pose as the photographer set up his camera. 'Very well done, Miss Gribble; and Salle, of course.'

The rain had stopped and the huge snowflakes continued to flutter down around them. Already, the top of the bridge wall was dusted white. Perhaps they would have snow for Yule after all, Arianwyn thought.

The phoenixes eventually appeared to grow bored of the attention. They each gave a low call before flapping their huge wings and taking off into the sky, where the grey rainclouds had lightened to a heavy white, promising more snow.

'Where will they go now?' Colin asked, glancing at Arianwyn.

'I don't know; I'm not entirely sure where they came from in the first place,' she said.

They watched as the two birds, who seemed to dance around each other in the air, flew out over the flooded meadow and high over Lull. As they disappeared, the snow seemed to fall thicker and faster behind them.

Somewhere a tune began to play, the sounds of an accordion and fiddle high and bright from within the town walls.

'We'll be able to go skating on the river tomorrow,' Salle said cheerfully. 'I can't believe we're finally going to have a real frost fair again! Come on, Colin, we'd better go and do our duties now. See you later, Wyn!' Salle grabbed Colin's hand and pulled him through the crowd by the East Gate.

He glanced back over his shoulder at Arianwyn briefly which only made her feel even more jealous that Salle had been chosen as the Winterthorn Queen. Not that she wanted to get dressed up in the silly outfit or have to do anything more – especially if it involved more singing! She had to admit that she was mainly jealous of how close her two friends had become.

'Well done, dear!'

Arianwyn turned to see Miss Delafield in a bright green raincoat, with festive brass bells pinned to her collar that jingled as she leant forwards to hug Arianwyn. 'That was superb!'

'Thank you, Miss Delafield. It was good of you to come.'

'I wouldn't miss it for the world, dear. Though I have to go back to Flaxsham before the feast starts . . . so I'll say goodbye now and Merry Yule.'

Arianwyn was aware that this goodbye was going to be for much longer than the usual few days before the next time she saw her supervisor. This was a proper goodbye.

She felt icy tears prick at the backs of her eyes. She sniffed and looked out across the frozen river. People were already taking careful steps out over the frozen water, loud whoops and cries of delight echoing back off the high honey-stone walls of Lull as the ice held firm.

'I'm going to miss you so much!' Arianwyn said, and reached forward to hug Miss Delafield. She really didn't know how she would cope without her trusted supervisor so close by.

'Now now, dear, I'm sure all will be well. We'll keep in touch and you can always give me a call on the phone. And I expect you to come and visit as

well. And I'm sure I'll be back . . . occasionally.'
Though she sounded far from certain. 'Well. I'll be
on my way, dear. Take care of yourself, Arianwyn.'
She sniffed then and swiped at the tears that glistened high on her cheeks. Then with a loud
'Cheerio, dear!' she marched past Arianwyn and
through the East Gate, swept into the crowd of
townspeople, and was gone.

The town square was full of light and music and
laughter. The snow had stopped falling and lay in soft
drifts around the square, the rooftops covered in a
thick white blanket. Long tables all covered in tablecloths filled the space between the buildings.
Lanterns and candles sat amidst huge steaming bowls
and plates of food. Arianwyn couldn't remember
when she had last seen such a feast. A raised wooden
platform stood before the town hall. The town band
had relocated here and were already playing lively
tunes as people rushed here and there finding seats at
the tables.

Salle and Colin sat on the platform in two massive
seats that were normally in the council chamber of
the town hall. These 'thrones' were covered in swags
of greenery and more of the mayor's favoured purple
material as well as twists of bright green and red.
They each held a large branch, again wrapped with

more winterthorn and miselberries whilst a steady queue of people moved towards them. As each person stood before Salle or Colin they were gently whacked with the branch. It was surely the oddest custom Arianwyn had ever seen. She hoped the 'wands' would last, as Salle seemed to be doing it with slightly more enthusiasm than Colin, who just timidly tapped people on the head or shoulder.

'Merry Yule, Miss Gribble!' people called as they hurried this way and that across the square, some with armfuls of gifts, or more plates full of food for the feast. Arianwyn could see Aunt Grace and Uncle Mat overseeing everything like conductors of an orchestra.

Arianwyn felt a tug on her coat and turned to see Mr Curry smiling at her. 'Merry Yule, Miss Gribble.'

'Hello, Mr Curry. How are you?'

'I'm looking forward to getting back to my house. Hoping now the temperature has dropped those nitherings will be on the run.'

'I do hope so,' Arianwyn answered, a little distracted as she watched the mayor.

He had a very satisfied smile on his face, watching everything. Meanwhile, Miss Prynce skittered about shouting orders at people, which they roundly ignored. And then the mayor's secretary spotted Arianwyn and charged over, brandishing her clip-board. 'Miss Gribble, what on earth are you doing here? Aren't you supposed to be attending to the kiln of wishes and sorrows?'

'Am I?' Arianwyn asked. 'I thought I just had to do the song and that—'

'No. Look, it says here, "Kiln – Arianwyn". I'm sure I told you about it the other day.'

Arianwyn shrugged. 'I'm sorry, Miss Prynce. I don't remember you mentioning it.'

'Well, you'd best hurry along then, hadn't you?'

'Now? But what about the feast?'

She pursed her lips. 'Oh, very well, but you promise me you'll go straight there after you've eaten – it's all set up on the bridge.'

'Yes, of course,' Arianwyn agreed. Though if she was stuck out by the bridge again, she was going to miss the best bits of the party, surely?

Salle and Colin came laughing towards her, swinging their Yule wands this way and that. 'That was fun, wasn't it?' Salle smiled to Colin as they reached Arianwyn.

'Well, you certainly looked like you were enjoying yourselves,' Arianwyn said, but it came out snappish and Salle and Colin both looked up at her, uncertainty clouding their faces. 'Sorry,' Arianwyn said quickly. 'Miss Prynce seems to think I'm manning the kiln right after the feast. I had no idea. Shall we just go and find a seat?'

'Well, we can come and help you afterwards, can't we?' Colin asked, looking at Salle who nodded enthusiastically. Arianwyn felt a flutter of hope.

Grandmother had already secured seats at the end of one of the tables, and Aunt Grace and Uncle Mat were there along with Arianwyn's father. Mr Turvy, Mrs Myddleton and most of her children were also at the table a few seats along. 'Merry Yule, Miss Witch,' Cyril Myddleton called from down the table. Arianwyn waved.

It took a while but soon everyone was seated. Occasional light flurries of snow swirled around them as the sun started to set. The braziers dotted between the tables kept everyone warm and the lights and lanterns and little electric strings of lights illuminated the town square until it looked quite magical.

Soon food was being passed around the table: huge bowls filled with creamy mashed potatoes and peas and carrots that gleamed like bright jewels; slices of chicken and beef; three different Yule pies and jugs full of steaming gravy made their way around until everyone's plates were groaning under piles of food. A huge wheel of Flaxsham cheese sat proudly in the middle of the table.

As the meal came to an end, Mayor Belcher stood on the platform where Salle and Colin had sat before. He turned on the microphone, his voice booming out across the town square, startling every-one. 'Yule blessings on you all, and now we shall invite the Winterthorn Queen and the Yule Lord to hand out the Yule gifts. And you can take your wishes and sorrow slips to the kiln out on the East Gate Bridge – Miss Gribble will be on hand there.'

'I guess that's my cue, see you later,' Arianwyn said as she got up from the table – but her friends didn't reply. Colin's offer of help was obviously forgotten as he and Salle were ushered once more to the heart of the party, and Arianwyn traipsed off alone. She made her way across the town square through the snow. The music was starting up again, people were dancing, children chasing each other in and out of the tables and snowballs were being thrown . . . but only the snowflakes swirled and drifted around Arianwyn as she moved from the bright warmth and cheer of the town square and back out to the East Gate.

The kiln was sat on the edge of the bridge just where it dipped down to the meadow. She hadn't noticed it earlier because of the crowds. She felt suddenly annoyed at all these strange country traditions that took her away from the fun. This wasn't how Yule was supposed to be. She suddenly longed for her grandmother's cosy apartment, decorated from top to bottom, candles everywhere, the radio burbling away as they sat and read together or planned their next walk through the snowy parks in Kingsport.

As Arianwyn crossed the bridge she could see that the snow was starting to fall heavier than before. She rubbed her hands together, wishing she had thought to go and fetch her gloves from the Blue Ox. Still, the kiln would keep her warm, wouldn't it?

'Except no one has lit it, of course,' she grumbled as she approached the stone-cold kiln.

It wasn't really a kiln at all. Instead, it was a large, shallow earthenware dish, as round and big as a dining table. A collection of branches and twigs had been dumped in but were now covered in snow.

'Are you ready yet, miss?'

Arianwyn turned to see a family standing on the bridge, all holding slips of paper in their hands.

'Just a sec!' Arianwyn said and turned back to the kiln. She sketched Årdra in the air over the damp kindling, and after a couple of attempts the twigs burst into flames, spitting and hissing. She gave it a few minutes before she beckoned the family on. 'There you go.' She smiled.

The little girl stepped up first and held her hand out above the flames, then she dropped the slip of paper which fell in amongst the fire and immediately started to curl. The paper turned from brown to black and vanished up into the air with sparks and smoke. 'Take my wishes and sorrows away this Yule-tide night,' she said quietly, then glanced at Arianwyn and smiled.

'Merry Yule.' Arianwyn smiled back.

Chapter 22
GIFTS FROM THE WINTERTHORN QUEEN

*A*rianwyn felt as though she had been standing beside the kiln for hours. Her fingers were numb. Her toes were solid lumps of ice. The kiln flames flickered up into the night sky, but just didn't shed enough warmth to take away the chill. The snow continued to fall, but now a stronger wind was buffeting it across the bridge.

Arianwyn had already relit the kiln with Årdra twice. It had been ages since anyone had been along to make an offering and all she could hear was the merry music coming from the town square. Arianwyn longed to be at the party again. How long did she have to wait here, anyway?

'Feeling lonely?' a bright voice asked from behind. She turned to see Grandmother, snowflakes dusting her hair like flower petals, her coat and bright yellow scarf pulled tightly around her shoulders.

'A little,' Arianwyn replied, smiling.

'Gosh, it's cold out here,' Grandmother said, moving quickly towards the kiln. Arianwyn noticed her drop a slip of paper into the flames. 'Take my wishes and sorrows away this Yuletide night.' Then she turned and smiled. 'Merry Yule, Arianwyn.' And she pulled her into a tight hug.

'Merry Yule,' Arianwyn replied.

'Why don't you go back to the party for a bit?' Grandmother offered, pulling her coat straight and wrapping Arianwyn's own scarf more tightly. 'Everyone is having so much fun. I can look after this.' Grandmother gestured to the kiln. 'Hurry back and get your Yule gift.'

Arianwyn kicked at the snow that was piling up now. 'Oh, it's only a daft apple, Grandma, and a sprig of something.'

'Rosemary,' Grandma said, taking a sniff of her own rosemary sprig and smiling. 'Makes me think of my grandmother's kitchen back in San Nevasto. She was always cooking something. Go on, run along, see your friends. I'll be fine here for a while.'

'You're sure?' Arianwyn felt suddenly light-headed at the prospect of returning to the party.

'Of course,' Grandmother replied.

'Thank you, Grandma!' Arianwyn beamed, turned

and raced back over the bridge, dodging a few people making their way to the kiln.

She was back at the town square in less than five minutes. Bob bounded across from the food tables, where the moon hare had no doubt been lurking in hope of a stray piece of cheese or pie, and ran in tight circles around her feet.

The crowd around Salle and Colin had died down a little and Arianwyn walked over slowly and watched as they handed out the apples and sprigs of rosemary. It was soon Arianwyn's turn and she stood before their thrones. 'Merry Yule!' she said as she approached them and held out her hand ready for her gift. She closed her eyes, and when she felt the weight of something in her palm she opened her eyes again.

But instead of the apple and sprig of rosemary she stared down at a small bundle of bright tissue paper and an envelope that had been decorated with draw-ings of stars and berries and snowflakes. Upon it 'ARIANWYN' was written in large letters in Salle's familiar handwriting. 'What's this?' Arianwyn asked.

'Gifts for you from the Winterthorn Queen, of course.' Colin smiled. 'And that one's from me.' He pointed at the small bundle.

'Oh, I . . .' Arianwyn stammered.

'Well, aren't you going to open them?' Salle asked, beaming at her.

Arianwyn carefully started to unwrap the small

tissue paper bundle first. As the paper unfurled like a blooming flower, she saw a small white object nestled in the middle. She carefully lifted it up and turned it over in her hand. It was a small carving of a moon hare. 'Oh, Colin. Where on earth did you get this?' Arianwyn asked. She looked up at him, saw his cheeks turn bright red as he coughed and looked away shyly.

'He carved it himself,' Salle said. 'He's *so* clever.'

'Look, Bob.' Arianwyn turned and showed the carving to the real moon hare. Bob sniffed at it twice and then gave a loud sneeze.

Salle laughed. 'I don't think Bob is that impressed with your handiwork, Colin.'

'Well, I think it's wonderful. Thank you, Colin,' Arianwyn said quietly. She could feel her own cheeks warming. She quickly turned to the envelope, tucking her moon hare figure safely in her pocket. 'And what's this?' she asked, looking at Salle.

She pulled the envelope open and tipped it up, catching the contents in her hand. It was a photograph of Arianwyn's mother in her uniform. Most of the photographs Arianwyn had were of her mother and father together. Or of them all when Arianwyn was just a baby. This was her mother as a recently qualified witch, her long curly hair falling about her shoulders, her broad grin shining out of the picture like a beacon.

Arianwyn could almost hear her mother's laughter as she looked at the picture. Her mother was always laughing.

'Thank you, Salle,' Arianwyn said, a lump in her throat.

'Colin helped me find it in the archives at the C.W.A. and then we tracked down the photographer who took the portraits for that year's graduates and he gave us a copy.'

'Has my grandmother seen this?' Arianwyn asked, a lump in her throat.

'No, not yet.'

Arianwyn wanted to show her straight away – wanted to show her both of these amazing gifts from her amazing friends. How could she have thought Salle and Colin would purposely try to be unkind? She felt bad now just thinking it.

'Thank you,' she said, reaching forwards and pulling them both into a tight hug. 'Merry Yule.'

And before she could pull away she felt herself being swung around by Colin and Salle, and they were all suddenly in the middle of a dance. Arianwyn tried to work out what was going on, but the steps didn't seem to ever repeat themselves and she gave in to being swept along by her friends, their laughter filling the air along with music, singing and snowflakes.

They twirled and skipped and stamped their way around the town square at least six times, the music growing faster and faster until it all ended and everyone collapsed into the snow with gasps and giggles.

It was the best feeling in the world. Bob, who had chased them around, raced over and gave them all a good wash as they lay laughing in the snowdrift beside the Blue Ox.

In the relative quiet the church bells sounded midnight.

'Oh, I've left Grandma with the kiln too long. I'll have to go,' Arianwyn sighed, getting to her feet and dusting off the light powdery snow. 'See you later, though.'

She waved as she hurried back across the town square and to the East Gate bridge. As she walked along Wood Lane towards the gate she could see a couple standing by the kiln, which had gone out again. But there was no sign of her grandmother. Maybe she'd gone back for an extra scarf or a hat, or to fetch a warm drink?

'Miss Gribble – we wanted to make our offerings,' the man said. He sounded rather disappointed.

'Sorry, I just went off for a dance,' Arianwyn apologized, and quickly relit the kiln with a spell.

The couple dropped their slips into the flames, muttered Yule blessings to Arianwyn and then hurried off back into town, the snow gathering in deeper drifts outside the town walls, the wind howling across the frozen meadow.

Arianwyn shivered and turned, wondering where her grandmother could have gone. And that was when she saw it. Just the other side of the bridge, already partly covered in snow, lay her grandmother's brilliant yellow scarf. Just as it had looked in the fire gazing. She darted forwards, her mind racing almost as much as her heart. She bent down to pick up the scarf, which already felt stiff with frost. She turned and looked along the river edge in both directions. But there was no sign of her grandmother anywhere.

Chapter 23
The SEARCH

*A*rianwyn pulled the scarf to herself tightly and raced back over the bridge. A few more people had wandered towards the kiln, slips of paper in hand, but she rushed past them, ignoring their questions. She had to find her father. He would know what to do.

Sergeant Gribble was sitting beside the roaring fire in the Blue Ox with Uncle Mat and Aunt Grace. They were all hugging mugs of hot tea and chatting cheerfully about the evening's festivities.

'Hello, Wyn,' he called. 'Come and have a seat.' He patted the chair beside him.

'Where's Grandma?' Arianwyn asked, and Aunt Grace must have read the panic in her voice as she got out of her seat, abandoning her mug, and moved towards Arianwyn quickly.

'I don't know. Why, what's the matter?' she asked.

Arianwyn felt as though she needed to move – to get out of the Blue Ox – but she didn't know where to go. 'I can't find Grandma,' she said, a sob bubbling up with her words.

Aunt Grace looked quickly at Uncle Mat – some unspoken message passing between them. He hurried away as Aunt Grace wrapped an arm around Arianwyn. 'She's probably just out dancing somewhere, don't you think?'

'No.' Arianwyn shook her head. 'I found this near the kiln, on the far side of the bridge. It's her favourite scarf in the world. She wouldn't have lost it.'

Aunt Grace's eyes widened. 'Um, OK, so you sit down there for a second and have some tea to warm you up and let's see what Mat says when he comes back.'

Arianwyn didn't want to wait. Even so she let Aunt Grace guide her into a chair.

'It'll be OK, love,' Sergeant Gribble said. 'She probably doesn't realize she dropped the scarf.'

Arianwyn glared at him. 'She got it travelling in Dannis; I remember her telling me there were weavers there so skilled that they could even weave memories.' A small sob escaped. 'She wouldn't have left this lying on the ground. Something bad has happened, I know it.' *And it's my fault for leaving her there, doing my job*, she thought.

Her dad squeezed her shoulder. 'Stay calm, Arianwyn. She'll turn up.'

She shook her head. He had no idea. He barely knew either of them any more. But she didn't want to argue so she kept quiet and waited.

After five long minutes of staring at the clock over the fireplace, Uncle Mat appeared with Mayor Belcher and Constable Perkins. They were all covered in snow. The mayor and constable both looked merry, bright-cheeked, and at the same time slightly annoyed to have been disturbed during the party. 'Now when did you last see your grandmother?' Constable Perkins asked.

'More than an hour ago, I think. Maybe more.'

'And where would that have been?'

'On the East Gate bridge, near the kiln. My grandmother was watching it for me while I came to the party.'

Mayor Belcher glared at her. 'The kiln was your responsibility, Miss Gribble—' he began to bluster, but Aunt Grace interrupted.

'Now's not the time, Josiah,' she said, folding her arms over her chest and fixing him with a stare that would scare off a horde of dark gruffits.

'And I found her scarf in the snow.' Arianwyn lifted the scarf, which had thawed by the fire and felt silky and warm now in her hands. She could smell her grandmother's perfume. 'It's her favourite, she'd never leave it anywhere,' she said again, giving her father another hard stare to make her point.

Constable Perkins looked at the mayor first and then scratched his head. 'I think we'd best get some people looking, Mayor Belcher, don't you? Especially with the snow coming down so heavy now.'

'Of course,' the mayor said. He reached out to place a comforting hand on Arianwyn's shoulder.

Everyone moved and started talking at once. 'Stay here,' Sergeant Gribble ordered as he pulled on his coat and scarf.

'No. I want to help,' Arianwyn said, moving after him.

'You should stay here. It might not be safe.'

'I am quite used to dealing with things that aren't safe, Dad. I'm a witch, in case you hadn't noticed!'

'Why are you always so argumentative these days?' her father asked.

'I'm not. Except for when I'm really worried about something,' she said quietly.

They stared at each other for a few moments, before Sergeant Gribble sighed and shook his head.

A few minutes later, Sergeant Gribble, Constable Perkins and the mayor led three search parties out of the Blue Ox.

Arianwyn watched anxiously from the window.

'Perhaps your grandmother might have gone to

the Spellorium to look for you,' Aunt Grace suggested gently. 'We could go and check there if you like?'

'Well, I don't want to be sat here doing nothing,' Arianwyn said. 'So yes, if that's all right?'

Arianwyn set off across the town square with Aunt Grace and Uncle Mat following close behind. The music and dancing continued and the snow still fell, and nobody took any notice of where the three of them were going, their faces so stony and etched with concern.

Arianwyn unlocked the door of the Spellorium quickly and they hurried inside, stamping the snow from their shoes and boots.

'Hello? Grandma?' Arianwyn called.

There was no reply.

'Shall we just check upstairs?' Aunt Grace asked, glancing at Uncle Mat.

As they made their way up the curving stairs Arianwyn took her chance. She turned and ran from the Spellorium, leaving the door wide open and letting the snow gust in behind her. She raced back towards Wood Lane and the East Gate, towards the kiln, determined to join the proper search for her grandmother.

The gusts of wind brought so much snow that she found it hard to see where she was going, occasionally stumbling over doorsteps or other things buried in the snow. But soon she was passing through the gate and on to the bridge. Why was no one looking there yet? It was the last place Grandmother had been seen! She hurried out over the bridge shouting 'Grandma!' over and over into the storm.

And then coming towards her, on the far side of the bridge, she could see a figure in the swirl of white.

'Grandma?' she called, wading forwards through the snow, which was now over her ankles in places.

But as the figure drew closer she could see it was not her grandmother. This figure was smaller, covered from head to toe in a long dark coat with a hood pulled low over its face. The figure moved quickly, despite the snow, with slightly erratic jerking movements, the hooded head searching this way and that as if trying to sniff something out.

'Hello?' Arianwyn shouted over the cry of the wind. 'Do you need help?'

At that moment the hood was thrown back by a strong gust, and Arianwyn saw it was Gimma.

Her skin was grey, her hair twists of dry white that looked like they might snap and shatter at any moment. A worrying fear churned in Arianwyn's stomach, colder than the snow and ice around her. She was shocked to see Gimma here – and yet perhaps part of her had known all along: wasn't this what her vision had shown her in the flames of the fire, and wasn't this what her grandmother had seen too? It all made sense. She had known this was going to happen.

'What have you *done*, Gimma?' Arianwyn asked. 'Where is my grandmother?'

Gimma carried on moving towards Arianwyn. Her dark narrow form sliced through the snow. She looked like a rift. But she still said nothing.

Arianwyn thought about running back into Lull for help but she stood her ground until Gimma was standing just a metre or so from her. 'Hello, Arianwyn,' Gimma said at last, her voice raspy and dry, as though she hadn't spoken for some time.

'Where's my grandmother?' Arianwyn asked again. Sudden tears tumbled down her cold cheeks.

Gimma glanced over her shoulder, looking back at her trail through the deep snow. Back to the Great Wood. '*She* has her.'

'Who?' Arianwyn asked, and was suddenly reaching out and grasping Gimma, her hands tangling in the heavy wool of the long coat she wore. 'What have you done with her?' she cried.

Gimma's black eyes stared ahead unblinking. 'I'm . . . sorry,' she said quietly, her eyelids flickering a little. 'I had no choice. She knows. She knows about the *Book of Quiet Glyphs*, Arianwyn. She knows the glyphs are inside you.'

'Who?' Arianwyn asked. Her mind felt fogged; she felt dizzy and suddenly sick. It must be the hex within Gimma. Where were her charms? The dark magic of the hex was stronger than ever.

'The . . . High Elder.'

'What?' Arianwyn asked, her mind spinning. It didn't make any sense. But then . . . hadn't her grandmother said that the High Elder was away, *travelling*?

It had all been a cover, she realized, the breath suddenly snatched from her lungs. The High Elder had been behind this all the time. *She* had been the one using glamour charms to disguise herself and threaten Gimma. *She* had been at the Alverston house, watching over Gimma from the window when Arianwyn had left! *She* had gone to the sanatorium in the guise of Elder Tully to talk to her father.

But what did any of that matter? She couldn't bring herself to care: she just wanted Grandmother.

'Just bring her back!' Arianwyn roared. She pulled Gimma towards her and the girls tumbled into the snow. Gimma tried to struggle free. She was strong: the hex had granted her a dark power. But Arianwyn's rage was strong too. She clung on hard and as Gimma brought her hand up – was she about to cast a spell? – Arianwyn reached out and smacked her across the face.

Gimma slumped to one side in the snow, a tangle of black in the white. She moaned.

'If you won't bring her back, then take me to her. Now!' Arianwyn said through her tears. She reached for Gimma, dragging her to her feet.

'Wyn?'

'Miss Gribble?'

Urgent shouts came from beyond the town gates. Her friends. She could hear the mayor and Salle and even her father. 'Arianwyn, where are you?'

'Here!' she shouted, but her voice came out as a dry squeak. 'I'm here with Gimma!'

She turned back as Gimma's eyes swam with the hex's darkness.

'She won't let me go,' Gimma mumbled and pulled back the long sleeve of her coat.

Her hand and arm were wrapped in a strange twist of metal that held small slivers of stone, hoops of silver and gold and several small charm orbs. Arianwyn recognized them at once – they were the ones she had made, but different somehow. The new components had altered the soft light from the charms. Now they pulsed with darkness. 'What's this?' she asked, reaching for the tangle of metal and the charm orbs, but Gimma snatched her hand away.

'It's how she controls the hex . . . and me.'

The High Elder was very interested in how I made those charms, Arianwyn remembered with a shiver.

'Take them off then,' Arianwyn said, reaching for the strange ties – but before she touched them she could feel the immense power of them, like a searing heat. She snatched her hands away.

'They won't come off,' Gimma said sadly. 'She was waiting for more of your charms to finish this.' Gimma shook her wrist. 'And you delivered them straight to Highbridge.'

Arianwyn felt like ice water had been poured over her body. *She* had done this. Her charms had been used to trap Gimma.

'Arianwyn!' came the shouts again from behind her.

'I'm here, on the bridge!' she called, then turned back to see Gimma retreating. She was already over the bridge and disappearing behind the snowfall, a sliver of black fading into the night. 'No! Wait!' Arianwyn shouted into the storm, but Gimma's retreating form only got smaller and smaller.

Fear, anger, hate bubbled up from deep inside Arianwyn. Before she knew what she was doing, she was summoning a glyph, the new glyph from the spirits in the Great Wood, the first one that sprung to her mind. She had drawn it into the swirling snow with her hand, and her strokes were strong and confident. The snow, already full of the frost phoenixes' magic, fed the glyph.

But Arianwyn, her mind clouded with confusion and fear, hadn't thought through the spell — the magic had no purpose. Before she could do anything else the glyph glowed brightly then vanished into the swirl of snowflakes. Seconds later, a new, stronger wind roared across the frozen meadow, bringing a blizzard, blotting out the view and surrounding her in a snowstorm. Ice stung her eyes, tears and snow blurring her sight. She'd made it worse. Gimma and

Grandmother were more unreachable than ever.

'Arianwyn!'

She turned and could just see her father hurrying through the snow towards her. 'What are you doing out here, you silly girl?' he snapped. 'We've all been worried sick!'

'Gimma . . .' Arianwyn mumbled. But Gimma's tracks were already covered by the heavy falling snow.

'What?' her father asked. 'What did you say?'

'Gimma?' Mayor Belcher loomed through the swirling white. 'No . . . it can't have been.'

Arianwyn gestured to where the bridge had been as Salle and Colin appeared. 'She has Grandma,' Arianwyn said to no one in particular, her voice almost lost to the winds.

'Who? Gimma?' Salle asked, wrapping a heavy blanket over Arianwyn's shoulders as the wind howled stronger than ever. She did feel incredibly cold all of a sudden.

'The High Elder,' Arianwyn said.

And she suddenly felt herself falling, everything swimming around her. She couldn't feel herself any more, as though her mind had drifted away from her body.

Everything was just white and white – and then black.

Chapter 24
The STORM

Arianwyn felt like she was swimming through deep, dark water. Somewhere high above her there was a glimmer of light, but she was surrounded by darkness.

Mumbled and muffled voices came from somewhere. There was a familiarity to the sounds but she couldn't pick out any definite words.

Where was she?

In the swirling darkness, which wasn't frightening but strangely comforting – like hiding under a blanket – she saw a form, a shape emerging. She knew at once that it was a glyph. A new quiet glyph.

'Not now,' she said to herself. 'Now's hardly the time.'

The shape was more complex than the other

quiet glyphs she had seen, its spiral longer, a sharp spear like a tail, it seemed bigger and bolder and its power throbbed and thrummed. It made Arianwyn feel a little sick.

She glanced around herself; the darkness and the glimmering light from above didn't seem to be changing at all — she was obviously not going anywhere anytime soon. So she reached towards the glyph, to see if anything would reveal itself about its power or . . . what was it Estar had called it? . . . intention.

But although it was clearly a powerful glyph it was also guarding its intention well. Very well, in fact.

'I suppose that's why you are quiet glyphs,' Arianwyn said to the glyph which was glowing a soft golden colour, like calvaria eggs. Like Yule decorations.

'Wyn?'

She heard her name called from somewhere and instinctively glanced up at the light. At the same time the glyph began to fade. She looked back at it, staring, trying hard to remember the shape, the colour and the feeling of it.

'Wyn, wake up.' The warm, familiar voice grew louder, tugging her from the darkness, pulling her free. 'She's waking up!'

It was Salle.

Arianwyn blinked, then opened her eyes properly. She was in a bed in Salle's room above the Blue Ox.

Several eiderdowns and a collection of different blankets were piled around her. Bob sat on the bed, watching her carefully. 'Hi, Bob.' The moon hare's blue eyes flashed with happiness.

The fire blazed. Salle sat beside the bed as Aunt Grace, Dr Cadbury and her father entered the room, expectant looks on their faces. Estar sat in a chair in the corner of the room, his yellow eyes glinting. He raised a hand in greeting.

But where was her grandmother? A sudden cold feeling filled her stomach, as realization dawned. 'Grandma?' she asked.

'We've not been able to find her—' Sergeant Gribble began to explain but Salle interrupted.

'Yet! We've not found her yet.' Salle fell quiet and glanced over at the window where a fluttering and gauzy light streamed in through the slightly drawn curtains. It was daytime – how long had she been asleep?

'Gimma,' Arianwyn said slowly, the memory of the night before slipping slowly through her mind. Gimma on the bridge. She had said the High Elder had her grandmother.

'Gimma?' Salle asked.

'She was there. On the bridge, when I went back. She said the High Elder took Grandmother. The High Elder *is* the traitor!' Arianwyn tried to get out of bed, but her father stepped forward and gently held her in place.

'You're to stay there, young lady.'

'But . . .' She didn't feel she had the strength to rise from the bed anyway, but she had to try, didn't she? 'But – Grandma.' She saw her grandmother's yellow scarf folded neatly over the end of the bed and her eyes suddenly swam with tears as she folded herself against her father's shoulder and sobbed.

'It's all right.' He rubbed her back and held her tight. 'We're going to find her.'

'But she's not *missing*,' Arianwyn said clearly. 'The High Elder has *taken* her. We have to go now and get her.'

Everyone started to talk at once, the voices in the room growing louder and louder as everyone tried to make their point heard.

It was Estar who brought calm back to the room as he pulled the curtains wide. 'Surely no one can go anywhere until the storm has blown over?' he asked, his voice high and fine.

Arianwyn blinked, waiting for her eyes to adjust. The window was laced with icy patterns all around the edges of each pane of glass, but she could see clearly enough that Lull and beyond was covered in the heaviest blanket of snow she had ever seen. More snow tumbled from the sky, swirling and flurrying in the gusts of wind. Nobody moved outside. Everything was white and perfect as though nothing really existed except for the immediate space of the room they were in and what looked like a half-finished sketch of the town square.

'It's been snowing all night and today,' Salle said.

Arianwyn glanced at the clock on the bedside table: it was three in the afternoon. She'd been asleep for hours and all that time the High Elder had Gimma and Grandmother. She had never felt so utterly helpless.

'We need to contact the C.W.A. And the council—' Arianwyn started.

'The phone lines are down,' Salle said in a tiny voice.

'And there's no electricity either.' Aunt Grace indicated the old lantern beside the bed which gave off a warm but slightly fluttery light.

'But we need to get word to somebody!' Arianwyn said desperately, searching the faces in the room.

'When we have power again, the constable will be able to send a message via his radio . . . but until then we are cut off from everywhere,' Aunt Grace explained.

There was a quiet in the room as everyone considered this.

Arianwyn glanced at Estar. He could teleport himself . . . But he seemed to know what she was thinking and was already shaking his head. 'I have tried, but the storm is not entirely natural, brought first by the frost phoenixes and then exacerbated by whatever it was you summoned?' His eyes glowed. 'A quiet glyph perhaps?'

217

Arianwyn nodded, feeling ashamed at her rash-
ness. She reached for her notebook and handed it to
Estar with the page open to show the last glyph she
had sketched, the gift from the Yule log spirits.

'Hmmm . . .' Estar turned the book this way and
that and then said. 'Well, that makes sense then.'

'What is it?' Arianwyn asked. 'Is it bad?'

'No,' he said quickly. 'But it looks similar to the
feyling word *mo'lkø*. It means abundance or exuberance. I suspect it amplified whatever magic was
already at work.'

'The snow from the frost phoenixes?'

Estar nodded. 'And it's now also blocking me from
leaving via my magic, or naturally I would have
sought help.'

'It doesn't make sense to me. Why would the
High Elder take Maria?' Arianwyn's father asked,
taking her hand.

'She wants *me*, because of the quiet glyphs. She
knows they're inside me,' Arianwyn said. 'She thinks
she can use Grandma to get what she wants.' She
blinked away her tears. She felt so angry with herself
for putting her grandmother in danger. And now to
make matters worse the glyph had caused the snowstorm that had cut off Lull, putting even more
people in danger. She was really outdoing herself.

Salle's hand flew to her mouth as she listened. 'I'll

go and fetch Colin,' she said, hurrying from the room.

'And I'll—' Arianwyn tried to sit up but was pushed firmly back down.

'Miss Gribble, you need to rest,' Dr Cadbury said. '*No* more excitement.'

'I'll keep an eye on her,' her father said.

'I'm fine,' Arianwyn protested, but she knew neither of them were listening. She scratched Bob's ears and the moon hare nudged up against her, flattening itself against the eiderdowns.

'I have other calls to make, several bumps and bruises and cuts from the ice and snow. Next it will be the cold keeping me busy, no doubt, and it takes so long to get about in this weather,' Dr Cadbury said as he started to pull on his coat and scarf and two pairs of mittens. 'Rest!' he said, pointing a woolly hand at Arianwyn. 'I'll be back later.' Then he turned and left, Aunt Grace following him out.

'We can't just sit here and do nothing, Dad,' Arianwyn pleaded with her father.

'I know,' he said firmly. Rising from the bed and pacing to the window and back, he stroked his chin as he walked. 'Let me think.'

The bedroom door flung wide and Colin and Salle rushed in. Sergeant Gribble spun and gave them both a sharp look. Colin stumbled to a halt at the foot of the bed. 'Oh, Wyn – Salle told me everything . . . Are you OK?'

She nodded. 'I'm just worried about Grandma.'

'You gave us all a fright,' Colin added. 'We didn't know what had happened when we found you on the bridge.'

Arianwyn explained about her encounter with Gimma, the warning about the High Elder and the strange charm contraption that had encircled Gimma's wrists.

'Well, what do you think it is?' Salle asked.

'They were my charms but ... twisted. It was definitely controlling the hex and Gimma at the same time.'

'She took your charms and turned them into something else,' Colin said quietly.

The room fell silent as they all looked at each other. Beyond the window the snow carried on tumbling down. Arianwyn pulled one of the eiderdowns about herself. It felt chilly despite the fire.

'We have to do something, and soon,' Arianwyn said, looking at her father. 'This isn't just about Grandma: everyone is in danger – don't you see? The High Elder wants the quiet glyphs, which basically means she wants me. It won't be long before she starts making demands. And anyone in her way will be in danger.'

Her father sighed and sat beside her. 'But I thought the High Elder was the head of the witches, one of the good guys?'

'I think ...' Arianwyn took a deep breath, the half-formed idea unfurling in her mind as everything fell into place. 'I think the High Elder was the one who released the hex into the Great Wood, the one who manipulated Gimma in the first place, trying to get her to steal the book before – so she could have control of the quiet glyphs. She sent us to find the book from the feylings' library. I think she even visited you in hospital, to find out about that Urisian witch. She's been using glamour charms to disguise herself. Maybe whatever she found out from you helped her figure out how to control Gimma?'

Salle and Colin's stony faces confirmed that they had come to the same conclusion.

Arianwyn's father looked a little surprised, but then he smiled. 'You took the photo? I wondered where it had gone.'

Arianwyn blushed, but her father didn't seem cross, for once.

'And now she wants you to tell her about the quiet glyphs,' Colin said quietly.

Arianwyn nodded.

'I won't let anyone hurt you,' Sergeant Gribble said quickly, coming back to the side of the bed and looking down at Arianwyn.

She knew he meant it. But didn't her father see that he couldn't protect her any more? She was the strong one. It was she who would have to protect him, and everyone else.

'I'll go and speak to the mayor now,' Sergeant

Gribble said and turned to head out of the room. 'You really should get some rest,' he said to his daughter, glancing pointedly at Colin and Salle.

The pair smiled at her. 'See you later, Wyn,' Salle and Colin said as they followed her father out of the room.

Estar remained in his seat, his eyes focused on Arianwyn and unblinking.

'What?' she asked.

'Another glyph?' he said. 'You saw it in your dreams, I think.'

'What? How did you—'

'Show me please?'

She reached over and grabbed her notebook and a pencil and quickly sketched what she could remember of the new glyph that had presented itself to her in the dark of her dreams. Then she handed the notebook back to Estar. He studied the page carefully.

Estar peered closer. 'It's a very ancient word,' he said. He glanced across the bed covers at Arianwyn, his lips pursed as he tried to recall it. 'It is known as Ðraxen. Some say it is the name for destruction.'

Arianwyn shifted uneasily under the covers.

'There is great power in this glyph. You must use it cautiously for it is like the shadow glyph and may have its own purpose and intentions that could sway a spell. Best keep it tucked away for now,' Estar said gently.

Arianwyn put her notebook away and slid down under her covers, but sleep wouldn't come. Her mind was too full of worries about her grandmother and the new glyph.

Mo'lkø – *The Glyph of Abundance*

Mo'lkø: The closest feyling word that matches this glyph means abundance, exuberance, glut – according to Estar. The glyph appeared when I encountered tree spirits in the Great Wood during the Yule log cutting ceremony.

I summoned the glyph in haste ... and it added to the magic the frost phoenixes had brought to Lull, extending the storm's power by loads.

I haven't dared to try and summon it again – though it was so easy to summon. I'm sure it could be really useful in the future as it adds so much to the original spell, even if the seam of available magic isn't great.

THE NEW BOOK OF QUIET GLYPHS BY ARIANWYN GRIBBLE

Chapter 25
AFTER THE STORM

*I*t was another two days before the snow eventually stopped falling. 'It's not snowing, look!' Salle said excitedly. She was standing beside the window, the curtains pulled back and they could see that the sky over Lull was bright blue.

Arianwyn scrambled out of bed and hurried to get washed and dressed, pulling on an extra two jumpers. Her mind was focused only on finding her grandmother.

'Wait for me!' Salle shouted as Arianwyn raced from the room and downstairs. 'I'll get Colin!'

Downstairs in the Blue Ox, Arianwyn was pulling on her boots beside the crackling fire when her father appeared in the archway. 'Where are you off to in such a hurry?' he asked, setting his mug down on a nearby table.

'To look for Grandma, of course,' Arianwyn said, tying an extra knot in her bootlace. She didn't look up at her father, even when Salle and Colin bounded in carrying bundles of food from Aunt Grace. 'We need to check again where I last saw her – out by the kiln. The High Elder must've taken her from there.'

'Hold on there,' Sergeant Gribble said, crossing to her. 'I think I'd better come with you.'

'It's fine, Dad. There's no need,' Arianwyn said.

'Just wait, young lady,' he said gruffly and stomped off to find his coat.

Estar came shuffling into the room, wrapped in his blanket and sporting a knitted hat that Aunt Grace had made for him as a Yule gift. He carried a small bundle of food.

'Where are you going?' Arianwyn asked.

'I should return to Edda now the storm has passed. Deep in the woods we rarely had snow. They will need me at home.'

Arianwyn sighed. She didn't want Estar to leave, but she knew he was worried about the other feylings.

'I'm sorry. I wish I could stay here and help you but I'll come back with help as soon as I can.'

'I know you will.' Arianwyn smiled. 'Do you want to walk with us to the wood?'

Estar nodded.

The large doors of the Blue Ox had been frozen

closed for three days so it took all four of them (and then some help from Uncle Mat and Aunt Grace) before they managed to pull the doors open.

Suddenly they were faced with the full consequences of the winter storm. All around the town square they could see other people shovelling the snow to make paths from their houses to the shops. Voices sang out and hands raised in greeting as people called across to neighbours and friends after being stuck inside for the last three days. Children were busy building snowmen or were engaged in fierce snowball battles. The snow reached as high as Arianwyn's hips and some tumbled inside the Blue Ox as they pulled the doors fully open.

'We might need a shovel or two,' Sergeant Gribble said, looking at Uncle Mat and Aunt Grace.

But Bob had no need. The moon hare leapt forward, straight into the snowdrift, disappearing with a soft *phlump* and a spray of snow, only to appear seconds later a few metres away. A brilliant white head, sparkling in the light, looked back at them, huge blue eyes blinking as though to say: *Well, what are you waiting for?*

Arianwyn was pulled outside and into the snow by Salle and Colin, their laughter ringing out across the town square. For a few blissful moments Arianwyn forgot all about her worries as they ploughed on, chasing after Bob and dodging a volley of snowballs thrown by a group of children from over near the grocer's on the corner.

They waded through the snow until they came to one of the already dug paths across the town square. It made it much easier to carry on their way towards Wood Lane and the East Gate. Estar and Sergeant Gribble joined them, a shovel leaning against his shoulder and a rucksack on his back. 'Extra supplies – just in case we get hungry on our way!' He smiled at Arianwyn.

And suddenly, even amidst the worry and terror of what might have happened to her grandmother, she was looking forward to this expedition with her father. He seemed more like his old self. It had always been like this in the past when he was on leave. He would take her on all sorts of exciting trips and excursions.

Each time they crossed paths with someone else they stopped to talk to them and heard their stories of the last few days:

'Snow up to the windows nearly!'

'We thought we might run out of food.'

'So good to be out and see everyone at last!'

'Our nitherings are all gone, Miss Gribble!'

'Haven't seen snow like this in fifty years, sixty maybe!'

As they made their way along Wood Lane, they could see the snow-covered land and the Great Wood through the partly open gate. They all paused for a moment to take in the sight of the never-ending white world. It was strange and new and beautifully terrifying.

Crossing the bridge, Arianwyn glanced at the spot where she had found her grandmother's scarf, where she had spoken to Gimma. The kiln was now lost under a drift of sparkling snow.

'It's OK, Wyn,' Colin said gently. 'I'm sure she's all right.'

'I hope so,' Arianwyn said.

At the edge of the Great Wood the group said farewell to Estar as he headed back to Edda and the other feylings and they went off in search of Grandma.

Arianwyn hung back a little, waving as her feyling friend made his way through the deep snow. It felt as though it was one goodbye after another at the moment. She swiped at frosty tears that fell as Estar was swallowed by the treeline. Then she turned and hurried to catch up with everyone else.

They had walked for only half an hour along the edge of the river, past the spot where the calvaria had laid its eggs and nearly eaten Gimma and Arianwyn, all those months ago. It seemed like a hundred years had passed, to Arianwyn. But there was no sign of anyone else here, now. And in some ways, Arianwyn was relieved: she had no idea what she was going to do once she found the High Elder. She couldn't exactly fight her, could she? Even with the quiet glyphs on her side, Arianwyn couldn't best the High Elder; she was too powerful and dangerous. And now wasn't she getting more people in trouble? Perhaps she'd made the wrong descison about going to find the High Elder.

'Are you OK, Wyn?' Salle asked, walking beside her and taking Arianwyn's mittened hand in her own gloved one. Arianwyn nodded. 'I'm hoping it might be time to break into Aunt Grace's supplies, soon!'

But then, up ahead, Colin and Sergeant Gribble froze in their tracks, Colin letting out a gasp of surprise. 'Arianwyn!' her father hissed. 'Arianwyn – what is *that*?' He pointed to the treeline before them.

Something hung in the air – something like a large, flat, mushroom-shaped balloon. But it was translucent, filled with swirls of colour and pulsating lights. Beneath the mushroom cap dangled tentacles of various lengths. It was like a gigantic floating jellyfish. Arianwyn stopped dead. She thought she had seen a drawing of one of these creatures once before but she wasn't sure where. Perhaps in her handbook . . . her handbook that was on the bookshelf back in the Spellorium! 'Snotlings.'

'It's a maudant,' Colin said, calmly but firmly. The moon hare had flattened itself against the snow and gave a low growl.

'A what?' Salle and Sergeant Gribble asked at the same time.

Arianwyn tilted her head to one side. Yes, it was a maudant. They were dark spirits, more common in the winter from what Arianwyn could remember. She'd never seen one before, and judging from the looks on everyone else's faces neither had they. The tentacles waved about, moved by the smallest breeze. The whole creature seemed to be moving forwards slowly. Very slowly. But certainly towards them.

'We should head back, I think. It's not safe to be here,' Colin said.

'But . . . Grandma,' Arianwyn said.

'Wyn, you know the maudant's tentacles are dangerous. If one of them touches us it could really hurt us . . . even kill us. And they rarely travel alone.'

'Right, that's decided then. Let's go,' Sergeant Gribble said, turning round and starting to move back towards Lull.

'Wait! But what about Grandma?' Arianwyn asked. 'We can't just give up! Isn't there a way round?' She looked at Salle who started to stare off into the wood.

'There might be a way around – perhaps,' said Salle. She pointed off to where the trees parted slightly. 'Could that be a pathway?'

Sergeant Gribble sighed and looked at Arianwyn. 'Please, Dad,' she said.

He looked back and forth between the path and

the maudant. 'OK, but if that thing gets too close, we head straight back, understand?'

Arianwyn nodded in agreement and they moved from the path to the relative cover of the Great Wood.

They could still hear the rustle of the maudant's tentacles several minutes later, but they were faster than the creature, gradually leaving it behind.

Sergeant Gribble continued to lead the way, with Arianwyn and Colin just behind him. Salle followed last, still glancing back every now and then. Despite the cover of the trees, the snow grew deeper, nearly up to their waists in some places. 'I think we should have a rest soon,' Sergeant Gribble called over his shoulder.

'Good idea, ready for a break, Salle?' Arianwyn glanced back at her friend. But she found Salle rooted to the spot, staring back the way they had just come. Standing on the path now were two figures wrapped in long dark coats and hoods.

For a second, Arianwyn thought it might be Gimma returned with her grandmother. And yet she knew that was not true. One of the figures *was* Gimma. But the other figure was shorter, stockier than her grandmother.

It was Constance Braithwaite. The High Elder.

Chapter 26
DEMANDS

'*W*here's my grandmother?' Arianwyn demanded, moving back towards the pair as quickly as the snow would allow until she could just see the High Elder's eyes under her dark hood.

'Hello, Miss Gribble,' the High Elder said calmly, as though they had just bumped into each other in the corridors of the C.W.A.

'Where is she?' Arianwyn asked again, her voice entirely calm, though inside she felt a storm was raging, a storm even more powerful than the one that had engulfed Lull.

'Somewhere . . . *safe*,' the High Elder replied. Before she knew exactly what she was doing, Arianwyn had a crackling spell orb in her cupped hand. 'I wouldn't suggest you do that now, Arianwyn,' the High Elder said, taking a step forwards. 'What might become of your grandmother if we didn't return?'

'Don't do it, Wyn,' Salle hissed behind her.

She let the spell orb fizzle away, bright sparks sizzling in the snow.

The High Elder smiled. 'Well, shall we talk now?' she said.

Arianwyn nodded once.

'Then you'll have to follow me. Alone.' The High Elder turned and started to walk away, gesturing for Arianwyn to follow. She started to, but Salle grabbed her arm, pulling her back.

'No, Wyn. You can't trust her – you know that.'

Arianwyn tugged away, glaring at Salle fiercely as she continued to follow the High Elder. She passed Gimma, who was still hidden by her hood and didn't speak or move. She just stood and watched.

The two of them carried on, walking the beaten path through the snow, the woods quiet around them except for the occasional far-off swishing noise of the maudant's tentacles.

'Well, this is better, isn't it?' the High Elder said as Arianwyn came alongside her on the path, moving ever further away from the others.

'I'm not sure anything about this is better.'

'Now don't be disagreeable, Arianwyn. I'm here to offer you something.'

'I don't want anything from you, except for my

grandmother,' Arianwyn said.

The High Elder paused and turned to face her. 'Exactly. And she is quite safe, you have my word. But there is something I will need from you in exchange.'

Arianwyn knew what she wanted. 'You want the quiet glyphs?'

The High Elder simply smiled, as if pleased that Arianwyn had worked it all out.

'Why?' Arianwyn asked.

The High Elder tilted her head. 'Because, as you have proven, there is great power in these new glyphs. Power I wish to have access to – for the good of the kingdom. Hylund needs the knowledge and the power of those glyphs to defeat our enemies.'

'What enemies? The war is over now.'

'Oh, for now.' The High Elder's eyes glinted.

'You think the war will start again?' Arianwyn asked. 'Why?'

'The Urisians have made a new discovery, one that could tip the balance in their favour.' She looked at Gimma pointedly.

Arianwyn followed the High Elder's gaze and something clicked into place: the photograph, the dark charms bound to Gimma's arms, the hex planted in the forest. 'You mean . . . the Urisian hex witches?' she asked softly.

The High Elder nodded. 'With the quiet glyphs in my possession and proof that we too can harness the hex, nothing will stand in our way. The King and the Royal Senate will see how indispensable the witches of Hylund truly are, and we will become a force to be reckoned with once again.'

Arianwyn's mind felt fuzzy, as though she was trying to work out a really hard sum in a maths lesson. 'What about Gimma?' she said quietly, her eyes drawn to Gimma's still, cloaked figure. 'Will you release her too?'

'Of course not.' The High Elder gave a small laugh. 'She is the perfect . . . *warrior*: powerful, yet obedient. Perhaps the first of many. Don't feel that you have to object, Arianwyn. I know you will, of course, even though my aims are perfectly logical. So let's make a deal. If you agree to share your discoveries with me, I will return your grandmother.'

A flurry of snow fell from the overhead branches. Arianwyn glanced back to Gimma and beyond, where her father and friends waited. Did she have any choice? All she could think of was her grand-mother. 'You promise?'

'You have my word. Hand over your little note-book and all's well.'

'I . . . don't have it with me now,' Arianwyn lied, stalling for time. Her mind was racing.

The High Elder raised her hand. 'It's quite all right. There is no rush. When you are ready to exchange, simply relight the kiln on the bridge and I will bring your grandmother back to Lull.'

Arianwyn stared hard at the High Elder, trying to see if she could trust her, even though she knew in her heart she couldn't or shouldn't.

But this gave her a chance, gave her the time to work out how to save her grandmother and Gimma and stop the High Elder.

'Arianwyn!' Colin shouted suddenly, pointing back through the wood to where the trees swayed violently. The maudant was coming! 'Get out of the way!'

'But please don't keep me waiting long, Miss Gribble,' said the High Elder quickly. 'My patience will not last for ever.' Then she called to Gimma, 'Come!'

Gimma turned and moved slowly towards the High Elder.

Arianwyn watched them walk back along the track, until the maudant's tentacles broke through the trees nearby and she turned and ran in the opposite direction to catch up with her father and friends.

Chapter 27
REPERCUSSIONS

*T*hey walked most of the way back in silence, only speaking to discuss directions once or twice. As they emerged from the Great Wood to the south of Lull about an hour later, the skies above the town had closed over with more white clouds and gentle flurries of snow gusting across the frozen meadow.

Salle saw the maudants first. 'Oh no! Look!'

Two maudants were advancing towards the town walls, their icy tentacles trailing across the meadow. 'What? No!' Arianwyn cried, hurrying forwards.

A group of people high on the town walls were shouting and pointing at the advancing spirits. Arianwyn and the others raced across the meadow towards the South Gate.

A few minutes later they had joined the group on the high walls of Lull, looking out across the expanse of frozen meadow and the advancing maudants. Mayor Belcher was amongst the party, dressed in a huge coat, with several scarves wrapped around his neck and a pair of bright pink earmuffs on his head. His face was thunderous as he marched towards Arianwyn.

'Oh, snotlings!' she mumbled. 'I'm in for it now.'

'And precisely where have you been, Miss Gribble?' the mayor shouted. Everyone turned and stared in their direction.

'We went to look for my grandmother, Mayor Belcher,' Arianwyn said, walking towards him.

'What?' the mayor asked. He looked past her at Salle and Colin, but they said nothing. Her father too stayed silent.

'I can explain—' Arianwyn began to say, but the mayor cut her off.

'No,' he snapped. 'You might be aware that we' – he gestured around himself to the town and everyone on the walls – 'are in something of a predicament.' He pointed at the maudants.

'I'm sorry . . . I had no idea—'

'No, because you weren't here. And we could have done with having you here to assist. Not just with whatever-they-are, but we also have people stuck in their houses because of the snow. Farmer Eames was asking for advice too about the qered. I could go on.' He glared at her.

'I needed to see if I could find my grandmother.' Arianwyn thought about mentioning Gimma, but now clearly wasn't the time for that.

'But it was entirely thoughtless of you, Miss Gribble, and rather selfish too, I hasten to add,' the mayor said, his voice rising. 'Hurrying off like that without speaking to me first.' Arianwyn tried to object, but the mayor raised a hand and silenced her. 'I am fully aware that your grandmother is missing. And of course she is well liked and respected here in Lull. *But* there are more urgent matters for us to attend to and we needed your assistance and you were not to be found! And in fact you placed yourself and three others in greater peril.' He looked entirely disappointed. 'Where would we be without our witch at such a time?' He blew his nose noisily into a handkerchief. 'And now with these . . . what did you say they were called?'

'Maudants,' Arianwyn offered quietly.

'Yes, maudants. With those hanging about, we really need to be coordinating our efforts.'

Arianwyn bit her lip and stared hard at the snow by her feet. Mayor Belcher was right, of course. She had been foolish and stubborn to rush off like that. Her grandmother would have gone bananas if she knew. 'I'm sorry, Mayor Belcher. Truly,' she said quietly.

'Now, how do we deal with these creatures?' His face was stony.

Arianwyn glanced away, her mind still full of the

High Elder and the quiet glyphs. She needed to check the maudants entry in her handbook, but she felt sure there was something about having to have more than one witch casting spells in unison to banish them. And she was on her own.

If only there was some quick way to contain a spell . . . Charms might work, but she didn't have enough stored up.

Then she had an idea. Across the street a brother and sister were busy attacking each other with snow-balls, each with a small pile beside a small snow fort. Perfect!

'Snowballs,' Arianwyn said. 'We need lots and lots of snowballs.'

There was soon a pile of spelled snowballs stacked against the walls, faintly glowing in the dimming light of the day – and still more were being made.

Each time there was a good pile Arianwyn would lean over them and cast a spell, drawing on Årdra and Erțe to spell them, imbuing them with a small amount of magic that she might add into a stunning orb.

'They're moving again!' someone shouted from further along the wall.

Everyone turned to watch as the two maudants began to drift again towards Lull. Then they looked back at Arianwyn expectantly. 'Well, don't wait for me – get throwing!' Arianwyn called.

The air was quickly filled with a volley of slightly glowing snowballs. They soared into the air above the meadow and towards the maudants as they floated ever closer.

The first few snowballs didn't quite reach, but as the maudants got closer and the throwers' aims improved with practice, there were bright flashes as the spells, hidden in the snow and ice, landed against the maudants' pulsating bodies.

As quickly as the townspeople were throwing the snowballs, others were making more and Arianwyn continued to cast the spell, drawing the glyphs into the drifts of snow on the high walls.

After several minutes of seemingly having no impact at all, the maudants started to drift off in the opposite direction, moving north, towards the river and away from the town! There was a small cheer from the group of townspeople on the walls.

The mayor smiled at Arianwyn and then seemed to recall he was angry with her and his smile vanished. 'Let's hope they don't return anytime soon then! You'll make sure there are sufficient snowballs available, in case they do?'

'Of course, Mayor Belcher,' Arianwyn offered quickly, desperate to make amends.

'Very good then,' the mayor snapped. Then he turned and stormed off along the walls.

Chapter 28
SHORTAGES

*A*rianwyn trudged back to the Spellorium, the snow clogged around her boots. Her feet were frozen and wet. Bob hopped at her side, but even the moon hare's cheerful disposition couldn't do anything to raise her spirits. She had colossally messed up this time, there was no doubt about that.

Once inside she crossed to the counter and fiddled with a collection of charm components that had been left there the last time she had been here. She'd lied to Salle, telling her she needed to go and collect some fresh clothes before going back to the Blue Ox. But she just wasn't sure she was ready to be with everyone after the eventful morning and afternoon.

Then she heard the bell charms over the door sing out. She turned, expecting to see a customer, but was surprised to see her father standing in the doorway. It felt slightly odd to have him here, in this place that had become *her* place alone. She stared at him, unsure what to say or do.

'Bad show today, eh?' Sergeant Gribble said softly.

'Are you going to tell me off now too?' Arianwyn asked.

'I think the mayor took care of that.'

'You could have stood up for me,' Arianwyn said quickly, wondering if that was the true source of her mood.

'But I think the mayor was right. We should have checked with him before we headed out. I know you are upset about your grandma, we all are—'

'Well, you have an odd way of showing it,' Arianwyn snapped. 'It's like you don't care at all.'

'Is that really what you think?' Sergeant Gribble asked.

It wasn't, but she was so angry, mostly with herself, that she didn't know what to say now. Arianwyn looked up but not at her father. She couldn't bear to look into his grey eyes. They seemed so full of disappointment these days.

'It just feels so hopeless, that's all,' she sighed.

Sergeant Gribble crossed over to her, his arms wide and a small smile on his face. Arianwyn allowed herself to be folded into a hug and she cried. Cried for her silly mistakes and for the fact that she had done nothing but cause more trouble for everyone else. She'd been selfish. The mayor was right; her father was right.

'Look,' Sergeant Gribble said after several quiet minutes. 'Things aren't so bad. Why not let me talk to the mayor? I'm used to dealing with these chaps in authority. Meet people just like the mayor all the time in the army, you know.'

Arianwyn couldn't quite imagine anyone else being quite like Mayor Belcher. But what did she know? Her father had travelled all over the Four Kingdoms and wider, so perhaps he really could help sort out this mess.

She nodded.

'I'll speak to the mayor then – see what can be done.' He smiled, his grey eyes sparkling in the wintry light. 'So, this is the famous Spellorium then? Are you going to show me around?'

When they returned to the Blue Ox later, everyone was just sitting down to bowls of winter vegetable stew and herb dumplings. Over dinner they all shared stories of snowbound Lull and what they had done that day. Everyone carefully avoided mentioning the trip into the wood, the encounter with

Gimma and the High Elder and the maudants. They all seemed to realize that Arianwyn needed distracting.

'The snow is so high in places you can barely get down the street,' Aunt Grace said, 'and there's no getting past the North Gate – it's snowed shut.'

'It'll be the flooding causing havoc next,' Uncle Mat said, taking a bite of dumpling. And everyone made sounds of agreement.

After dinner, Arianwyn was helping to wash the dishes with Colin and Salle and she was quietly washing a bowl when Salle nudged her, saying, 'So what are you going to do next, Wyn?'

'What?'

'About your grandma!'

'I don't know. I want to speak to Miss Delafield, but with the phone lines down I don't know how.' She put the bowl she had been washing on the drainer. She had to notify *someone* in the council or the C.W.A. – but who else could they trust? 'Miss Newam!' Arianwyn said, almost dropping the large pot she was holding. 'We could try and get word to her to warn her and others about the High Elder.'

The kitchen fell quiet.

'But how?' Salle asked.

'If you hadn't noticed, we're quite snowed in!' Colin added pointing through the kitchen window to the snow-covered courtyard beyond.

They fell silent again as they all tried to think of ways to get a message out of Lull somehow.

The very next morning, as soon as the breakfast things were tidied away, Arianwyn pulled on her coat, scarf, hat and extra gloves and stepped out on to the snowy town square. Thankfully the snowfall overnight had not been enough to cover over the pathways that had been so carefully dug out the day before.

'Where are you going?' Salle called from the doorway of the Blue Ox. She was fastening her own scarf with Colin beside her, buttoning his coat.

'I have to go and see the mayor and see what jobs he has for me today,' Arianwyn said quietly. 'And I need to spell more snowballs too, just in case.' She was still feeling bruised from the day before. She didn't want to give anyone any more excuses to tell her off.

'Let us know if you need our help with anything,' Colin offered. 'Or we'll just be busy building snowmen and drinking hot chocolate.'

Arianwyn knew he was joking but she felt a pang of jealousy that Salle and Colin would get to spend the whole day together and she would be busy at work. 'Try not to have too much fun without me then,' she called back as she headed out across the square towards the town hall, where a small group of people had gathered by the doors.

'We're worried about running out of firewood, Miss Gribble,' one person said as she approached the crowd. 'Should we go to the Great Wood to fetch more?'

'No, it's not safe!' Arianwyn said quickly, thinking about the maudants.

'And we're running out of food,' a young man added. He held tightly to two small children. 'When will the shop open again?'

'I don't know about that, I'm afraid,' Arianwyn started, but at that moment everyone started to ask yet more questions, all at the same time.

They pressed in around her, all asking things she didn't know the answer to at the same time. She found herself backed up against the town hall doors with everyone crowding in closer and closer. What could she do?

Just as it began to feel too much, the huge doors behind her swung inwards, sending her toppling backwards on to the marble floor of the entrance hall. Miss Prynce stood over her. 'What on earth are you doing on the floor, Miss Gribble?' she asked, and at the same time the crowd surged forwards, turning their focus on Miss Prynce and starting their questions afresh.

'One at a time, one at a time!' Miss Prynce shouted as she was surrounded by the crowd.

Arianwyn seized the chance to duck past her and rushed upstairs to the mayor's parlour.

'Oh, Miss Gribble. What on earth was all that commotion?' the mayor asked, glancing up from his paper and a plate of small Yule pies topped with thick cream. It seemed the mayor had not started to run out of provisions like others had! 'Would you like one?' he asked, lifting the plate.

'No thank you, Mayor Belcher. There's a small crowd of people downstairs worrying about food running out and when the electricity might be back on – and some other things as well,' Arianwyn said.

'I see,' the mayor replied. He eyed the Yule pies longingly but got to his feet. 'Well, hopefully we can resolve all the issues this evening – I've decided to hold a special town meeting,' he said, fiddling with his sash, which he wore over two cardigans instead of his usual suit. Arianwyn noticed that there was only a small fire burning and the stack of wood beside it was quite low. 'You'll come, of course?' he asked.

Arianwyn nodded.

'I wonder if whilst you are out on your other errands today if you might help spread the word as well? Perhaps Miss Bowen and Mr Twine might assist you?'

Arianwyn nodded in agreement.

'Well then, shall we take a look over what we need to get done today?' The mayor smiled a little.

Perhaps he had forgiven her for the nightmare yesterday had been. Arianwyn smiled back and moved around the desk.

Standing side by side they leant over the list to see what the day had in store.

Chapter 29
The TOWN MEETING

*A*rianwyn had only been inside the town's main hall once before and she was impressed with its grandness all over again. The floor was huge flagstones, smooth and polished from thousands of footsteps. Wood panelling ran around the lower parts of the walls and above this hung portraits of various lords and ladies from Lull's past. High above them carved wooden arches held the roof aloft.

A high platform had been erected at the far end of the hall with a long sturdy table and a few seats lined up behind it. Miss Prynce was busy directing people into the seats, most of which were already occupied, and the mayor was greeting people as they streamed in from the cold. Most of the town appeared to be there. People were standing at the back, partway down the aisle between the chairs and in the hall beyond. Arianwyn could see Millicent Caruthers who owned the boutique next to the Spellorium, Aunt Grace, Uncle Mathieu, Mrs Myddleton and her four children as well as many other people she had come to know since she arrived in Lull.

'Good evening, everyone,' Mayor Belcher began. 'As you know we have been facing significant challenges since the recent storm, and as such, many of you have concerns. After taking advice I decided a town meeting would be the best way to proceed and to pass on information and also to hear your concerns.'

The mayor continued with a longer than usual speech, the room soon growing uncomfortably warm. Everyone began to fidget in their seats; people looked beyond bored. Arianwyn stifled her own yawn behind her hand and sat straighter in her chair, fighting the urge to close her eyes for just a few seconds.

'And now, does anyone have any questions?' the mayor asked at last.

It looked to Arianwyn as though every single hand in the hall went into the air. *We'll be here all week!* she thought.

But after the first few questions the hands started to fall quickly.

'Are we going to run out of food?'

'When will the shops open again?'

'What happens if those giant jellyfish creatures come back?'

'We might run out of firewood – can we get more?'

The mayor answered all of these as well as he could and thankfully without imposing his own personal thoughts and feelings into the answers.

Arianwyn decided to ask a question herself. She'd been thinking about how else they might send a message to Miss Newam and thought she'd come up with the perfect plan . . .

'Yes, Miss Gribble?' the mayor indicated Arianwyn.

'I just thought that, well, could we try and get to Flaxsham for help?' Arianwyn suggested. The trip would serve two purposes, she thought. They could fetch help and supplies as well as calling or telegramming Miss Newam at the C.W.A.

There was a general murmur of agreement from the crowd. But the mayor's face grew stony. 'Well, that's quite out of the question. We can't get any vehicles out of the town, Miss Gribble: the snow is too deep. And from what we understand, the roads are quite impassable.'

He smiled and then looked into the crowd, hoping perhaps for another question. But Arianwyn continued to speak: 'But surely someone could go on foot?'

The mayor looked as though he might be considering this for a moment until Arianwyn heard her father say, 'No. Absolutely not. Out of the question. That would be incredibly dangerous.'

She turned and looked across at her father. He was standing near the platform, staring not at Arianwyn but at the mayor, who seemed unsure how to respond. 'Yes – perhaps not wise,' Mayor Belcher said slowly. 'We don't want to risk putting anyone in harm, Miss Gribble.'

'But aren't we going to run out of food?' Arianwyn asked. She regretted it as soon as she had said it. There were gasps from the assembled crowd and then everyone started to talk at once. Loud shouts filled the air as the mayor tried his best to calm the room and answer the questions.

'Perhaps I could go on my broom – it wouldn't take that long,' Arianwyn offered quickly.

'Absolutely not,' Mayor Belcher called over the rising voices, but when they didn't die down he stamped his foot on the boards of the platform. 'We need you here, Miss Gribble. You are our witch!'

The room fell silent but Arianwyn's ears rang with the mayor's words. She was fuming.

'Rest assured I do not take this decision lightly,' the mayor said at last. 'And I have taken advice on the matter. Therefore, until further notice, we will be instigating a strict curfew.'

'Advice from who?' It was Aunt Grace who called

above the grumbled sounds of disagreement.

'Why, from Constable Perkins and . . . Sergeant Gribble as well.'

Arianwyn looked quickly at her father. This had been *his* suggestion? She'd thought things were getting better after their afternoon in the Spellorium – she'd really felt like they'd turned a corner . . . And now *this*?

The mayor continued, 'The curfew will take effect from sunset to sunrise. And the gates will be locked and guards posted at all times.'

The excited chatter died away, filled with shocked silence.

'We must keep the town and all of you safe at all costs,' Mayor Belcher added quickly. 'Journeying beyond the safety of the town could have very serious consequences.'

'You're wrong,' Arianwyn said in the silence that followed, before she had even thought through what she wanted to say. 'This . . . isn't a good idea at all. You're putting everyone in more danger by doing *nothing*!' She was on her feet and moving towards the platform. She caught the amazed looks from Salle and Colin. 'We need to send for help!'

Mayor Belcher was turning an interesting shade of purple. 'Well, I think that is all we have time for this evening. THANK YOU!' he shouted. Everyone looked rather bemused. 'Good evening!' the mayor said loudly and then climbed down from the platform.

The room started to slowly empty, everyone filing towards the doors and heading back out into Lull. Arianwyn, unsure what else to do, had just joined the back of the queue when she felt someone grab her arm. She turned and came face to face with her father. 'I can't believe you've done this,' she said.

'What?' her father said.

Does he really not see it?

'Told the mayor to do nothing. So we're stuck here with no help! Grandma needs help, Dad.' She shook her head. 'We *all* do!'

Sergeant Gribble pulled her to him, saying angrily, 'I know what I'm doing, Arianwyn. I've been in worse situations than this, time and time again, and the best course of action is to hunker down and wait it out. The snow will melt. We could risk far more doing something foolish and stupid.'

It felt like he had slapped her across the face. *Foolish and stupid*. 'Is that truly what you think of me?'

'No, wait – I didn't mean—'

'I think you did,' Arianwyn replied as she tugged her arm free. 'You think that what I am doing here, what I am trying to do, is stupid and foolish?'

'That's not what I said, Wyn.' His cheeks were red as he stomped a few steps away. 'Why won't you listen to me? I know what's best!'

She could see it then, what really angered her father. This was why he was always so out of sorts. It was because *she* was the one who was asked and consulted, not him. 'Nobody always knows what's best all the time,' Arianwyn said. 'And you're wrong now.' She was suddenly aware that everyone was watching them.

'That's enough!' her father shouted. His voice was so loud that it made her jump. 'You will not speak to me like that in front of everyone. Get back to the Blue Ox, now.' He pointed to the door.

Embarrassment, hurt and anger all welled up inside Arianwyn like water boiling in a kettle. 'You can't just turn up after years and years and start to boss me about, Dad. I'm not a child. I have responsibilities as well, and whilst you might not think so, I do actually know what I'm doing.' Then she was crying and she didn't want to be there with everyone glaring. She shoved her way out of the town hall, through the crowd, and ran down the steps and across the snowy town square as fast as she could.

The lights of the Blue Ox looked inviting, but that wasn't where she wanted to be. She turned down Kettle Lane and was soon unlocking the door of the Spellorium. It was freezing inside; icy patterns laced the inside of the huge bowed window, but it still felt more comforting than anywhere else right then. The smell and the feeling in the Spellorium, even though it was dark, felt like home. It felt safe and welcoming.

She walked slowly across to the counter and let the tears fall down her cheeks.

She wasn't certain how long she had been sitting in the dark for when she heard a tapping on the door, followed by the sound of Bob scampering across the floorboards of the Spellorium and Salle calling, 'Wyn? Are you here?'

She didn't turn to look. Perhaps they would leave if she didn't answer.

Bob jumped up at Arianwyn, pawing at her legs with tiny cold paws and making a gentle whimpering sound.

She heard more footsteps and guessed Colin was with Salle and Bob. Nobody said anything, but she suddenly felt comforting arms being wrapped around her and the weight of two bodies, two friends, leaning against hers.

A few minutes later they were all sat upstairs, the fire crackling away and milk warming on the pot-bellied stove for hot chocolate. A few candles and lanterns lit the small space. They were all wrapped in blankets and eiderdowns and sat cross-legged on the floor in front of the fire. Bob stretched out and munched on a ginger biscuit.

'Well, now we're really stuck, aren't we?' Arianwyn said. 'It could take a week or more for the snow to clear or for the electricity to come back on. The maudants could come back at any point. And the

High Elder will want the glyphs soon. And now we're prisoners in Lull.'

She noticed a brief look pass between Colin and Salle. 'What's going on?' Arianwyn asked.

'I think Salle has a plan,' Colin said quietly. He smiled and patted her hand.

'I do indeed.' Salle grinned, sitting back against the armchair and looking very pleased with herself.

Chapter 30
CANTICLES

'We thought what everyone really needed was something to cheer themselves up after the last few days,' Salle said in her most charming voice.

They stood in the mayor's parlour the next day, having snuck past Miss Prynce who was busy gossiping with her friend when they entered and hadn't noticed them at all. Arianwyn hung back, still embarrassed by the argument the night before. This was all Salle's grand plan, so she was leaving it up to her.

'Hmmm,' the mayor said, not entirely listening and searching through a stack of envelopes and folders on his desk.

'And we thought,' Colin added brightly, 'that it

might be nice to have everyone come to the town square to sing Yule songs. It would raise everyone's spirits.'

The mayor glanced up at them and pouted. He was considering it, which was a good sign at least. 'I do think that, sadly, morale is low, especially with the curfew and . . . *everything*.' The mayor glared at Arianwyn, clearly thinking about her argument with her father from the night before. Then he quickly looked away again. 'Yes, I suppose it's not a bad idea. But I really don't have the time to be running about organizing things so I'm leaving it all up to you three.'

'Excellent!' Salle said quietly as they left the mayor's office. 'That was just what I was hoping he would say!'

'What exactly is the plan? You were a little sketchy on the details?' Arianwyn asked as they headed out across the town square.

Salle tapped her nose and winked. 'Don't you worry about all of that, Wyn. Just be ready for a bit more singing in the town square tomorrow afternoon!'

Word quickly spread around Lull that there was to be a concert and singing in the town square the next afternoon, and everyone's mood lifted as a result. At three o'clock Arianwyn headed to the town square, wrapped in extra jumpers and two scarves. The square was packed with people and a carnival atmosphere filled the air. On the steps of the town hall, the band were playing Yule songs, the music drifting out over the heads of everyone there. People danced and laughed. Arianwyn stared in wonder. However had Salle managed this? The change in mood was like magic!

'Wyn!'

'This is amazing, Salle. I'm so impressed!'

Salle glanced around herself as though she was seeing it all for the first time herself. 'Oh, this – well, yes, I suppose so . . .'

'Arianwyn.' It was her father's voice from behind her. She looked at Salle and Colin for help but they both suddenly found something fascinating to look at on the ground. Slowly Arianwyn turned. 'Hello,' her father said quietly. 'How are you?'

She was still so angry that she didn't know what to say. She felt that her father had betrayed her, had embarrassed her in front of the whole of Lull and there was no way she could forgive him so simply, not after that. Couldn't he see that? 'Excuse me,' she said quietly and walked away.

One song slipped into another as the sky above Lull began to darken. Lanterns and candles were lit here and there as the first few stars began to twinkle in the velvety blue sky. 'Come on,' Salle said as a song ended. She reached for Arianwyn's hand and pulled her away from the steps of the town hall as the band struck up another song.

'Where are we going?' Arianwyn asked.

'Shush – just follow me,' Salle said as they wove their way in and out of the crowd.

The next thing she knew they were standing in the middle of Meadow Street facing the South Gate. The street was empty, everyone still in the town square except for Colin, Aunt Grace and Uncle Mat, and Bob who all waited further down the street. 'What's going on?' Arianwyn asked. She cast a nervous look back, worried that someone might be watching as a feeling about what might be happening crept over her.

'We're going to Flaxsham,' Salle said quietly as they carried on down the street.

'All of us?' Arianwyn asked.

'No, just you and me and Colin – oh, and Bob as well.' She smiled.

'But the curfew? The gates?' Arianwyn gestured ahead.

'The South Gate isn't being watched whilst everyone is in the square,' Colin said.

A thrill of excitement tickled along Arianwyn's spine. Salle had known that would happen. But at the same time it was tinged with worry and fear. 'I can't ask you and Colin to put yourselves in danger, to get in trouble by doing this,' Arianwyn said quickly.

'I think it's already too late for that,' Aunt Grace said with a smile. She held out a knapsack. 'Food for your little expedition.'

'It'll take you about twelve hours or so to walk from here to Flaxsham, maybe a bit longer because of the snow,' Uncle Mat said as they walked towards the gate.

'We'll get our messages sent and bring back help,' Salle said as she hugged her aunt and uncle.

'Take care, and don't get yourselves into any danger,' Aunt Grace said, then she hugged Colin and Arianwyn as well, tightening Arianwyn's scarf and straightening Colin's woollen hat. Bob skipped about them as they waited. Uncle Mat checked quickly that no one was looking and then opened the smaller door in the huge wooden gate.

'Quickly,' he said as they hurried through and out into the snowy, frozen meadow.

'We'll be back as soon as we can,' Arianwyn said.

Aunt Grace smiled as the smaller door closed, and then the three friends and the moon hare stood staring up at the high stone arch of the South Gate.

They skirted the town wall, heading for Flax Road which would lead them straight to Flaxsham and much-needed help, they hoped.

They walked on in silence, each lost in their own

thoughts. Even Bob wasn't as excited as usual to be out in the meadow and followed close beside Arianwyn through the snow. They joined Flax Road and as the land rose up a little they all paused and turned to look back at Lull as the sky darkened. A few flecks of snow flew on the air that also carried the words of a song being sung in the town square.

'*And while winter birds sing to the high frosted moon,*

Here in our hearts we'll hold you, till you're home again soon.'

They turned and carried on their way.

Chapter 31
NIGHT-TIME WALK

The snow grew deeper the further they travelled from Lull, and it was so dark that Arianwyn had to summon a light orb to float over their heads. Occasionally she led them off the path by accident, suddenly confronted with a snarl of frosted brambles, an icy ditch or a thick line of trees heavy with snow, and they had to double back the way they had come.

They passed a few houses and farms, half buried in deep drifts, but most of them seemed to be abandoned. No lights shone at the shuttered windows, no paths of cleared snow led out from the doors.

It grew colder and colder and colder as they walked on. After about an hour the snow began to fall again, little flurries whipped up by the wind, stinging their faces as they stumbled on through the dark.

They had been walking for a couple of hours when Arianwyn felt a tug on her sleeve. It was Colin. 'I think we need to stop to have some food, Wyn.' He gestured back to where Salle stood shivering further down the road, leaning against a fencepost.

'Oh, Salle,' Arianwyn said, moving quickly to Salle's side and wrapping her arms around her friend.

'I'm fine, Wyn,' Salle said through chattering teeth. 'Honestly!'

A couple of moments later they had left the road for the shelter of the wood, the trees shielding them from the biting wind and swirling snow. 'Here,' Arianwyn said, offering her own scarf to Salle. She refused at first, but then gratefully wrapped the long red woolly scarf around herself.

'And here's some soup,' Colin said, passing Salle a steaming tin cup.

Salle sipped on it gratefully, staring off into the dark wood. Colin offered Arianwyn a cup next and sat next to her on the fallen tree. They all ate quietly as Bob wandered in and out of the trees, occasionally digging furiously in the snow.

'We'll have to get moving again soon. Will you be OK, Salle?' Arianwyn asked.

Salle nodded, but then gave a gasp and dropped her cup, the dregs of the soup splashing into the snow. She pointed off into the trees, where a fluttering shifting light moved like sunlight dancing through water.

Arianwyn felt the definite tingle of unadulterated magic but at the same time she could smell the stench of something darker.

'What is it?' Colin asked.

Bob growled, the hair on the moon hare's back standing on end.

'Whatever it is, I don't think it's good,' Arianwyn said. She stood, dusting snow from her coat, and moved cautiously forwards, sending her light orb ahead of her.

Here at the edge of the wood the trees grew so close together that it was slow going. She could hear Salle, Bob and Colin following her. It wasn't safe, but she knew there was no point in telling them to stay back. The stench of dark magic grew and grew, until Arianwyn thought she might be sick. She held one hand over her mouth as she used the other to move branches and brambles from the path, following the light.

And then she was in a small clearing. A small stunted tree, twisted and weak from the lack of light, stood on the opposite side. Hex was wrapped around the tree: Arianwyn could see its defined, twisted ridges.

'Oh no,' Salle said, coming to an abrupt halt beside her.

But something else was happening. The fluttering, shifting light they had glimpsed before danced behind the hex-ridden tree.

'What is that?' Colin asked, just as the spell light hovering by Arianwyn's head began to pulse brighter and brighter, its perfect sphere bulging and wobbling as though it was being moulded by invisible hands. It started to flash through different colours, bright sparks flying from it in every direction.

Arianwyn thought back to her train ride and the encounter on the bridge. 'It's a seam of magic,' she said, pointing ahead as the ribbon of magic passed into the clearing.

'But how can we see it?' Salle asked, her eyes wide with wonder.

'It's the hex affecting it. Because it's so near. This is just like what I saw on the train.'

'Should we try and stop it?' Colin asked.

'I wouldn't even know how,' Arianwyn said quietly.

Just as the seam of magic touched the tree (and the hex) there was a blinding flash of light and a burst of energy that sent Salle, Arianwyn, Colin and Bob flying back through the trees a short distance. Thankfully the deep snow broke their fall and they lay gasping where they landed as brilliant flashes and bursts of magical energy flew overhead.

After a few moments they crawled carefully forwards so they could see what was happening. The seam of magic had surrounded the tree now and the two magics were reacting with each other – bursts of energy flew out in every direction, flashes of light and magic exploding against the nearby trees and bushes. Bright specks of magic melted into the snow. 'I think we should get out of here!' Arianwyn said quickly. Bob sneezed in agreement and scampered on ahead.

It must have been the middle of the night when the trees of the Great Wood ended and the land opened up into snow-covered fields. Arianwyn guessed they were about halfway to Flaxsham. Her feet felt like lumps of ice, snow had settled on her hair and she couldn't remember what it was to be warm any more. Salle and Colin trudged ahead of her.

There was a sudden movement in the snow, and Salle and Colin stopped dead. They looked back at Arianwyn.

'What is it?' Salle squeaked.

Arianwyn had a crackling spell orb ready in her hand in seconds and moved in front of Salle and Colin, placing herself between her friends and the danger.

But then Bob suddenly darted between her legs and rushed forwards at the shifting shape, giving a loud squeaking call of excitement.

And then there were two Bobs.

'Whoa!' Colin breathed as the two moon hares stepped carefully towards each other. It looked as though Bob was staring into a mirror. And then the two moon hares were chasing each other round and round in circles, darting in between Arianwyn, Salle and Colin's legs, iridescent scales flashing in the faint light of Arianwyn's spells. Snow sprayed up behind them like stars as they raced about.

How could this be? Arianwyn wondered. The other moon hare was slightly larger than Bob, though its ears were a little shorter and after the initial excitement and running around, it was rather cautious of Arianwyn, Salle and Colin. It kept its distance from them but bounded about with excitement whenever Bob raced nearby. They couldn't even tempt it with Bob's favourite ginger biscuits.

They watched as the two moon hares sniffed at each other again and then continued to run in their strange patterns across the open field. Arianwyn could feel gentle waves of magic radiating towards her from the two spirit creatures. It was wonderful to see them with each other.

But the wind was picking up again now and the snow falling thicker and faster. They were all very exposed in the middle of the fields. 'We'd better get going,' Arianwyn said reluctantly. 'Come on, Bob!' she called, but the moon hares carried on their strange chasing dance.

'Bob!' she called again and this time rattled the packet of ginger biscuits. But Bob only stopped and turned to look at Arianwyn. The moon hare didn't seem to want to leave its new friend.

'Bob, please, we're all freezing here. We have to go,' Arianwyn said as she traipsed across the field towards the moon hare. Bob skipped towards her and she knelt briefly in the snow, thinking she might scoop the moon hare up. But Bob hopped forwards and tugged on Arianwyn's scarf with its little teeth, as though trying to pull her across the field, towards the other moon hare.

'We really need to be going, Bob,' Arianwyn said sadly. 'You'll have to say goodbye to your friend . . .'

She often wondered how much the moon hare understood what she was saying, but such a look of sadness passed over the moon hare's white face that she knew she had been understood. Bob glanced back at the other moon hare. Then it looked up at Arianwyn and made a sad mewling sound.

It made Arianwyn's chest ache as Bob looked again back and forth from the other moon hare to Arianwyn. Then it took several quick steps away from Arianwyn before coming back again and rubbing its soft white head against her gloved hand, the mewling sounds continuing.

Bob looked at Arianwyn; they looked at each other, both understanding what was happening and yet hoping it could be different somehow.

The moon hare was leaving.

Arianwyn leant forward and Bob leapt into her arms, 'I'll miss you,' she said through icy tears, hugging the moon hare closer.

They sat like that for a little while, until Bob wriggled free and bounded back across the field towards the other moon hare, pausing once or twice to glance back at Arianwyn, blue eyes full of hope and sadness. She lifted a hand in farewell and then the two moon hares were swallowed up in the snow and darkness.

It felt as though a small part of Arianwyn had gone as well.

Chapter 32
SECURE CHANNEL 736

*T*he hours slipped past as the chill wind whipped at their faces, snow blinding them as it drove towards them, gusting across the open land.

Arianwyn had given up trying to see ahead and the whole world now consisted of her boots moving forward through the snow, and endless, endless white. She felt a hollowness inside: Bob gone, her grandmother in the clutches of the High Elder, Gimma lost to the hex, and a father who just seemed to misunderstand her and not see how she had changed from the little girl he had left behind so many years ago.

Salle and Colin walked close by her side; she knew they were keeping a careful eye on her and heard them whispering occasionally. She was thankful they were there, her two best friends, the very best friends she could ever have hoped for.

'Look!' Salle said, her words almost snatched away on the wind. She pointed a gloved hand ahead to where the snow-covered road, which had offered nothing but fields and hedges and walls for the last who knew how many hours, suddenly revealed a scattering of houses and two street lights casting their orange glow out across the snow.

'We must be nearly there,' Salle called.

But the first few houses, like so many they had seen on their walk that night, were abandoned and empty of life. Curtains drawn or shutters closed, no lights, no people. It was as if everyone in the whole silent, white world had vanished except for Salle, Colin and Arianwyn.

'Where do you think everyone is?' Salle asked.

'They must have moved into town for safety,' Colin said.

They carried on, finally passing a sign that said 'Welcome to Flaxsham, the Heart of the South' just as the sun was rising, the darkness chased away by a soft pink light.

Not long after this, as they made their way to the town centre, they encountered their first person: a police officer patrolling the street. He stopped as he saw the three of them, clearly surprised. He must have realized from their snow-covered clothes and

tired expressions that they were not from Flaxsham.
'Where have you three come from then?' he asked,
puffing out his cheeks in puzzlement.

'Lull,' Salle said, pulling her scarf from her face.
'We've come from Lull.'

The police officer, who introduced himself as PC
Walters, took them quickly to Flaxsham police
station which was just a little further down the
street. A small fire was burning in his office and he
helped them take off their frozen, stiff coats and
damp, cold scarves. He fetched a pot of tea and a
plate piled with hot buttered toast. They ate and
drank in silence, grateful for the warmth in their
bellies and to be out of the snow at long last. It was
better than any feast.

'Now, how's about telling me just what's going
on?' PC Walters asked. He picked up a pencil and
held it over a notebook on his desk as he took a bite
from his own pile of toast.

They all started to talk at once, babbling about
everything that had happened – from Gimma to
Grandma's abduction. Even Bob meeting the other
moon hare. This last piece of news made PC Walters
scratch his head, but Arianwyn noticed him write
down 'Moon Hares?' on his notepad.

'We really need your help,' Arianwyn said finally

as they reached the end of their tale. 'We have to get word to the C.W.A.'

PC Walters sat back in his seat and took a big gulp from his mug of tea. Then he glanced towards the window which was all frosted over, the snow piled on the window ledge outside.

'Well, it's not quite so simple, I'm afraid,' he said gloomily. 'You might have noticed we've not exactly escaped unscathed from the storm ourselves. We're just as cut off as Lull is. Our power is intermittent at best. Our telephone lines are down and telegrams aren't working either.'

The office fell silent as the news sank in.

What could they do now? They'd come all this way and were no better off because of it. Flaxsham had been their hope, their only chance.

PC Walters cleared his throat. 'But our radio has been working on and off – it's on a battery. See.' He pointed across to a large black metal box on a cabinet in the opposite corner of the room. 'We're trying not to use it too much, though . . .' the police officer said, but Colin was already on his feet and moving across the small office towards the radio. He bent over the black metal box and started to fiddle with some of the dials and switches on the front. Three small windows suddenly became illuminated on the front, needles twitching this way and that.

'Hang on a second!' PC Walters started to object, but Colin wasn't taking any notice.

He pulled on the pair of headphones and continued fiddling with the dials and switches on the radio. 'This is Flaxsham police station to C.W.A. Headquarters on secure channel seven-three-six. Over,' he said firmly.

Arianwyn glanced at Salle as Colin focused his attention again on the dials. He seemed to know exactly what he was doing, but it was so early in the morning: would anyone be monitoring this channel at the C.W.A? And wasn't there a risk that it might be someone loyal to the High Elder?

There was a sudden urgent beeping sound from the radio. 'What's that?' Salle asked. Two red lights on the side began to flash at the same time as the machine beeped loudly a second time.

And then it stopped again almost as quickly as it had begun. Only to start again seconds later.

'It's an emergency message,' PC Walters said. Snatching up a piece of paper and a pencil, he lingered by the radio beside Colin, waiting for the beeping to start again.

When it did, he started to write something down in the notebook, his eyes flicking briefly to Arianwyn. A cold weight sank in her stomach and even though she couldn't see the piece of paper or understand the beeping message she felt instinctively that it was about Lull.

'What is it?' Arianwyn asked. She got up from her seat and walked across to PC Walters.

'Not got the full message back yet, hold on.'

They waited as over the next few minutes the radio continued its beeping message and pauses of aching heavy silence. Eventually, PC Walters turned his notebook towards Arianwyn and she read the message:

URGENT. LULL IN GRAVE DANGER. PLEASE SEND ARIANWYN GRIBBLE BACK AT ONCE. URGENT ASSISTANCE REQUIRED. OF UTMOST IMPORTANCE. PLEASE RESPOND. REPEAT. LULL IN GRAVE DANGER.

Arianwyn glanced at Colin and then at Salle. 'It's Lull. I have to go back,' she said quickly. She flipped the pad over so that Colin and Salle could read the message.

There was a flurry of movement as Salle raced across the room to look at the notebook. She gasped as she took in the writing and the weight of the words settled on her. She reached out to take Arianwyn's hand. 'What do we do?' she asked.

But Arianwyn didn't know what to say; she just knew she had to go back. 'I have to go,' she said and she moved to pull on her coat and scarf.

'Wait,' Salle said. 'Don't we need to talk about this?'

'Yes, Wyn. Wait and see if there's more information,' Colin added from his perch next to the radio.

'I don't think we can take that chance, though. Or

lose any time. Jinxing-jiggery, I should have brought my broomstick!' Arianwyn moaned. 'Has anyone got a car that might get through the snow?' she asked, already knowing it was a useless idea.

PC Walters gave a little cry of excitement. 'Oh, we have a broomstick you can use! Miss Delafield always made sure the local stations had one – in case of emergencies.' He disappeared into a large cupboard and emerged moments later with a broom covered in cobwebs and dust. 'Don't think it's been used for a while, though.' The police officer smiled, trying to give it a dust.

'Good old Miss Delafield!' Arianwyn beamed, taking the broom from PC Walters and smiling. She turned to her friends. 'Now, you two stay here and carry on trying to get hold of the C.W.A. Or whoever else might be able to help.' She headed for the door.

'Just wait a second, Wyn. It might not be safe for you to go back on your own,' Salle said. 'At least let me come with you.'

'I'll be quicker flying on my own,' Arianwyn said, taking Salle's hand. 'Stay here and wait with Colin until he gets through to Miss Newam or somebody.'

'No,' Salle said, pulling on her coat. 'I'm coming with you.'

Arianwyn could see from Salle's face that there was going to be no arguing with her at all. She sighed. 'All right then, but don't be a back-seat flyer, OK?'

Salle nodded.

'Will you be OK here, Colin?' Arianwyn asked.

'Yes, of course.' He nodded, and then quickly repeated his message again. 'Should I reply to the message to let them know you're coming back?'

'Yes,' Arianwyn said quickly, before she could think about it any more. 'Thank you for your help,' she said to PC Walters.

'Well, I don't feel that I've done all that much,' PC Walters replied. 'And now you've got more worries. I hope we can get some assistance back to you soon as possible. Do tell the mayor in Lull that we will come and assist as soon as we can.'

Arianwyn nodded. She turned and waved to Colin, who was relaying his message again, then she and Salle left the office and followed PC Walters back outside into the street.

There were a few more people outside now, and Arianwyn noticed a few curious glances as she and Salle mounted the broomstick. She kicked off from the ground and the broom shot forward, low to the ground but at a good speed.

As they left Flaxsham, Arianwyn hoped it would be fast enough.

Ðraxen – The Glyph of Destruction

This glyph is linked closely to the
feyling word for destruction and
Estar believes it to be a strong and
powerful glyph, of similar power to
the shadow glyph. It seems big and
bold, its simplicity hiding its real
nature perhaps?
I first encountered this glyph when I
was unconscious and dreaming. It
made me feel sick then, and I'm really
scared to try and use it without
knowing its intention.

THE NEW BOOK OF QUIET GLYPHS BY ARIANWYN GRIBBLE

Chapter 33
RETURN TO LULL

*H*alfway back to Lull, they clambered off the broom for a quick break, Salle stretching her legs out and twisting this way and that. Arianwyn could feel the muscles around her shoulders and back; they felt knotted and stiff. She stretched and turned to Salle. 'Sorry, I think I was getting grumpy there. I'm tired.' She smiled.

'That's OK,' Salle said. 'Me too.' She glanced around herself, then exclaimed: 'Isn't this where we saw that seam of magic thingy!' She pointed to the tracks in the snow leading off to the line of trees.

'I think you're right,' Arianwyn said, and she let her senses reach out, seeking for the feeling of magic or the roughness of the hex that had ravaged the trees.

But there was nothing. No tingle of magic, no roughness of hex.

'Strange,' she said as she moved towards the tree-line.

'Where are you going, Wyn?' Salle asked. 'Don't we need to be getting back?'

But something strange had occurred here, that much Arianwyn was certain of – she couldn't help thinking it might be important somehow. The feeling of the magic and hex had been so strong before – where had it gone? Curiosity tugged her along.

In the daylight it was easier and quicker, and they were soon in the little clearing that was mostly bramble and thorn and snag vines surrounding the hex-infested tree. Dappled light flooded in from above.

'Where's the tree gone?' Salle asked as she ducked under a thick vine hanging between two trees.

Arianwyn pointed to the tree ahead of them. 'There.'

'No,' Salle laughed. 'That can't be it. It's—' She stopped, stepping forward.

'Not infested any more,' Arianwyn said, finishing her friend's sentence, though she could barely believe what she was seeing herself.

The tree was free of hex.

The bark was just bark, a little scarred here and there where the hex had obviously broken through it, but the wood beneath was clear and healthy and pale, like a newly healed wound. Even the branches showed the first shoots of greenery.

'How is that even possible?' Salle asked. She let her hand brush the bark and Arianwyn didn't stop her. She couldn't feel any trace of hex at all within the immediate vicinity and certainly nothing was affecting the tree now.

Her mind whirred. What had they seen? The strange seam of magic, reacting to the hex-infested tree. The hex had made the seam of magic visible to them all and had caused some flashes and pops of magic as it had passed over the tree. But had it done much more than that?

'I think the seam of magic might have . . . got rid of the hex.' A small laugh burst from Arianwyn's mouth as she realized how ridiculous that sounded. 'Could it?'

She looked at Salle, who shrugged. 'Don't ask me, you're the witch!' Salle giggled.

Arianwyn thought back to the train and the seam of magic she had encountered there, its strange behaviour and random properties that had caused all sorts of upsets on the train. The seam they had seen here the night before had had similar reactions when it got near to the tree and the hex. The more she thought about it, the more certain she became she was right.

'So, let me get this right now. You really think that the natural deposits of magic can cure the hex? That a seam of magic passed over the tree and took away the hex?' Salle asked, her head to one side as she tried to figure it out.

Arianwyn nodded slowly, her mind bursting with what this could mean.

They fell silent, the only sound the wind dancing through the trees, the occasional creak of a trunk or branch followed by the cascading sound of snow sliding to the ground.

This could mean so much in terms of curing the hex in the Great Wood. If they could find a way to control or position the seams of magic . . . It might even be something that could help Gimma in time!

The thought of Gimma brought Arianwyn back to earth with a bump. 'We should be getting on our way,' she said, the dread of what awaited them in Lull returning, spoiling the moment of excitement.

They slowly walked back to where the broom lay waiting in the snow beside Arianwyn's backpack. Within a few minutes they were whizzing away again over the snowy track, roughly following the path back to Lull and whatever was waiting for them there.

They could see a small group of people waiting by the West Gate. Arianwyn was sure one of them was Mayor Belcher, his purple sash visible even from a distance, but everyone was so wrapped up in coats and scarves and hats that it was a little hard to tell exactly who was there.

As the broom flew closer Arianwyn saw Mayor Belcher raise his hand. 'We got the message. What's happened? Is it the maudants?' Arianwyn asked as she brought the broom to a graceful stop just before the mayor.

Mayor Belcher shook his head. 'No, Arianwyn, it's not that.'

She looked around herself, hoping for some clue as to what the problem was and what she needed to do to fix it.

'It's the High Elder,' Mayor Belcher said. 'You left the town unprotected when you . . . disappeared, and it was easy for the High Elder and' – he paused and swallowed – 'Gimma to get into town.'

'What?' Arianwyn asked, her voice dry, her throat tight. The High Elder had made her feel safe, promising that there was no urgency, that Arianwyn could decide when they would meet again. And Arianwyn had left the town unprotected. Then another thought occurred to her. 'Is my grandmother with them?'

The mayor nodded once.

'Where are they?' Arianwyn asked.

Arianwyn and Salle followed the mayor through

Lull. They all stayed silent. There was nothing now that anyone could say. No words of comfort. No brilliant ideas. There would be no more going for help, no more waiting for someone – or some miracle – to save them. It was quite possible that nobody would come at all now. The day had come and the choice had to be made one way or the other.

The town square seemed drained of all its colour, the buildings damp and grey. People were clustered in small groups by doorways or peering through windows. Arianwyn could see her father and Aunt Grace and Uncle Mat waiting by the door of the Blue Ox. As she walked towards the town hall they followed her. The building seemed to hulk over the town like some giant, menacing and threatening. Three figures waited on the steps of the town hall: the High Elder, Gimma and Grandmother.

Arianwyn paused on the edge of the town square.

'Are you OK?' Salle asked, squeezing Arianwyn's hand.

But Arianwyn didn't know how she felt. Everything felt numb, as though this was all more of a dream than real life. As though the cold had consumed her entirely.

She could feel the weight of her notebook in her pocket.

But it was like a lump of lead.

They moved on again, drawing closer to the town hall. They reached the steps at the same time as

Sergeant Gribble, Aunt Grace and Uncle Mat. They all stood in a small semicircle behind Arianwyn as she faced the High Elder. Arianwyn glanced quickly at her grandmother who looked all right, but tired, her hair tangled about her face. Her coat was muddy and torn near the shoulder; her face looked a little bruised.

Arianwyn felt herself shake with anger.

'Hello, Arianwyn,' the High Elder said. 'I gather you've been on a little trip?' Arianwyn didn't say anything. 'Trying to summon some help from the C.W.A? That's rather disappointing, I must say. Though not entirely surprising,' the High Elder said. 'You took advantage of my generosity. I should have known you would be plotting something when you didn't respond as soon as you got back to town.'

Salle squeezed Arianwyn's hand a little tighter.

'The town's been cut off. We need food and help getting the power back,' Arianwyn replied. She turned to Mayor Belcher. 'PC Walters promised to come to help as soon as possible,' she said quickly.

'Indeed,' the High Elder said, but she clearly didn't believe a word. 'Well, Miss Gribble, perhaps now you are ready to share your discoveries with me?' Her eyes slid across quickly to Grandmother.

Arianwyn flashed a look at Salle. Her friend's face was set and stony, her eyes wide. She gave Arianwyn the smallest of nods.

Arianwyn stepped forward, her hand slipping free

from Salle's. She reached into her pocket and pulled out her notebook. It had been a gift from Salle and Colin. It was beautiful, the leather gleaming even on the grey morning. She was sad to think the High Elder would soon have it, aside from having access to the new quiet glyphs she had discovered and recorded on its pages.

It felt as though it took a year to make the last few steps. The High Elder and Gimma towered over her. The High Elder reached out her hand towards Arianwyn, the faintest of smiles drawing across her face as she reached for the notebook. 'You have played a part in the history of the Four Kingdoms and ensured the witches of Hylund be recognized as *leaders* of this country. Not *servants* of the King and Royal Senate.'

'Constance, you are deranged,' Grandmother said quietly.

'Deranged? Far from it, Maria. The witches of Hylund dragged this country out of the dark ages and ushered in an era of culture, art and *magic*. We were queens once, leaders, revered and honoured. Now we wear a uniform and fill out forms or spend our days banishing snotlings and brownies from broom cupboards. We're just *servants*. Slaves of the kingdom and nothing more, so don't delude yourself, Maria.'

'And you think you'll change all of that with the quiet glyphs and by inflicting hex upon us?' Grandmother demanded.

'The hex has made Gimma stronger than any witch in the Four Kingdoms. And with the new glyphs she will have even more power.' The High Elder sniffed and turned away.

'It's possessed her, it's feeding off Gimma,' Arianwyn said.

'A small sacrifice for our cause, don't you see? Now hand over the glyphs!'

Arianwyn passed the notebook over, her hands shaking. She locked eyes with her grandmother, her heart racing, and allowed herself a small smile at the thought that they would soon be back together; although this wouldn't be over, at least she would have Grandmother by her side again.

The High Elder examined the book. 'Hmmm,' she said, flicking through the pages. Then she looked up at Arianwyn and said flatly, 'That's all?'

Arianwyn nodded. She felt a small moment of triumph. The High Elder had clearly thought there would be more. Perhaps her struggles with the glyphs hadn't been such a bad thing, after all.

'Well, it will do, I suppose . . . at least for now.' Constance Braithwaite closed the book. 'Thank you, Arianwyn.'

It felt as though everyone watching in the town square had held their breath and now they all seemed to sigh with a kind of relief.

Grandmother made to move, away from the High

Elder, down the steps. She tried to lead Gimma away as well, but something wasn't right. Arianwyn realized that Gimma had a tight grip of Grandmother's wrist and she wasn't letting go. Arianwyn reached towards her instinctively and Grandmother pulled harder, trying to move Gimma.

'You're not going anywhere, Maria. I am sorry,' the High Elder said as she tucked the book away under her long dark coat.

Arianwyn felt her heart plummet as the realization gripped her. 'But you promised!' she shouted.

The High Elder cocked her head to one side and gazed at Arianwyn. 'You're far more naive than I suspected. Maria is my . . . insurance. I know there will be more glyphs, Arianwyn. In time. And when they reveal themselves you will notify me before passing the knowledge to anyone else.'

Arianwyn felt a cold dead weight in her stomach, but she couldn't pull her gaze away from the High Elder's face.

Grandmother tried to pull herself free now, but Gimma and the hex were too strong.

'No!' Arianwyn cried, reaching for her grandmother. But the High Elder stepped forwards and grasped Arianwyn by the shoulders with her strong hands. 'Now, you listen to me,' she hissed. 'If you know what's good for you, you'll do nothing. Let this happen and nobody will be harmed – that's all you want anyway, isn't it, Arianwyn?' the High Elder asked, her voice sour and unkind. Her eyes scanned the people in the town square, her threat clear. Arianwyn would do nothing or she could harm everyone she loved.

The anger pulsed through her like a current. She could feel her fingertips crackle with energy, even though she had not summoned a glyph.

Should she fight back?

How?

There was no witch here to help her; the High Elder had seen to that. Miss Delafield was gone. Grandmother was helpless. Gimma was under the High Elder's spell. The High Elder could hurt Grandmother or anyone else before Arianwyn had a chance to summon a spell. She couldn't take that risk.

So she stepped away, her legs wobbling.

And she did nothing.

She felt sick.

The High Elder pulled the hood of her coat up as rain and snow-flecked wind whipped across the town square. She beckoned to Gimma who turned to follow, dragging Grandmother along with her.

Grandmother glanced back at Arianwyn, her face – usually so composed and sure – a mask of fear and worry. It twisted Arianwyn's heart until she thought she might die from sadness.

'Grandma!' Arianwyn cried as the three figures moved off across the town square, everyone giving them a wide berth.

Arianwyn felt suddenly dizzy; she stepped back and half stumbled. But Salle and her father were there, strong and loving arms holding her, supporting her, even as it felt as if the sky was tumbling down on them all.

Chapter 34
FAITH & FAILURE

*A*rianwyn wasn't sure what happened next, but she found herself sinking to the floor, Salle and her father holding on to her as best they could. She couldn't move. She didn't know how to. Wouldn't the world just end right there and then and put her out of her misery?

'Wyn, please,' Salle begged. 'Don't sit here in the cold . . .'

She felt Salle tug on her arm, trying to pull her up. She glanced across the town square to see where the High Elder was leading Grandma away; they disappeared across the square and turned on to Meadow Street.

'They've gone,' Arianwyn said sadly. She glanced up at her father. 'I got it wrong, I know.' She looked away, unable to meet his grey eyes. 'You don't have to give me a lecture.'

Sergeant Gribble dropped into a crouch beside Arianwyn. His hand rested on her arm. 'I'm not going to give you a lecture,' he said softly. 'I'm not going to say anything unless you want me to.'

Arianwyn sniffed and looked up at him. 'I'm so sorry,' she said quietly, a huge tear coursing down her cheek.

'So am I,' her father replied, glancing away for a moment. 'For everything.' He took a deep breath. 'I should have come home more. I should have made more effort to see you and your grandmother. But I think I was running away from . . . everything. And I think what happened in the Uris has affected me more than I thought. I'm' – he took a huge shudder-ing breath – 'frightened now, and I was never frightened before.'

It felt strange to hear her father talking like that. Arianwyn didn't know what to say and then she recalled her grandmother's words after they had once faced a night ghast: 'Fear is with us all at some time or other. It's nothing to be ashamed of.'

Her father gave a small chuckle. 'I remember your mum saying that to me once.' He smiled. 'You know you look more and more like her, every day.'

He reached up and brushed a curl from her face. She felt an odd sensation around her heart; it was a warmth, a flutter. She couldn't remember the last time her father had said anything like this or if he ever had. Arianwyn felt for the photograph that Salle had given her. She had kept it in her pocket since that night, hoping it might bring her luck somehow. 'Look,' she said, drawing it out. 'Salle gave it to me for Yule.'

'You're more like her than you know,' Sergeant Gribble said quietly, his fingertips resting lightly on the photograph.

'I'm nothing like her,' Arianwyn said. 'I mean, I look like her . . . but she was so much braver and better than me.' She couldn't bring herself to look down at the photograph.

'But don't you see that you *are*, not just to look at. But your good heart, your striving to do the right thing, to help. Putting yourself in danger to help others—' He fell suddenly silent and looked away. Arianwyn saw him bring his hand up to his eyes. He turned back, his eyes glinting with tears. 'You haven't let anyone down, Arianwyn. I was wrong to say that the other day. I was angry, and you're my little girl—'

'But I'm not a little girl any more, Dad,' Arianwyn said.

'I know, I know. And it took me a while to see that. I've heard all the great and amazing things you've done. I've seen how everyone here looks to you for help. And they're right to. You are a fine witch. Just like your mum.'

She glanced down at the photograph at last. Her mum smiled out at her, her long curly hair tumbling about her face. Her eyes were bright, her smile wide. One hand was raised in a wave. 'Oh, Mum,' Arianwyn said and it made her suddenly ache for her mother in a way she hadn't in a long time. 'I've let you down,' she whispered to the photograph.

'What did she say?' she heard Mayor Belcher ask.

'She feels like she's let her mum down,' Salle explained quietly.

'And Grandma and everyone else,' Arianwyn said, unable to stop the tears from coming now.

Sergeant Gribble wrapped his arms around Arianwyn and hugged her tightly. After a few moments he sat back and smiled. 'Now then, what do you need us to do to help? I'm at your command.' He gave her a small salute.

Arianwyn shook her head. 'We can't risk putting the town in danger. We have to hope that Colin got through to Miss Newam at the C.W.A. and that they can get help here as soon as possible.'

'Or perhaps your friend Estar will return with help. He seems like a resourceful fellow,' Sergeant Gribble added.

'But you have to go after her, now,' Salle said.

Arianwyn glanced across the town square in the direction the High Elder and Gimma had taken Grandma. 'But I can't ask the town to put itself at risk like this. My job is to protect Lull not to keep putting it in danger. Who knows what the High Elder might do?'

'Nonsense!'

Arianwyn looked up; it was Mayor Belcher who had spoken. And she assumed she had misheard him.

He knelt down in the snow at Arianwyn's side. 'Just you listen here, young lady,' he said. 'You are our witch and we are *very* proud of you. Lull will stand by you now, to help you bring your grandmother back safely.' She looked up at the mayor. He smiled gently. 'For all the times you have put yourself in danger to help us, let us help you now.' He grasped her hands in his own. 'Let us do this for you, Arianwyn. Please.'

'But I don't know what *to* do,' Arianwyn said, her voice small and useless.

'Mere details — I'm sure you'll think of something,' Mayor Belcher said patting her arm.

Arianwyn looked quickly at her father and the mayor. She glanced at Salle but didn't dare meet her eyes for fear she would burst into tears. She could feel determination spreading through her like warmth.

'You're right,' she said; her voice sounded small, like the seeds from a dandelion that might just evaporate and disappear in a strong gust of wind. She felt small in the vast space of the town square. 'We have to stop the High Elder!' She shakily got to her feet and looked at her family and her friends and her friends who had become her family.

'We can rally the townspeople, Arianwyn. Don't worry about that,' Mayor Belcher offered calmly, stepping towards her. She could see his hands shaking a little. His face was white. 'Just send a signal when you need our help. Go and rescue your grandmother . . .' He gave her a warm smile and rested his hand on Arianwyn's shoulder. '*Help Gimma . . .*'

Salle stepped forwards and adjusted Arianwyn's scarf. 'We're all behind you,' she said, and hugged her tight.

Arianwyn turned, the cold tears already swimming in her eyes, then she raced across the town square, following the well-trodden paths through the deep snow.

Her mind was fixed, clear. She didn't even feel nervous about what she was about to do. She turned down Meadow Street. And ahead, through the high arch of the South Gate she could see the frozen lands beyond Lull. *Where was the High Elder going now?*

Her boots slipped a little on the packed snow that glinted beneath her. She saw the worried looks on people's faces as she hurried past. As she reached the gate she could hear the urgent shouts of the mayor, 'Miss Gribble requires *our* help now. All our help. Grab anything you can that might help in a fight and follow us.'

She felt a small smile spread across her face and dashed onwards through the gate. Her eyes flicked to the treeline of the Great Wood. Was Estar really there? With other feylings? They were well hidden if they were. A glimmer of hope shone through the darkness of the day, though her mind rumbled with questions that rolled like storm clouds.

She could see the High Elder now. Behind her, Gimma was forcing her grandmother along through the snow. The icy wind dragged across the meadow, tugging at coats and scarves and strands of hair.

'STOP!' Arianwyn shouted as loudly as she could as she ran, slipping and sliding after them.

She saw them pause. The High Elder glanced back across her shoulder. She was slightly ahead and separate from Gimma and Grandmother.

This was her chance. Arianwyn hurled a crackling spell orb in the direction of the High Elder. The snow before her exploded, sending her flying to one side with the force of the blast. For a second, everything was white as chunks of ice and billows of steam flew back across the meadow at Arianwyn.

Arianwyn quickly assessed the scene. The High Elder was on the ground a metre or so away, Gimma and Grandma off to one side on a slight slope. 'Gimma, Grandma, run!' Arianwyn shouted.

But Gimma stayed put, her hold on Grandma firm. She remained under Constance Braithwaite's control. The High Elder was rising to her feet – but before there was time for her to attack, Arianwyn summoned Oru and Årdra.

The spell flare that Grandmother had taught her was ready and she launched it skywards, praying it was enough and that everyone in Lull would spring into action. Though who knew what that action might be.

The High Elder shrank back from the bright spell as it shrieked upwards and flared high in the sky. She looked slightly frightened, and that made Arianwyn glad. *Now you know how it feels*, she thought.

But the High Elder quickly gathered her wits. Now she crouched low in the ice and snow covering the frozen river. She already held a crackling ball of angry energy in her right hand and her face was full of rage. Now it was Arianwyn's turn to be afraid.

What was I thinking! I can't hope to win in a fight against the High Elder!

Arianwyn bunched her hands into fists. She had made a right boggin' mess out of this and no mistake, she was on really thin ice this time — but she wasn't going to give up, not this time.

She hoped her friends were ready to fight too.

Chapter 35
FRACTURE

'You're a fool, Arianwyn. I warned you. But you wouldn't listen,' the High Elder growled as she got to her feet, her spell orb, a dark green, crackling in her hand. She looked across at Gimma and Grandma, frozen like ice statues, watching everything unfold before them.

The High Elder made a simple hand gesture and Gimma began to move forwards as though the High Elder had pulled strings or turned a switch. But Gimma had only taken a few steps when a barrage of snowballs flew through the air, pelting the High Elder in the chest and face. As each ball of snow exploded, Arianwyn felt a tingle of magic.

These were the leftover snowballs she had spelled to chase away the maudants! Arianwyn turned to look up at the high walls of Lull. She could see Mayor Belcher, snowball in hand, leaning over the wall edge. There were other welcome faces too, including her father, Salle, Cyril Myddleton and Miss Prynce all armed with spelled snowballs. And amongst the familiar townspeople were different faces, faces covered in midnight-dark feathers, or pale as bone. Even one that was blue with lamp-like eyes that glowed, even in the morning light. They gave a loud cheer.

'Estar!' Arianwyn breathed; a wave of relief and hope rushed over her and an unexpected laugh escaped her at the sight. Her heart swelled with love and thanks for her friends and for Lull.

But it didn't last long as the High Elder gave a loud screech of frustration and threw her pulsating green spell orb up at the wall and the people there.

'NO!' Arianwyn cried, but she needn't have worried as the faces quickly vanished as the orb sailed high over the walls.

'Your aim isn't what it used to be, Constance,' Grandmother said as more snowballs were launched by eager townspeople.

'Do something!' the High Elder screamed at Gimma, who released Grandma and then turned and unleashed a burst of black lightning that forked across the snow towards the walls of Lull. Arianwyn spun, sketching Aluna into the air. She sent the nearby snowbank shooting upwards like a high white wall. But Gimma's spell was much stronger and the ice wall shattered into a spray of snow and water that covered them all. The cold made Arianwyn gasp, breathless for a few seconds.

The High Elder formed a new spell orb and aimed it straight at Grandma, who had collapsed, weakened from her ordeal, into the snow.

There was nothing Arianwyn could do; there was no time. But then there was a flash of bright blue light and Estar was suddenly beside Grandma. His hands moved quickly in the air as the High Elder's spell surged forwards – and then it slammed into an invisible wall and evaporated into nothing more than sparks.

Arianwyn let out a gasp of relief and smiled in thanks at her feyling friend. There was another burst of blue light and both Estar and Grandma vanished.

Her grandmother was safe for now, Arianwyn thought, her heart racing with excitement. She was elated, light with relief! She turned back towards the High Elder and took a deep breath. It wasn't over just yet.

'Enough of this!' the High Elder spat, scrabbling back to her feet. She reached under her coat, covered in snow from the attacks, and pulled out the notebook which she shook at Arianwyn. 'You have caused this, Arianwyn. This is all your doing. All your *fault*!' She flicked quickly through the pages and then paused, her eyes alight with danger.

'NO – wait!' Arianwyn called, a sick feeling rising in her stomach. She could sense the High Elder's next move and it terrified her.

When the High Elder looked up again, her eyes briefly locked with Arianwyn's before she glanced back at the book and then pressed her hand into the snow beside her. A look of cruel triumph spread across her face.

Arianwyn started to run towards her. 'Stop!' But the High Elder's hand moved quickly, more quickly than Arianwyn could run in the snow and slush that pooled around her feet. As she drew nearer, she saw the High Elder's eyes shining in the light of the glyph sketched into the snow between them.

The High Elder's eyes widened, and a frightening grin spread across her face that was all teeth.

'What have you done?' Arianwyn asked, reaching out as though she might be able to undo the spell.

'You have only yourself to blame.' The High Elder's grin widened.

Arianwyn stared down into the space in the snow where the High Elder had sketched the glyph. It flashed and flickered there, and Arianwyn felt her heart stop for a second and she rushed forwards in panic. 'That's . . . the glyph of destruction – you . . . *idiot*!' she snapped.

'I warned you. And now you will have to face the consequences. You and your friends in Lull. It could have been so different, Arianwyn – we could have worked together.'

The ground beneath them seemed to rumble and shake and it was difficult for Arianwyn to keep her balance. The glyph glowed brighter and brighter. She could just see the High Elder through the spell's brilliance as she shifted, channelling the power of the glyph. But the magic wasn't as Arianwyn had expected it to be – there was no darkness to it, though she could feel that it was there behind the spell, feel the High Elder's intentions mingled with the magic.

The High Elder thrust her hands out, but not towards Arianwyn.

Towards the town.

Towards the high, safe, honey-coloured walls of Lull. Arianwyn's home!

From where the High Elder stood, straight across the snowy ground a jagged tear opened. It zigzagged through the snow, splitting the earth below into a narrow ragged gap. As it reached the walls there was a sound of stone grating against stone. The break in the ground snaked its way up the wall and the grating sound grew louder and louder.

Then suddenly about halfway up the wall, two huge chunks of stone, almost as large as Beryl, tumbled out and fell into the snow. More stone collapsed inwards, but still the crack grew larger. A moment later another massive lump of stone fell, and by now Arianwyn could see through the gap into the town, the rooftops and walls of houses and buildings she knew well. Townspeople high on the tops of the wall cried out in fear and panic. She saw people and feylings rushing about, running away from where the wall was weakening.

She hoped they would be in time. But she could do nothing to help – all she could do was watch.

'You have brought this all on yourselves!' the High Elder shouted.

There was a loud pop and the familiar flash of blue light and Estar was next to her again.

'What do we do?' Arianwyn asked as they both stared up at the huge chasm in the walls. 'She's destroying Lull!'

'Watch,' Estar said, his yellow eyes glinting through the dust.

'Estar—' Arianwyn began.

'*Watch!*' he said, and again he gripped her shaking hand in his own. It was strangely warm on this cold day so full of fear and terror.

Where the ground was split something now moved, shifted.

It snaked along the ragged tear in the snow. And suddenly bursting through were thick green tendrils, shoots.

Something was growing in the midst of the destruction.

'What is that?' Arianwyn asked Estar.

He smiled. 'The glyph!'

More shoots were springing out of the space in the town walls; they bulged and rippled, thickening in seconds, turning from bright green to dusky brown, casting out branches and leaves and more shoots.

'TREES?' the High Elder screeched.

Arianwyn turned, as surprised as the High Elder at what was unfolding before them.

'What is this?' the High Elder demanded.

'The power of the glyph,' Estar explained simply.

'But it was supposed to be a spell of destruction,' she spat angrily, stomping a little further forwards. 'You said so in the notebook!' The High Elder glared at Arianwyn as though this were all her fault.

'Indeed,' Estar replied. 'Ðraxen is a powerful glyph. It is a feyling word for destruction . . . but also for change and transformation. For to undergo our greatest transformation things sometimes must be destroyed, like a seed bursting open to form a shoot that grows into a mighty tree!' He gestured back to where all along the route of the spell's path trees were growing, twisting up through the snow and reaching for the high cloudy sky. 'A seed bursting into a shoot might look like destruction to someone who knew no better.' He grinned wide.

'You tricked me!' the High Elder spat.

Arianwyn could feel herself shaking; it was terror, but excitement as well. She glanced at Estar – he had known all along what the spell would do.

'The feyling magic isn't dark, High Elder. It's only your intention that makes the spell that way. But even you cannot undo the ancient magic in the quiet glyphs.'

'I will destroy Lull and everyone in the wretched town!' the High Elder shouted.

But before she could say or do anything more, everything seemed to jolt to one side. The ground beneath them gave a terrible lurch and groaned, and Arianwyn was suddenly stumbling and sliding as the world pitched.

What was happening now?

All around them the frozen ground was shifting, huge lumps of ice breaking apart as though struck with a huge hammer. Cracks spread out in every direction. The spell was still at work, Arianwyn realized. It was causing some sort of earthquake. For a moment, there was stillness.

'Enough!' The High Elder was standing over her, her eyes wide. She grabbed Arianwyn's coat and pulled her to her feet. 'You've always been decidedly too tricky a witch for your own good, Arianwyn Gribble. Well, I won't put up with it any longer.' The High Elder aimed a strong kick at Estar, sending him flying back across the fractured ground with a small cry.

And then there was a terrific cracking sound that filled the air around them. The High Elder's grip was tight around Arianwyn's uniform coat, but there was panic in the older witch's eyes. It sounded as through the whole earth was splitting in two, lurching and shifting even worse than before, large chunks of the ground sliding over each other.

Arianwyn realized with a sickening feeling that it wasn't the ground at all . . . She glanced around herself. The land rose up a little to her left. There was the East Gate bridge. That meant . . .

They were in the middle of the frozen River Torr. Except it wasn't frozen any more!

As more of the ground – no, the ice – split open, steam rose up into the air around them, obscuring the view.

There was another lurch of the ice under her feet and Arianwyn stumbled backwards, out of the High Elder's grip, and felt her head crack against a large solid something. A sharp pain spread out from the back of her head. Her vision blurred and was filled for a few moments with bright blasts and flashes of colour. The edges of her vision grew dark as she lay stunned, the coolness of the ice a relief against her back. But under her coat she could feel the ice moving. She tried to get up but her arms and legs felt too heavy. Any moment though, she knew she would slide through into the river below or the water would surge over the ice and claim her. It didn't feel as terrifying as she had imagined it should, but perhaps that was because she had just whacked her head.

Sure enough, she could feel the chill pull of ice water running under and around her at last.

And then she felt hands on her arms and shoulders and she was being pulled, then dragged then lifted. The steam and snow flying about in the air kept everything shrouded in a veil of white. 'It's all right,' said a raspy, dry voice near her ear. 'It's OK.'

She could feel herself being dragged away. Arianwyn had lost all sense of where she was, even though she tried to look about herself. Again the raspy voice said, 'You're safe now.' She saw a grey hand move past her face and she quickly scrabbled to her feet. Gimma was standing before her, the High Elder's charm ripped free from her wrist at last, her skin torn and sore. Estar was at her side.

'Gimma?' Arianwyn said, brushing ice and snow from her coat. 'Estar?'

'He removed the charms,' Gimma said, her voice still dry and hushed.

Arianwyn could see the red raw marks on Estar's hands, where the magic had worked against them both. *It must hurt so much*, she thought. 'You should put some snow on that,' she offered, still feeling a little muddled after the blow to her head.

But before she could say anything more there was another cracking, wrenching sound as more large chunks of ice were suddenly tipping up on end, cracking and slipping under the fast-flowing water. Arianwyn moved forwards, searching for the High

Elder. But Gimma reached out and held her back. 'There's nothing you can do, Wyn,' she said quietly. 'She's gone.'

They watched the water surge past, tumbling the huge broken slabs of ice as though they were nothing more than leaves in a stream.

Chapter 36
HEALING

*A*rianwyn hurried along the busy street towards the Civil Witchcraft Authority building. She weaved in and out of the people on the pavement as cars, buses and vans sped past on the road. A boy stood on the side of the road selling newspapers, thrusting them into the arms of passers-by as he called, 'New Council of Elders to be elected today!'

As she neared the high black gates at the front of the C.W.A. building, Arianwyn realized that one of her shoelaces was undone. She'd have to stop to tie it up before she fell flat on her face. As she knelt, she heard a booming bright voice call out over the sound of the busy street, 'Arianwyn, *dear*!' Turning, she saw Miss Delafield striding across the road, oblivious to the traffic hurtling past and around her. Her coat flapped out behind her, arms wide in greeting. 'Hello! Hello!'

'Miss Delafield!' Arianwyn leapt up from the pavement and straight into Miss Delafield's open arms. 'It's so good to see you.'

They held each other tight for several long moments as the world whizzed around them. 'So, what do you think is going on?' Arianwyn asked as they walked, arms linked, towards the C.W.A. gates. 'I had a call from Grandmother yesterday asking me to come straight away – my train only got in an hour ago.'

Miss Delafield grinned, twirling her satchel in a wide circle. 'And I've been recalled from my posting out in Hagley Bottom.' She laughed.

Arianwyn came to a halt and turned quickly. 'Really? Are you coming back to Flaxsham?'

Miss Delafield laughed again. 'Sounds like it, dear. Certainly the Director has retracted the previous posting, along with several other daft decisions that were signed off by the High Elder.' She looked thoughtful for a few moments. 'How were we all so easily fooled?' As they carried on inside she continued, 'Who knows, dear, I might take a well-earned holiday whilst I'm waiting to hear what they want to do with me.'

They passed through the doors of the C.W.A. and into the reception area which was packed full of witches all in their identical navy uniforms. Some were rushing here and there while others stood in small groups talking quickly and quietly. A few glanced across as Arianwyn and Miss Delafield entered.

'Is every witch in the kingdom here?' Miss Delafield asked.

They'd only gone a few metres when Colin and Miss Newam came rushing forwards from the crowds. They both waved and Colin called, 'Wyn!'

'Hi, Colin, Miss Newam,' Arianwyn said as they all came together amongst the waiting witches.

'Miss Gribble,' Miss Newam said. Her voice was lighter than usual, but she still wore her usual ill-fitting black suit, thick spectacles and a slightly sour expression. 'And Miss Delafield, back from . . . where was it that you were re-stationed?'

'Don't ask!' Miss Delafield said quickly. 'So, what's going on, any news?'

Colin raised an eyebrow and motioned to a small alcove in the far corner of the reception hall, tucked out of the way of the other witches. When they were all assembled he said, 'Director Coot has been in the council chamber all day with the remaining members of the council who didn't resign after the news of the High Elder's . . .' He hesitated, searching for the correct word.

'Treachery!' Miss Newam spat.

'Yes,' Colin agreed. 'So, they've been in there all

morning nominating and voting new members of the council.'

'But there has been a lot of disagreement, I can tell you,' Miss Newam added. She looked rather pleased about this.

'My grandmother sent word for me to come,' Arianwyn explained.

'Yes, she wants to see you in a while, but first of all . . .' He paused and glanced at Miss Newam. His cheeks bore two bright spots. He shifted from foot to foot.

'Miss Alverston has asked to see you,' Miss Newam said in her matter-of-fact way.

'A lot,' Colin added.

'Oh. Gimma,' Arianwyn breathed.

A few minutes later they all stood in a corridor looking through long glass doors into a small courtyard garden. Bright purple and yellow crocuses prodded up through the earth. A man and woman sat on a bench talking with a young girl with the palest of pale blonde hair that looked like high clouds at sunrise.

She was chatting happily with the two witches as they drank from mugs. Her skin, though washed-out, was no longer grey and the black film was gone from her eyes.

Arianwyn felt a surge of relief, flooding her like warm sunlight. 'It's the seam of magic, isn't it?' Arianwyn asked, looking at Colin and Miss Newam. 'It really worked!'

Colin nodded and smiled.

'Your theory was correct, Arianwyn,' Miss Newam said softly. 'The seam of wild magic does purge the hex from living matter.'

'We tested it a lot before trying it with Gimma,' Colin explained quietly.

'Silas and Judith have been working with Gimma for the last few weeks. I've been carefully supervising them myself,' Miss Newam added.

Gimma was free of the hex at last?

Without waiting a second longer, Arianwyn opened the doors and stepped into the courtyard.

'Gimma . . .' Arianwyn said quietly.

Gimma glanced up at Arianwyn, the two girls' eyes locking on to each other. The black film of the hex no longer present, Gimma's bright blue eyes shone back again.

'Arianwyn!'

'Hi, Gimma.'

Gimma looked at Judith and Silas and Miss Newam, who had followed Arianwyn into the courtyard, and said, 'Um . . . d'you mind?' Arianwyn smiled at this hint of the old, superior Gimma.

'Colin said you'd been asking for me,' Arianwyn said, once they had left.

Gimma looked like she was considering her words carefully before she spoke. Eventually she said, 'I wanted to say . . .' She took a deep breath. 'Thank you.'

Arianwyn felt her cheeks warm. 'You don't have to thank me, Gimma.'

'But you stopped the High Elder. And worked out about the hex and the seam of magic.'

'Not on my own,' Arianwyn said, smiling. 'And you pulled me from the river before I drowned. I should be thanking you too.'

Gimma fixed her eyes on her again. 'You didn't give up on me, though. You tried to be my friend . . . despite everything.'

'I'm a bit stubborn like that.' Arianwyn smiled.

'In a strange way, I think you're the only friend I've ever really had, Arianwyn Gribble,' Gimma said quietly, glancing down at her hands. Scars from the hex were still visible, but the heavy blackness was gone. Now the swirls and twists were pale under her skin, which was flushed pink once more.

Perhaps she would always bear the scars.

'You can always make more friends. It's not as hard as you might think,' Arianwyn said gently. Gimma seemed to consider this for a while in silence, until Arianwyn asked, 'What will you do once they finish treating you?' deciding it was better to look forward than dwell on the past. 'Will you ask for a new assignment somewhere?'

Gimma shook her head. 'I have no idea.' She studied the crocuses in the patch of garden. 'I'm not sure I can go back to being a witch and working for the C.W.A. – not after . . . everything. Besides, I never really wanted to be a witch anyway.'

'It's all I ever wanted to be,' Arianwyn said, trying to think of what her life would have been like if she hadn't been born a witch like her grandmother and mother. What would she be doing now?

'I know. And you're the best witch there is. And it's not just me that thinks that, you know.' Gimma lifted her head towards the glass doors, where everyone else was waiting.

'She's right!' Miss Delafield said and blushed.

'Absolutely right,' Colin agreed.

'Possibly the finest witch of her generation,' Miss Newam added quietly.

Arianwyn could feel her cheeks flushing.

'But I do need to try and make up for what I've done, somehow,' Gimma continued.

'Gimma, that wasn't your fault, it was the hex,' Arianwyn said.

Gimma gave a small laugh. 'No, well, not just that. But from before the hex. I've not been a good person, Wyn, you know that and . . . well, I can't blame that all on the hex, can I?' The courtyard was quiet again for a moment and then Gimma said, 'I have to be different now.'

'You can be whatever you want to be, Gimma.

But whatever it is, I hope we can be friends now?'

Gimma nodded and then smiled shyly, reaching out her own hand and taking hold of Arianwyn's. The two new friends sat quietly in the courtyard, bathed in bright spring sunshine.

Chapter 37
The NEW COUNCIL

en minutes later Arianwyn and Miss Delafield walked through the huge double doors of the council chamber. The room was flooded with light from the long windows that filled the far wall. A cluster of witches stood in the middle of the room in quiet conversation. 'Only twelve of them so far, dear,' Miss Delafield said quietly. 'They've not selected a full council yet – or a new High Elder, it would seem.'

The witches were surrounded by administrative staff from the C.W.A. Director Coot stood slightly to one side, talking intently to Grandma.

The chatter in the room fell to a hush as Arianwyn and Miss Delafield approached them.

Arianwyn had no idea what was going on, but she

assumed she was about to be quizzed over her various encounters with the High Elder. 'Ah, Miss Gribble,' Director Coot called. 'So good to see you again.' He shook Arianwyn's hand. His felt rather sweaty. He leant in closely and said quietly, 'You've come a long way since your evaluation and the last time we met, haven't you? Quite the rising star in our midst, it would seem.' He smiled and looked at Grandma. 'You must be remarkably proud of her, Elder Stronelli.'

Grandma smiled broadly. 'I always have been.'

'Now then,' Director Coot said, clapping his hands, 'if I can have everyone's attention, please.'

The chatter in the room died down again and all the assembled witches and C.W.A. staff turned to look at Director Coot. 'Miss Delafield, if you could come forward please?' He pointed to a patch of floor just in front of him.

A small thrill passed through Arianwyn. She glanced at Grandma, who smiled and winked. Was Miss Delafield about to be asked to join the Council of Elders? One of the elders stepped forward and bowed her head for a moment. Miss Delafield shot Arianwyn a look of wide-eyed excitement. What was happening?

'Jucasta Delafield,' the other witch said calmly. 'For your loyal service and ability. Your hard work and dedication to honouring the magic within the Kingdom of Hylund, we' – she gestured to the assembled witches who had closed in around her, forming a horseshoe shape – 'proudly invite you to join our Council of Elders.'

There was a loud clatter of applause from everyone. Arianwyn felt warm tears of joy on her cheeks and gave a loud whooping cry that rang out through the council chamber.

Miss Delafield had brought her hands to her mouth, her eyes wide.

The witch who had spoken then opened her palm, and in it rested the silver-and-gold star badge of the council. 'Do you accept this position of service and devotion?'

'I accept it willingly, dear,' Miss Delafield said, her voice shaking a little.

There was more applause as the council closed in to surround their thirteenth member. Arianwyn saw a flash of silver and gold as the badge was pinned to Miss Delafield's jacket. Then Grandma moved forward and handed her a folded talma of bright silver cloth. Miss Delafield wiped at her eyes and then turned to beam at Arianwyn, who was wiping away her own tears again.

After several minutes of excited chatter in the room, Arianwyn suddenly found herself standing facing the horseshoe of council witches. She felt paralysed, frozen to the spot. So now came the interrogation!

She glanced at her grandmother who didn't look

worried at all, just excited and proud: always the look of pride shining in her eyes.

A witch stepped out of the group and approached Arianwyn slowly. 'Arianwyn Gribble, after much discussion and in light of what you have done for the kingdom, the new council has decided to extend to *you* the opportunity to join us.'

Arianwyn wasn't sure she had heard correctly; surely there had been some sort of mistake? She hadn't just said what Arianwyn thought she had said.

Had she?

Arianwyn glanced across at her grandmother who smiled. At Miss Delafield, who stood open-mouthed. Colin gave her a double thumbs-up as the elder witch continued formally, 'Arianwyn Gribble, for your loyal service, for your skill and bravery, your dedication to upholding the magic of the Kingdom of Hylund and for your kindness, we, the new Council of Elders, invite you to join us.' She reached out her hand, and there nestled in her palm was a badge, a silver five-pointed star brooch, larger than the one she wore now and edged with gold.

The badge of the council. Just like the one her grandmother wore, just like the one Miss Delafield now wore as well.

'I . . . I don't know what to say,' Arianwyn said, her words hushed and whispery, her throat dry with nerves. She stared down at the badge again, the lights from above blinking off it.

'You would be the first witch in recorded history to be made an elder at such a young age,' Director Coot said proudly. 'But we feel that your skills at this time would be an advantage to the new council as it forges ahead, putting the recent past behind itself.'

What should she do? And what did this mean? Arianwyn let her eyes rove around the room, falling on the faces of the rest of the council, the other thirteen witches, including Miss Delafield and her grandmother. Some looked expectant, excited. Others looked uncertain, nervous. No doubt this had been a difficult decision for the council to make; she felt sure she was certainly not everyone's first choice.

'Perhaps we should allow Miss Gribble some time to think this over,' Miss Newam said from behind her, where she had been standing all this time like a sentry.

Arianwyn felt suddenly terribly grateful for her. 'Thank you,' she said quietly as the council filed out, leaving her alone with Grandmother, Colin and Miss Delafield in the chamber.

'Are you all right?' Grandmother asked, pulling her into a tight embrace.

'I don't know. Why do they want me?' Arianwyn asked. She looked up into her grandmother's pale eyes, suddenly nervous that she had pulled some strings, just as she had once before to secure Arianwyn's original posting in Lull.

'There are many reasons to have you join the council and many reasons not to. The council feels that your knowledge of the quiet glyphs is important for our future, for the protection of the Four Kingdoms, not just Hylund,' Grandmother said.

'It is a huge honour to be asked to join at such a young age,' Colin said.

'An honour that you deserve,' Miss Delafield added.

The room was quiet for several long minutes. Arianwyn walked slowly across the room, not really paying attention to where she was going or what she was looking at. Thoughts drifted in and out of her mind. Mainly about her mother who had died too young to become an elder witch. She slipped out the photograph Salle had given her for Yule. It was a little crumpled now; she really should get it framed soon. Her mother smiled up at her. She would have loved to serve on the council, she was sure of that. But did that mean that Arianwyn had to do the same?

Her mind drifted back to Lull and the Great Wood, to Estar and the feylings. They still needed her help as much as the rest of the kingdom, didn't they?

'I can't accept,' Arianwyn said, breaking the silence at last.

'What?' Miss Delafield looked up.

Arianwyn heard her grandmother sigh but didn't know if it was a good sigh or a bad sigh. She looked at Colin who smiled at her.

'It is a great honour to have been asked. And I know other witches would give their broomsticks to have this chance. But I never wanted to be on the council. And I don't think I'd make a very good council member either. I want to go back to Lull. To carry on helping there. The hex still threatens the Great Wood, the feylings need help establishing their new home. I want to understand more about natural magic and how it combats the hex. I don't want to be in meetings, cooped up here all the time. I want to be in Lull.'

She saw her friends smiling at her. She had not made the wrong decision, she was sure.

'And that is precisely why the council needs someone like you,' Grandmother said a little sadly. 'I support your decision, of course. Though I'd have rather loved to have my granddaughter on the council beside me.'

'And perhaps one day you will,' Miss Delafield said. 'Arianwyn will have her chance again. Of that you can be certain!'

Grandmother smiled. 'But of course.'

Chapter 38
A STRANGE SPELL

'Thank you, Miss Gribble.' Mrs Myddleton smiled as she packed away a parcel of charms and ushered her collection of children towards the Spellorium door.

'Bye, Miss Witch,' Cyril called cheerfully as they stepped out into Kettle Lane, already busy with people coming and going.

A warm spring breeze stirred the door charm, the red ribbons fluttering, the six silver bells singing gently. Arianwyn turned back to the newspaper that lay open on the counter top. At the top of the page was the article she had been reading before Mrs Myddleton had appeared to collect her order:

COUNCIL OF ELDER WITCHES
SELECTS NEW LEADER

Nearly three months since the Hylund Council of
Elder Witches declared their previous leader,
Constance Braithwaite, missing presumed dead,
they have now elected a new High Elder from
within their ranks.

During a secret ballot and after three days of talks,
interviews and discussion, Eloise McGiven, an elder
witch from Occlestree, was selected by eighty-five
per cent of the witches' council, which was itself
dramatically reconstructed following revelations
of corruption led by Elder Braithwaite . . .

Arianwyn looked up as a sudden clatter of footsteps sounded by the doorway and Mayor Belcher
burst through, panting, his cheeks shiny and bright
red. 'Oh, Miss Gribble!' he wheezed. 'There you
are!'

'Ssssh!' Arianwyn said quickly, casting a glance
back to the counter. In a small wicker basket tucked
to one side Bob was sleeping. 'The kits are fast
asleep!' she hushed the mayor.

Bob had returned quite unexpectedly just a few
days before, but what was more remarkable was that
Bob had returned with two tiny moon hare kits.

'Oh, I am sorry!' Mayor Belcher's voice fell into a

slightly too-loud whisper.

'Is she there?' A sharp voice cut through and a woman emerged from behind Mayor Belcher. She wore sunshine-yellow trousers and a jumper covered in a busy pattern, almost as bright as the spring day outside.

It took Arianwyn more than a few seconds to recognize her. 'Miss Newam?' she said a little uncertainly. She looked quite different free of her ill-fitting dark suits!

'Arianwyn!' Miss Newam called.

'Hush, my dear – the baby moon hares!' Mayor Belcher said, pointing to the basket and placing an arm around Miss Newam's shoulders, his eyes wide and full of wonder as he peered into the basket.

Bob stretched a little and set about washing the babies for a few moments and then yawned and went back to sleep.

'Yes, quite sweet I suppose, if you like that sort of thing.' Miss Newam sniffed, but Arianwyn noticed that she gazed just a little longer at the moon hares curled around each other inside the basket, the smallest of smiles on her lips.

'Miss Newam, I didn't know you had arrived already.' Arianwyn came round from behind the counter, smiling.

'It was rather late last night.' Miss Newam sniffed again, but then smiled too as Arianwyn pulled her into a slightly awkward hug. 'I was hoping Colin would be here?' she added as they pulled apart.

'He went down to the meadow with Salle to start recording the . . . transformation,' Arianwyn explained.

They emerged through the South Gate a few minutes later and into the meadow that surrounded Lull.

The flooding had receded at last and the grass was lush and green. It rippled a little in the spring breeze, where it had started to grow long. The qered herd, returned from Bridge Farm, moved about, their happy calls singing out across the meadow.

To Arianwyn, it looked so different. And it still took her breath away.

Where the High Elder's spell had worked its strange magic, a curving line of trees had sprouted and now ran from Lull back to the Great Wood in a huge sweeping arc. She could see ash, silver birch, oak and sycamore – and more besides that she didn't know the names of but recognized. There were some more unusual specimens as well: one with dark purple bark and another with branches bursting with white buds that glowed at night time. There was another tree closer to the river that made a beautiful sound as its long branches moved with the breeze, but it was too far away to hear just then.

And what had been the chasm in the high walls of Lull was now also bursting with life. The trees that had grown there had twined and twisted and grown together, forming a brown and green mesh in the space, mending brick and stone with bark and leaf. It looked almost as though Lull had become a part of the Great Wood.

'It looks quite . . . spectacular!' Miss Newam gasped.

'It really does!' Mayor Belcher agreed as they made their way over the small bridge near the pond and towards Colin and Salle, who were sat beneath one of the purple-barked trees.

'Hello, Mayor Belcher, Miss Newam.' Colin and Salle waved as they approached. 'Hi, Wyn.'

Colin held a camera in one hand and had a pile of notebooks in the grass at his side. Salle was holding on to a map of the meadow and was brandishing a long wooden measuring stick.

'Isn't it amazing?' Colin asked.

'It certainly is,' Miss Newam said, turning to take in the full sight before her again. Then she leant over to look through Colin's notebooks and at the map in Salle's hand. 'Are the . . . new trees having any adverse effect on the others?' she asked.

'It doesn't appear so,' Colin replied quickly.

'And have you managed to identify them at all? Catalogue them?'

'Some, thanks to our visit to see Estar in the

feyling settlement a few days ago. He promises to come and help us as soon as he can.'

'The feylings are busy building their new city,' Arianwyn explained. 'It's amazing how much they have done: there are houses already being constructed, all sorts of strange shapes and sizes, some high in the tree branches with others like huge burrows under the ground.'

'And no matter what or where they build it's all beautiful and unique,' Mayor Belcher added.

'You've been to see the feyling camp, Josiah?' Miss Newam asked, unable to hide the shock from her voice.

Colin flashed a quick look at Arianwyn, amazed at how relaxed Miss Newam was being with the mayor. It seemed her dress sense wasn't the only thing to have lightened up.

The mayor lifted his chin and said proudly, 'Indeed I have. And very glad I am to have done so. You won't believe what they can build, Hortensia. It is truly astounding.'

'Really?' Miss Newam smiled. 'I look forward to seeing it then.'

'And the mayor is going to establish a trade agreement with the feylings, and Lull will be the first town in all of Hylund to host a feyling market once a month to trade goods and food,' Salle added, breathless with excitement.

'We will show . . . our friends,' the mayor said after

considering for a second, 'that they are welcome here whenever they wish. They helped to defend Lull in our darkest hour. We owe them our friendship.' He looked directly at Arianwyn as he said this.

She smiled back at him. Hearing the mayor speak like that when he had been so against the feylings at one point made her heart warm.

'Would you like me to show you some of the most interesting specimens?' Colin asked Miss Newam.

But before she could reply, the mayor stepped forwards and said quietly, 'I will show Miss Newam if you like. Why don't you three run along?'

'Are you sure?' Colin asked.

'Yes, of course. Off you go.' The mayor smiled and shooed them all away.

At first they raced back across the meadow, whooping and laughing. Salle stopped to do a hand-stand which Arianwyn and Colin tried to copy, but they collapsed into a pile of giggles amongst the early daisies peeking up through the grass.

Getting to their feet they walked more slowly back towards the South Gate.

'Where's your dad today?' Colin asked.

'He's gone to visit some friends he knows who just moved to a new house on the other side of Flaxsham, then he's going back to Kingsport tomorrow for an interview.'

'He doesn't want to stay here in Lull then?'

Salle asked.

'I think Lull is just big enough for one Gribble.' Arianwyn smiled. 'He'll be happier in Kingsport.'

'Won't you miss him, though?'

Arianwyn thought about it for a moment. When her father had first mentioned his plans, she had felt a pang of fear and an ache that she would miss him. But then she realized she'd not lived with her father for so many years and she had sort of stopped missing him in an odd way. And now she knew he wouldn't be returning to the army she felt more hopeful that she would see more of him.

'He said he's going to visit, lots,' she said, and she noticed that Colin flushed a little.

She glanced back over her shoulder and saw the mayor and Miss Newam wandering off to inspect the curve of the trees. He had his hand placed gently on her back as they walked along. And Arianwyn was surprised to hear Miss Newam's laugh drift across the meadow, back towards them.

They all paused for a moment on the little bridge over the marshy pond near the South Gate. The shadows were lengthening and the sun was sliding down towards the treeline. It would be dark soon. The breeze had a cool edge to it.

'OK?' Colin asked, quietly moving a little closer to Arianwyn.

'I was just thinking how the meadow used to look. It's so different now. Changed beyond all recognition. Changed more than anyone ever thought it might or could,' she said. It was exciting, but strange and different.

'But changed for the better?' Colin asked, and his voice sounded slightly worried.

'I hope so. Yes,' Arianwyn said. 'Look – it's flourishing!' She swept her free arm across the view before them, the strange new trees as beautiful as the oak and birch trees that grew right beside them. All side by side and reaching up into the sky which was flecked with the first few stars.

'And all thanks to you,' Salle said quietly. She slipped her hand gently into Arianwyn's. It felt warm and secure.

'What do you mean?' Arianwyn asked, glancing back at the meadow and the trees again.

'You've been like a wonderful, strange magical spell for Lull. You've changed it beyond what it was,' Salle said, smiling.

'And all for the better,' Colin added. His hand was now slipping into Arianwyn's free hand.

They quietly turned, and hand in hand the three friends walked back up the short slope towards the South Gate and back home to Lull.

GLOSSARY OF GLYPHS

Årdra is the fire glyph. Its strength is immense, as is its ability to destroy at the hands of an inexperienced witch. It also contains properties for light and protection.

Briå, the air glyph, is summoned for spells that require delicacy. It is used in broomcraft and for transformation. Its defensive properties are limited but can be wielded by a witch with high skill.

For spells of strength and protection it is best to use Erte, the earth glyph. Strong and resourceful, it is the easiest of the glyphs to summon but the most difficult to master.

Aluna is the water glyph, useful for spells of healing and for those skilled in the arts of divination. Like water, it can appear weak but has a hidden strength.

L'ier is the banishing glyph and contains at its heart a sliver of dark magic for it summons a small rift, opening a portal from the human world to the void to which a dark spirit is returned.

Oru is the simplest glyph to summon and creates a light spell orb. It is usually the glyph and spell a witch would first learn, before the age of five.

SPIRIT CREATURE GLOSSARY

Extracts from

A WITCH ALONE: A MANUAL FOR THE NEWLY QUALIFIED WITCH

FEYLINGS

These rare magical creatures feature heavily in the mythology of the Four Kingdoms and beyond but no two descriptions ever match. Some believe they are a cross-breeding of spirit and dark spirit creatures – others believe they are something altogether different.

FROST PHOENIX

Frost phoenixes are now a rare sight in the Four Kingdoms, with fewer sightings reported each year. The records that do exist indicate huge but fast and graceful spirit creatures with white, shimmering plumage and wings edged with brilliant ice-blue. They are believed to summon the first snowfalls of winter. Frost Phoenix feathers are considered to be lucky, and contain healing properties.

GANT

Standing at over seven metres tall, Gants are gentle spirit creatures that live primarily along coastal regions. They use their two long trunks to communicate and find food, mostly crustaceans and seaweed. Their dung can be utilized for various magical purposes.

HARVEST BOGGLIN

The skin of these dark spirit creatures, that have not been seen for seventy-five years, is toad-like and camouflaged, though their bright red eyes will often give them away. Extremely territorial, they are known to claim whole fields, preventing crops from being harvested.

MAUDANTS

Maudants have the appearance of huge airborne jellyfish. They have been known to reach more than ten metres in diameter with tentacles of well over one hundred metres. A maudant's tentacles are incredibly dangerous; the touch of one can cause paralysis and even death. Maudants generally travel in small pods of between two and seven creatures. The spells required to banish them are complex and must be carried out by two witches in conjunction to take effect.

MOON HARE

These rare spirit creatures were once a common sight across the Four Kingdoms and beyond. They are neither male nor female and are believed to be born from eggs. Partly scaled and partly covered in pure white fur they are naturally shy but incredibly intelligent.

NIGHT GHAST

No recorded sightings for nearly a thousand years. These extinct dark spirits stood at over three metres tall, with a single orifice serving as eye, mouth and nose. They were extremely violent and hungry for living creatures, possessing a distinctive insect-like call.

NITHERINGS (Ice Imps)

Nitherings are one of the smaller forms of ice imp, prevalent throughout most of the Four Kingdoms. They are active from late October until mid-March and build ice crystal nests in small spaces and tight corners, usually in occupied buildings. Nitherings are incredibly fast which makes them hard to spot or catch. Their skin colour is normally frosty-blue with mottled ice-white patches. They have large eyes and a large beak-like nose. They warn off predators by hissing and dropping their temperature to well below freezing in a matter of seconds.

PANGORBAK

Pangorbaks are dark parasitic spirits that thrive on attention. When they attach themselves to a host, they resemble a slug. Over the course of a few hours they will grow tentacles and expand rapidly. If they are not removed quickly they can cause serious damage or death.

QERED

Standing at over three metres tall, these horse-like spirit creatures are scaled with long flowing manes and tails. Gentle herbivores, their call is similar to that of whales and can carry for over seventy miles. They live in large herds and mate for life.

RAZLOR

These rarely seen dark spirit creatures are winged, dog-like beasts, with oily black skin and bony but strong bodies. They are expert hunters and usually do so in small packs of three to five creatures. They were once hunted for sport.

SKALK

No recorded sightings for seven hundred years. Adaptable to most conditions, these dark spirit creatures were easily identified by their large bony beaks, dark matted hair and scuttling movements. They were fast and incredibly dangerous.

SNOTLINGS

Common and pesky dark spirit creatures that build hibernation nests in shadowy, sheltered places. She-snotlings have thick crests of spines, are generally larger than the males, and can deliver a sharp and painful bite. If you spot signs of a nest it is best to deal with it at once.

STAGGET

These sacred spirit creatures guard forests and moorland and generally live in large herds. They resemble deer and are often mistaken for them, but they are much larger and their antlers are usually gold or silver.

VELASTAMURI commonly referred to as 'shrieking ritts'

These spirit creatures have small bird-like bodies, but a massive three-metre wing span. They emit a high-pitched shrieking noise whilst in flight, which is often mistaken for their call, but is actually a result of the air passing through their wings.

WILD BRUNKUN

These gentle spirit creatures grow to no larger than ten centimetres in height and nest in thistle patches. Wild brunkun are entirely covered in thick brown hair, which they shed and regrow every month. They have a fondness for sugar.

WINGED GRIPPETS

These dark spirit creatures stand around forty centimetres tall, have hoglike faces and tusked mouths. Each of their four legs ends in many-fingered, dextrous hands. They are not terribly dangerous unless they swarm, when they can cause considerable damage and disruption.

ACKNOWLEDGEMENTS

I have a tendency to get a *bit* gushy at this point – and I can hear poor Laura at Chicken House wondering how on earth she can squeeze in the acknowledgements without making the font so small you'd need a microscope to read them. But, simply put, books are created by more than just the author and there is never going to be enough space to say thanks for all the minuscule and massive things that people do in the course of a book being written, published and beyond.

My thanks always and for ever to the wonderful Kate Shaw, my heroic agent. She's so cool, funny, kind and brilliant. She deserves a medal – no, actually, the silver and gold star of an elder witch for sure!

If I was going to face a night ghast or a skalk then I'd want my two fine writer friends, Vashti and Lorraine right beside me. They are true rocks and it's fate that writing should have brought us together. #YPRForever

To the wonderful team at Chicken House, Rachel H, Elinor, Rachel L, Jazz, Laura S, Laura M, Sarah, Esther and Lucy, lots of love to you all for your ongoing support and belief in me and my stories. It's an honour to work with you all! And of course, Barry Cunningham, who is surely a little piece of magic in human form!

I'm also hugely grateful to the many teams and publishers around the world who have brought Arianwyn to new readers over the past few years, especially to

Helena at La Galera in Barcelona, Nick, Sam, Lauren and the team at Scholastic in New York and Anya, Maike and (superfan) Kathi at Chicken House Germany in Hamburg.

To Luis, Leo and Camille who have all brought the books to life in Spain, the USA and France with their stunning illustrations. It's been an honour to have your work linked with my stories. And most especially, Daniela Terrazzini, who illustrates the UK covers, thank you so much for beautifully imagining Arianwyn and making her fly!

Thank you, Elizabeth Knowelden for superbly reading the US audiobooks and for being such a huge supporter, fan and friend! I don't know how you do it but it's wonderful!

To the army of booksellers, librarians and teachers out there in the world who help the books find their way into the hands of eager readers, you are all heroes and make the world a better, more bookish and wonderful place. Keep it up!

Thank you to the reviewers and bloggers who have championed Arianwyn and helped her to reach new readers. Your enthusiasm for books is infectious!

There is a wonderfully supportive community of children's writers out there and I'm so thrilled that many of them are now good friends. It's great catching up at festivals, events and the occasional party or just by email or a desperate tweet! Thanks for your love, support and friendship.

Thanks for the continued support of Imogen and the whole Golden Egg Academy Family. I'm so proud I sprang from that nest!

All my love to my family and friends – who are all very patient with me being permanently busy one way or another. For putting me up as I dash to events, for still being so proud and so excited and for being my own unique set of crazies! Special thanks to Kathleen and Martin Westerman as much of this book was edited in their spare bedroom and garden in the midst of the worst house move in history! And not forgetting Julian – who is a marvel and a treasure. Thanks for giving me the best writing room in the world (it's even better than the dishwasher!).

There are not enough words to express how really wonderful my editor Kesia is. Always calm, always positive. Adds just enough ☺ to keep me going when it feels like I'm swimming through spaghetti or trying to knit chain mail. She is brilliant and yet the most humble person in the world. It is a pleasure working with you. You are a total star, the books wouldn't be the same without you – thank you for everything.

Last but never least, thank you readers of this book and the series. It's lovely to meet you at events and to get messages saying how much you enjoy Arianwyn's adventures. You are my inspiration and you are the very best!